Praise for *Murder on the Île Sordou*

"Charming."—Marilyn Stasio, *The New York Times Book Review*

"[T]horoughly delightful . . . Longworth deftly handles what is in effect a locked-room mystery, but the book's real strength lies in the backstories she creates for each of the distinctive characters. The puzzle's answer, buried in the past, is well prepared by what has come before."

—*Publishers Weekly* (starred review)

"Longworth once again immerses readers in French culture with this whodunit, which will delight Francophiles and fans of Donna Leon and Andrea Camilleri. The setting will also appeal to readers who enjoy trapped-on-the-island mysteries in the tradition of Agatha Christie's *And Then There Were None.*"

—*Library Journal*

"Longworth's novels, set in the south of France, are mysteries for foodies, with the plot providing a table upon which the enchanting meals and accompanying wines are served."

—*Booklist*

"[A] charming read with a well-crafted mystery and characters as rich and full bodied as a Bordeaux."

—*Milwaukee Journal Sentinel*

"A splendid read."   —*Mystery Scene*

"Longworth's maritime version of a country-house cozy offers genuine pleasures."   —*Kirkus Reviews*

T0200939

Praise for *Death in the Vines*

"Judge Antoine Verlaque, the sleuth in this civilized series, discharges his professional duties with discretion. But we're here to taste the wines, which are discussed by experts like Hippolyte Thébaud, a former wine thief, and served in beautiful settings like a 300-year-old stone farmhouse. So many bottles, so many lovely views. A reader might be forgiven for feeling woozy."   —Marilyn Stasio, *The New York Times Book Review*

"Though the plot is hair-raising, what keeps you glued to this mystery is its vivid portrait of everyday life in Aix, which deftly juxtaposes the elegance of the city . . . with quotidian woes and pleasures."   —Oprah.com

"As much as the mystery intrigues—in this case some intertwined crimes involving a local winery, a missing elderly woman, and a rich man's suspicious construction project—what really make Longworth's books enjoyable are the atmosphere and details that she includes of the South of France."

—*Seattle Post-Intelligencer*

"What follows is a lovely, almost cozy police procedural that deserves to be read with a glass of wine in hand. Longworth paints such a loving picture of Provence that it's likely you'll start planning a vacation trip to France the moment you set the book down."   —*The Denver Post*

"This is an intelligently written police procedural with the warm comfort of a baguette with banon cheese."

—*Ellery Queen Mystery Magazine*

"Enjoyable . . . the book's real strength is its evocation of place."
—*Publishers Weekly*

Praise for *Murder in the Rue Dumas*

❧

"Fans of European sleuths with a taste for good food . . . will have fun."   —*Publishers Weekly*

"What really makes Longworth's writing special is her deep knowledge of French history, landscape, cuisine, and even contemporary cafés and restaurants. This is that rare atmospheric mystery that is street-wise and café-canny."

—*Booklist* (starred review)

"Longworth's gentle procedural succeeds on several levels, whether it's for academic and literary allusions, police work, or armchair travel. With deftly shifting points of view, Longworth creates a beguiling read that will appeal to Louise Penny and Donna Leon fans."   —*Library Journal*

"French-set mysteries have never been more popular [and] among the very best is a series set in Provence featuring Monsieur Verlaque, an examining magistrate, and his sometime girlfriend, law professor Marine Bonnet."   —*The Denver Post*

Praise for *Death at the Château Bremont*

❧

"This first novel in a projected series has charm, wit, and Aix-en-Provence all going for it. Longworth's voice is like a rich vintage of sparkling Dorothy Sayers and grounded Donna Leon . . . Longworth has lived in Aix since 1997, and her knowledge of the region is apparent on every page. Bon appétit."   —*Booklist*

"A promising debut for Longworth, who shows there's more to France than Paris and more to mystery than Maigret."

—*Kirkus Reviews*

"Mystery and romance served up with a hearty dose of French cuisine. I relished every word. Longworth does for Aix-en-Provence what Frances Mayes does for Tuscany: You want to be there—NOW!"

—Barbara Fairchild, former editor in chief, *Bon Appétit*

"*Death at the Château Bremont* is replete with romance, mystery, and a rich atmosphere that makes the south of France spring off the page in a manner reminiscent of Donna Leon's Venice. A wonderful start to a series sure to gain a legion of fans."

—Tasha Alexander, author of the Lady Emily mysteries

"Longworth has a good eye and a sharp wit, and this introduction to Verlaque and Bonnet holds promise for a terrific series."

—*The Globe and Mail*

"*Death at the Château Bremont* offers charming French locales, vivid characters and an intriguing who-done-it."

—Kevin R. Kosar, author of *Whiskey: A Global History*

"Here's hoping the series lasts for years."   —*RT Book Reviews*

"Your readers will eat this one up."   —*Library Journal*

M. L. LONGWORTH'S PROVENÇAL MYSTERIES

A PENGUIN MYSTERY

The Mystery of the Lost Cézanne

M. L. LONGWORTH has lived in Aix-en-Provence since 1997. She has written about the region for the *Washington Post*, the *Times* (London), the *Independent*, and *Bon Appétit* magazine. In addition to the Verlaque and Bonnet mystery series, she is the author of a bilingual collection of essays, *Une Américaine en Provence*. She divides her time between Aix, where she writes, and Paris, where she teaches writing at New York University.

The Mystery of the Lost Cézanne

A VERLAQUE AND BONNET MYSTERY

· M. L. LONGWORTH ·

PENGUIN BOOKS

PENGUIN BOOKS
An imprint of Penguin Random House LLC
375 Hudson Street
New York, New York 10014
penguin.com

LIBRARY OF CONGRESS CATALOGING-IN-PUBLICATION DATA
Longworth, M. L. (Mary Lou), 1963–
The mystery of the lost Cézanne : a Verlaque and Bonnet mystery / M. L.
Longworth.
pages ; cm.—(Verlaque and Bonnet mysteries ; 5)
ISBN 978-0-14-312807-6
1. Art thefts—Fiction. 2. Murder—Investigation—Fiction. I. Title.
PR9199.4.L596M97 2015
813'.6—dc23
2015004005

Printed in the United States of America

Set in Adobe Caslon Pro • Designed by Elke Sigal

Pour Sophie et Philippe

Author's Note

Paul Cézanne did have an affair "with a mysterious Aixoise" in 1885, a curiosity I first read in a *New Yorker* article, later confirmed when rereading *Paul Cézanne: Letters,* edited by John Rewald in 1976. Cézanne's good friends Émile Zola and Philippe Solari did, of course, exist, but all the others have been invented by the author.

The Mystery of the Lost Cézanne

❧

Chapter One

La Fête des Rois

January was his favorite month. He loved Provençal winters; they were cold and dry, often with bright-blue skies. The ancient plane trees—so essential in summer to block the sun—now, without their fat leaves, looked like tall knobby sculptures. But their winter bareness revealed the Cours Mirabeau's soft golden architecture: mansions of the seventeenth century, now banks, law offices, cafés, and the twenty-first-century addition of American chain stores. But most of all, January meant that the commercialism and strain of Christmas was over, and the routine of work, cigar club, and being with Marine could begin anew. This year he would be a better boss, a better friend, a better lover. Or try to. *Like hitting the refresh button on my computer*, he thought.

Antoine Verlaque paused in the middle of the Cours, leaned against one of the trees—its multicolored gray and pale-green bark like army fatigues—and relit his cigar. He slowly puffed on his Partagas, and while he smoked he watched his fellow Aixois filing up and down the wide avenue. Three teenage girls—with identical haircuts and expensive, giant leather purses—walked arm in arm, speaking so quickly that it was near to impossible for him to eavesdrop. There was something about the trio that reminded Verlaque of his own youth, spent in Paris; perhaps it was their obvious wealth—always flaunted in Aix, and in certain arrondissements in Paris—or their easiness with one another, their self-assuredness. He had had friends just like these girls in high school, but their faces were now a blur. What remained were their names, names that reflected their parents' good taste and education, or their Catholicism: Victoire, Mazarine, Josephine, Marie-Clothilde.

An old woman came in the opposite direction. She appeared to be wearing her slippers and bathrobe. Verlaque felt his chest tighten in sadness; when she got closer he was relieved to see that she was wearing a winter coat, albeit flimsy and weather-beaten. But she was indeed wearing her slippers.

She stopped to take a rest, and leaning on her cane she looked up at the judge and smiled. *"Bonne journée, monsieur,"* she said slowly and carefully. Her accent was Parisian, educated.

"Bonne journée, madame," Verlaque answered, smiling and slightly bowing in respect.

The woman took a deep breath and looked up at the sky. "Blue, and clear," she said.

"The only blue sky in France today," Verlaque answered. "I looked at the weather report earlier this morning." He stopped himself from adding "on my computer." Verlaque imagined she had an old boxy television in the corner of a room, the kind with a rabbit-ear antenna.

"Humph," she replied, clicking her teeth. She readjusted

her cane to get ready to walk on. "And Christmas is finally over."

Verlaque laughed out loud. "Thankfully."

She nodded in lieu of saying good-bye, and walked away. Verlaque turned to watch her go, and he wondered where she lived. Was her apartment a small, squalid bed-sit? Or was she an eccentric noblewoman, who lived with too many cats in a grand bourgeois *hôtel particulier*? One thing was clear to him, though: she lived alone. At least his parents still had each other—even if they rarely spoke—and a team of servants to look after them.

He walked on, heading south on the cobblestoned side of the Cours, toward his favorite pâtisserie. A couple walked toward him and he tried not to frown. They were the sort of Aixois couple he despised: she, too thin, too made-up, and sporting the same haircut and expensive bag as the teenage girls. She walked on impossibly high heels, and pushed a baby buggy almost as big as his 1961 Porsche. Verlaque couldn't imagine how she interacted with the infant inside; it was an accessory. He realized he was probably being unfair. *Try to be a better person, Antoine.*

Usually he looked in peoples' eyes to grasp something of their character, but husband and wife both wore enormous sunglasses, the kind that made the wearer look like a fly. Dolce & Gabbana. They both had the same colored, streaked hair (or was it possible to have natural hair with a dozen shades of red and blond?), and *he* wore a leather motorcycle jacket that was covered in brand names and insignias. Verlaque tried not to be angered by their obvious posing; he knew that Marine hardly noticed others around her. He took a drag of his cigar and vowed to be more inward thinking, like Marine.

"Another damn resolution," he mumbled. And then he saw the queue. "What the—?"

A lineup, at least twenty people long, flowed out of Michaud's and onto the sidewalk. Verlaque pulled out his cell phone and checked the date. "*Merde!*" The phone then rang and he answered it, almost yelling. "*Oui!*"

"Good morning, sir. Am I interrupting you?"

"No, no," Verlaque answered. "Sorry, Bruno. I'm standing on the Cours, hungry, in front of Michaud's, and forgot that it was January sixth."

Aix-en-Provence's commissioner laughed and then coughed. "Sorry, sir. Are people queuing up to buy their *galettes des rois*?"

"Of course they are!" Verlaque said as he got in line. "Do people actually like those things?"

Bruno Paulik coughed again. "Well," he said, "yeah."

"I just want a brioche; I didn't have time for breakfast," Verlaque said. "I'll be a while getting back."

"Sir," Paulik began, "since you're in the queue—"

"You want a brioche, too? No problem."

"No, actually," Paulik said, "I'd promised Hélène and Léa that I'd buy them a galette, for this evening."

"*Oh mon dieu,*" Verlaque said.

"A medium-size one will do," Paulik said, ignoring Verlaque's comment. "Don't forget the paper crown," he continued. "Léa will go berserk if there isn't the crown."

"I know about the crown, Bruno," Verlaque said, inching forward toward the shop's front door. He stepped up onto the first step of the shop and set his cigar on the window ledge, planning on picking it up on his way out. The smell of butter and warm sugar made his stomach growl. "I can't remember the last time I had a galette des rois. I've never cared for almond paste—"

"In fact," Paulik continued, as if he hadn't heard a word,

"we're having a Fête des Rois this afternoon at the Palais de Justice; I forgot to tell you."

Verlaque held his cell phone away from his ear and looked at it, bewildered at his rugby-playing commissioner's enthusiasm.

Paulik continued, "And Léa asked me this morning if you and Marine could come to our place tonight to celebrate."

Verlaque smiled, touched by Léa's earnest invitation. But the thought of having to eat an almond paste pie, twice in one day, turned his stomach over. "We'd love to come," he found himself answering, thinking of Léa Paulik's bright ten-year-old face. "I have my cigar club tonight, but I can show up late."

"Great. How was court this morning?"

"Well worth our effort, Bruno," Verlaque answered. "Kévin Malongo will be behind bars for the next twenty years."

"Perfect. See you soon."

Verlaque was finally inside Michaud's. Stainless steel racks had been pulled out of the back room and filled the interior of the shop, each one stacked high with the flaky galettes. Those customers still in line strained to see the cakes, already selecting their favorite. Verlaque winced; they all looked the same to him. Other customers, ahead in the queue, pointed to their chosen cake, and a black-and-white-uniformed Michaud salesgirl carefully lifted the cake and placed it in a shiny red box. The prices Verlaque could hear being rung in at the cash register astounded him. Thirty euros? There was just a bean hidden in the cake, not a bloody diamond. And why was there going to be a party at the Palais de Justice this afternoon? He tried to picture his group of police officers, gathered around the cakes, with the youngest officer—Jules?—sitting cross-legged under his desk, calling out names. Verlaque sighed; sometimes he loved the traditions of his country, and sometimes . . .

"Monsieur le juge?" a saleswoman asked. Verlaque recognized her; she had been working at Michaud's as long as he could remember. She obviously knew him, too.

"Un galette des rois, s'il vous plaît, et deux brioches," he answered.

"Which one?" she asked.

Verlaque looked at the cakes. The ones lower down looked too small, and he eliminated the cakes that looked lopsided or messy. The saleswoman shifted her weight and he finally pointed to one on the top shelf. If they were to be five that evening, Léa would want a big cake. "Don't forget the crown!" he called after her.

Natalie Chazeau had been watching Antoine Verlaque from the window. L'Agence de la Ville was Aix-en-Provence's most luxurious real estate office, or it had been until that summer when John Taylor Realtors opened a branch across the street. Mme Chazeau, a handsome, tall woman in her early seventies, was the company's owner, and had built it up from scratch with her husband, who had died of a heart attack twenty years earlier. They were young newlyweds when they bought the office, prestigiously located on the Cours Mirabeau, and for years had lived frugally while paying back the loan. It was now worth a fortune.

Mme Chazeau was adding new color photographs of two estates for sale—one just outside of Aix and the other in the Luberon—in the office's large plate-glass window, where the Aixois could stroll by, see the photos, stop, and dream. People who ended up buying estates sold by L'Agence de la Ville rarely did so by seeing the photographs in the windows; more often than not they hired scouts to find them the perfect (often second or third) home. But the agency was known for its window display, as was Pâtisserie Michaud across the street, whose queue Verlaque was now impatiently standing in.

She pinned up the last photograph and looked at the judge, who had his head bent, speaking on his cell phone while trying to puff on a cigar. The queue moved slowly. He reminded her of her only child, Christophe, a friend of the judge's and a fellow cigar smoker, who had recently moved to Paris to open his own agency. Had she been a younger woman she would have done everything she could to work her way into Antoine Verlaque's arms. But those days were over, and she knew that the judge saw her as others did—a distinguished, hard-working old woman who probably dyed her thick black hair (she didn't). She looked at Verlaque's wide back, clothed in a black coat that she guessed was cashmere, and she reached up and twisted one of her diamond earrings—a gift from Christophe.

Her office phone rang and she answered it, and by the time it got dark, just before 6:00 p.m., she had had more than fifteen calls. She left her office and told Julie, her secretary, that she could leave for the day. Mme Chazeau herself would lock up after tonight's meeting. She thanked Julie for her hard work, adjusted the thin wool scarf around the young girl's neck, and then stood looking out the glass door at the lineup across the street. The judge had long gone; she hadn't seen how many cakes he had bought. Mme Chazeau wished she could go home, put on her slippers, call her half brother Franz, and tell him about Michaud's famed galettes des rois. But tonight she would be working, hosting a meeting of apartment owners who owned flats in the four-story apartment at 23 rue Boulegon. There had been a time, when sales were easier to get, that she had refused to work as a *syndic*. Smaller, less prestigious Realtors could take on the headache of dealing with the often-daily problems in running a small apartment building. Especially apartments that had been built in old Aix and were themselves often more than five hundred years old. But finding clients—French or foreign—to buy estates worth more than two million euros was getting harder to do, so she agreed to represent the owners at 23 rue Boulegon, if only for the prestige: it was a beautiful, well-kept building, and it had been Paul Cézanne's last residence.

A thud brought her out of her reverie; René Rouquet had walked into the glass door. Startled, she opened the door. "M. Rouquet," she said, "you should walk with your head up. Welcome. You're the first here."

Rouquet mumbled a good evening, walked in with his head still down, and stood with his back to Julie's marble-topped desk, fidgeting with his wool hat. Mme Chazeau smiled, pleased that the gruff retired postman had remembered his manners and removed his hat. The tiny bell that hung above the door rang again and she turned around; it seemed that the rest of the owners had all arrived at the same time: Pierre Millot, who came with the new owners of his top-floor apartment, a young couple whom Mme Chazeau hadn't yet met; Dr. Pitavy, a podiatrist who owned a two-room office on the ground floor, to the left of the building's entrance; and Philomène Joubert, who owned and rented out the two apartments on the second floor, above Dr. Pitavy's office.

"Did you see the queue at Michaud's?" Mme Joubert said as she walked in, blowing on her hands, wishing she had not left her apartment on the rue Cardinale without gloves.

"I bought my galette this morning," Dr. Pitavy said, smirking.

"I made my own," Philomène Joubert said, glaring at the doctor. *What a pretentious bore,* she thought to herself.

Pierre Millot turned to the young couple, Françoise and Eric Legendre, who had just moved to Aix, and explained. "Michaud's is an institution," he said. "Cézanne even bought his pastries there."

"Let's go upstairs to the meeting room, now that everyone is here," Mme Chazeau said. She turned the door's lock and left a large set of keys dangling in it.

"*Et le Belge?*" René Rouquet asked as they mounted the stairs.

"*M. Staelens*," Mme Chazeau slowly said, "called me this afternoon. He's at home in Brussels and sends his best wishes."

Mme Chazeau closed the conference room's door, out of habit, once everyone sat down. She went to the head of the table and opened a red file. "Pierre, why don't you introduce the new owners of your former apartment?" she asked, sitting down. She didn't add that she thought it odd that Pierre Millot was present that evening, as he no longer owned an apartment at number 23. But she had seen it before—some people had a hard time letting go, even once all the documents had been signed. One seller, years ago, had such remorse that he drove every evening to his former house and parked in the street, looking at the grounds that he had lovingly tended for thirty years. When he began to wander around the yard, the new owners had to get a restraining order.

Pierre straightened his back and began. "I'd like to introduce Eric and Françoise Legendre, who moved into my former apartment six days ago. They are returning to France after spending over ten years in New York."

"New York?" Mme Chazeau asked. "How was that?"

"Expensive," Eric Legendre flatly replied.

"So I've heard," Mme Chazeau replied. "Welcome to Aix. If you have any questions about the city, I'm always available."

"Thank you," Françoise Legendre quietly replied, looking at her husband and smiling.

Mme Chazeau picked up a pen. She would act as secretary that night. "First on the agenda is the hall and stairway cleaning. The price is going up fifteen euros a month. Does everyone approve this?"

"What choice do we have?" Dr. Pitavy asked.

"Change companies," Mme Chazeau said. "Which means interviewing them. And I've already looked into it. The one we're using is still the cheapest, even if they raise the fee."

"In that case, I approve," Mme Joubert said, raising her hand.

"So does M. Staelens," Mme Chazeau said. "We went over this evening's agenda on the telephone." She looked at the Legendres and explained, "Jan Staelens owns a large apartment on the third floor. He uses it for vacations. What do you think about the cleaning fees?"

Eric Legendre looked at his wife and shrugged. "We approve, I guess."

"So do I," Dr. Pitavy said, sighing.

"M. Rouquet?" Mme Chazeau asked.

René Rouquet looked up. He had been twirling his hat in his hands, thinking of other things. More important things.

"We were voting on the fee increase for cleaning the building's common areas," Mme Chazeau reminded him. "Everyone has approved it."

"Oh, okay, then," Rouquet said.

Mme Chazeau tapped her pen on the table.

"I approve," René said.

"Thank you," Mme Chazeau replied, taking notes. She had expected more of a fight from René Rouquet, who was notori-

The Mystery of the Lost Cézanne • 11

ously cheap. He usually paid more attention. "Second on the agenda—"

"The mysterious storage room," Dr. Pitavy interjected.

"Yes—"

"I'm willing to pay rent for its use," Dr. Pitavy went on. "It's right across the hall from my office. I have equipment I need to store, and paperwork that the tax man and medical fraternity insist we keep for ten years. If I don't have somewhere to put all of that I'll have to move my office. And, as you all know, it's quite nice having a quiet podiatrist downstairs, instead of a dentist, who's drilling, or—horror of horrors—a snack shop, frying meats . . ."

"Who *is* using the *débarras?*" Philomène Joubert asked. "One of my students, the one who's renting the smaller flat, asked if she could put her bicycle in it." Mme Joubert loved renting her two apartments on rue Boulegon to students— always female—and she treated them like family (especially the ones who went to Mass). She no longer had to list the apartments at the university; they passed down through friends, sisters, and cousins by word of mouth.

"The clothing store at 21 Boulegon," Dr. Pitavy answered.

Mme Chazeau sighed and set down her pen. It seemed that the podiatrist had taken over the meeting.

"They use it to store extra stock," Dr. Pitavy continued. "And they won't say who they're renting it from!"

"M. Rouquet," Mme Chazeau carefully said, looking at René. "Since the subject of the ground-floor storage room has never before been an issue, only today did I look at the deeds, and I discovered that it belongs to you. Would you be willing to rent it out to Dr. Pitavy?"

René Rouquet looked at her, surprised, and then glared at

Pierre. He grabbed his coat and got up, knocking over a chair in the process, mumbling as he opened the door. Eric and Françoise Legendre looked at Mme Chazeau, bewildered. Philomène Joubert took out her wool and needles and began knitting.

"Please don't leave, René," Mme Chazeau called after the ex-postman.

"I'll talk to him," Pierre Millot said, getting up and quickly putting on his coat. "René's just being—"

"René," replied Mme Chazeau, as she heard the front door open and close, its little bell ringing. She stood up and walked to the large window that overlooked the Cours Mirabeau. There was still a queue at Michaud's, and René and Pierre had stopped in the middle of the sidewalk. René was gesturing wildly and Pierre reached up to the old man's shoulders, only to have his hands brushed away. "Where were we?" Mme Chazeau asked as she turned back around to the now-smaller group.

Chapter Two

❧

Pierre's Request

You know you look foolish wearing a gold paper crown while driving a Porsche," Marine said, glancing over at her boyfriend.

"Really?" Verlaque asked, feigning surprise. "Do you mean to say that if I was driving a different vehicle, say, a newer-model Peugeot, or a battered pickup truck, I'd look better with the crown?"

Marine laughed out loud. "You had fun, didn't you?"

"I always have fun with the Pauliks," Verlaque answered. "And as much as I dislike the cake, I do get a kick out of the youngest person in the room sitting under the table, calling out names. It was always Sébastien who got to do it at our place."

"And it was always me at ours," Marine replied. Marine Bonnet, a law professor, was an only child, born to a family doctor and his theologian wife. She went on, "Léa was tickled pink you were served the slice with the bean."

"My loyal subject."

"I think she was more excited to see how ridiculous you'd look wearing the crown."

"You'll be sent to the tower for that remark."

Marine smiled and looked out of the car's window; even when it was dark out, they both insisted on taking the narrow, winding Route de Cézanne instead of the straighter Route Nationale. The Porsche's lights lit up the shimmering silver leaves of the olive trees as they passed. Every time she was on this road she thought of Aix's famous son Paul Cézanne, and how he would walk this road daily, his easel strapped to his back. He died on this road, too, caught in a sudden storm and contracting pneumonia, dying a few days later at the age of sixty-seven.

"It's amazing when Léa sings for us, isn't it?" Verlaque asked, smiling as he drove.

"Mmm," Marine said, frowning. "But I worry about the amount of time the music conservatory takes out of a young person's life."

"Didn't you see her face?"

"Yes," Marine slowly replied. "Of course she was happy singing. She had a captivated audience."

"So you think her happiness wasn't genuine?" Verlaque asked, glancing at Marine.

"She's the kind of little girl who'll do anything to please her elders."

Verlaque geared down to first gear and swung his 1961 Porsche around a hairpin turn. "How do you know?"

Marine tried to smile. "Because I was that kind of little girl."

"And look at you now."

"Exactly. Careful, there's a sleeping policeman coming up."

Verlaque slowed the car down to slowly pass over the speed bump. "Thank you," he said. He had been happy listening to Léa sing, and so he was frustrated that Marine was putting a black cloud over the evening. They entered the outskirts of Aix, and the olive orchards gave way to small houses and low-rise apartment blocks. This was Aix's quiet La Torse neighborhood, almost as expensive as the Route de Cézanne itself. Every time he met people from La Torse they bragged that they could walk downtown and yet were only a three-minute drive from the highway, *plus* they could park their cars right in front of their houses or apartments. He hated La Torse.

"Let's get back to Léa," Verlaque said. "Don't you think that Bruno and Hélène would stop her from all of the music lessons if they saw that she was suffering?"

Marine bit her bottom lip. "I don't know them well enough to say."

"But you claim to know their daughter."

"Oh just forget it, Antoine."

"What's bothering you? Why are you in such a gloomy mood? You've been acting weird lately."

"I'm okay," she said quietly.

Verlaque turned right onto *le périph*—the ring road that surrounded Aix's old town—and then quickly turned left and drove down the steep and narrow rue Emeric David, which almost dead-ended into the great white neoclassical Palais de Justice.

"You don't sound convinced," he said, glancing over at her again.

"I don't like sounding whiny," she anwsered. "I know that I should be happy: I have a good academic job that challenges me and that I enjoy—well, except for the numerous pointless meetings. My parents are both alive, and healthy. I bought my apartment before the new TGV station brought trainloads of Parisians to Aix, flooding our real estate market. And," she said, reaching over and rubbing Verlaque's shoulder, "I'm in love with a wonderful man. But tonight I have the blues, and I don't know why. I'm almost ashamed—"

"Are you mad at me?"

Marine sighed. "Honestly, Antoine." She almost added "not everything revolves around you," but she kept that thought to herself. Antoine wanted an explanation—words, and answers. But despite being surrounded by words and arguments all day at school, tonight Marine couldn't describe her feelings. She could only describe what she saw: the Pauliks in their three-hundred-year-old farmhouse, laughing about the leaking roof in the dining room; Léa singing, her brown eyes lighting up when she looked at Antoine; and Antoine, despite being one of the moodiest people she had ever met, laughing like he hadn't a care in the world. She didn't understand it, and she hated being emotional over something she couldn't explain. She had overheard Antoine, while washing the wineglasses with Hélène Paulik, tell Hélène of his parents in Paris. He'd said, "I think they pass each other in the hallway once a week." But he had said it in a light enough way—imitating his mother's permanent frown—that Hélène had laughed. It had taken a year of dating before Antoine had even told Marine his parents' names.

"The city is more beautiful at night," Marine said, looking out the passenger window. "At least in the winter. At night the buildings are more than just gold; they're luminous."

"Wow," Verlaque said. "What a way to change the subject." He slowed the car down to pass over another sleeping policeman on the rue d'Italie. "We're almost at your place, and you're not getting out until you tell me what's wrong." He turned right on the rue Fernand Dol and stopped in front of Marine's green door.

"Please don't tell me what to do, Antoine."

"What?" he asked, turning on his hazard lights. A Volkswagen Polo blaring loud, thumping music pulled up behind him. Verlaque winced and said, "Marine, I'm trying to understand how this conversation about a happy little girl turned into you admitting that *you're* not happy."

The Polo beeped its horn. Marine opened her door and quickly got out. Verlaque got out of his side and ran to her.

"It's late, Antoine," Marine said, fishing for her keys at the bottom of her purse. "We can talk about things tomorrow."

"What things?" he asked. "What's wrong?" The Polo beeped again and Verlaque swore and walked over to the car, motioning for the driver to roll down his window. "Hold your horses for two seconds," Verlaque said to the driver, a young man with diamond earrings and neck tattoos. The driver looked up at Verlaque and laughed.

"I spent a few hours this morning putting someone who looks just like you behind bars," Verlaque told him. "Twenty years."

The Polo driver shrugged, still smiling, and Verlaque heard a door thump closed. He swung around and saw that Marine had gone. "*Putain de merde!*" he shouted, resisting the temptation to bang his fist on the VW's roof. He walked back to his car and got in, putting it into first gear, and slowly drove away. The cigar club was to be at Jean-Marc and Pierre's apartment, not far away, on the rue Papassaudi. There was no point in going back to Marine's. He'd sleep across town at his place tonight, and tomorrow, when he had gone over every detail of the evening, he'd try to figure out what was wrong. Had he said something at the Pauliks' to anger Marine? Did he pay too much attention to Léa? It was true, he loved Fauré's hymns, and Léa sang them beautifully. Marine liked jazz, especially Brazilian, and so didn't take part in their classical-music conversations. Had she felt left out? Verlaque realized that he had also spoken a lot to Hélène, who, as a winemaker, did something that he had always secretly wished was his profession. Perhaps working with grapes would have been an easier *métier*, and possibly more rewarding, than prosecuting all the Kévin Malongos of Aix. He looked in his rearview mirror and saw that the Polo was no longer behind him.

Verlaque slowed down, spotting a parking spot up ahead; he didn't have time to drive to the other side of the old town, where, unlike the La Torse folks, he rented a parking spot. He drove slowly toward the rare empty spot, but just as he was about to signal to pull in, a Mini turned left from a cross street just in front of him. He slammed on the brakes and cursed. The Mini—a car he particularly hated, and this one had red and white racing stripes up its sides—pulled quickly into the spot.

"Son of a—" Verlaque exclaimed in English. He turned around to try to make eye contact with the driver but couldn't see him or her. He drove on, past the Collège Mignet, which had been Cézanne's and Zola's high school when they had still been friends and dreamed of changing the world. "*Salut, les gars*," he whispered to their ghosts. He was about to give up and head for his parking garage when he saw a spot, the last one before the road curved and the parking spots ended. He signaled and quickly pulled in, turning off the car and grabbing his travel cigar case out of the glove compartment. He locked the car and walked quickly up the rue Laroque, past the cinema, and alongside Michaud's, where he half expected to still see a lineup. The bakery was closed for the evening, but the smell of butter still permeated the street.

The Cours Mirabeau was quiet on a winter's evening, and despite his rush, Verlaque dipped his hand into the steaming La Moussue fountain, feeling the warm, thermal-fed water run through his fingers. He turned up the rue Clemenceau, which would eventually lead him to the cigar club. His fellow Aixois smiled as he passed. He found himself smiling back.

He buzzed at Jean-Marc and Pierre's building at number 19, and the heavy wooden door made a thudding noise, opening about an inch. He pushed against it and walked into the foyer, making sure the door closed well behind him; thefts in the old town were rampant. He skipped up the building's worn stone steps two at a time, past the architects' offices on the first floor, on up to the second floor that Jean-Marc and Pierre shared with their neighbor, a retired tax inspector who listened to his television too loudly—despite several pleas from the other tenants—and never seemed to leave.

The apartment door—still sporting a small Christmas wreath—was ajar and Verlaque walked in to a cloud of cigar smoke. He breathed in and said, "Good evening, my friends. What a lovely smell."

Jean-Marc Sauvat stared at Antoine Verlaque with an open mouth, and his partner, Pierre, began to laugh. Gaspard Baille, a law student and the club's youngest member, put his hand on his heart and knelt before the judge. The club's president, Fabrice, who owned a string of plumbing stores across southern France, was the first to speak. "*Mon roi,*" Fabrice said, bowing slightly and shaking some ash off his generously proportioned stomach. "We are your humble servants."

Antoine Verlaque immediately realized what had happened.

"So that's why people kept smiling at me," he said, reaching up to his head.

A flash from a cell phone temporarily blinded Verlaque, and he quickly removed his prize, folding the paper crown and putting it in his coat pocket.

"What's it worth to you for me *not* to send this photo to the newspapers?" asked Julien, slipping his iPhone back into his pocket.

Verlaque looked at Julien—a gregarious, *très gourmand* luxury-used-car salesman whom he would trust with his life—and laughed. "My firstborn?" Verlaque asked.

"Deal," replied Julien. "But I think your beautiful Dr. Bonnet might have issues with that promise."

The group laughed and Jean-Marc glanced nervously at his good friend the judge. Never had Antoine Verlaque mentioned marriage, or children, with Marine Bonnet, nor with anyone else for that matter.

"Did you eat dinner, Antoine?" Jean-Marc asked.

"Yes," Verlaque said, rubbing his stomach, which in turn reminded him of his New Year's resolution. "Thanks."

"Would you like a whiskey?" Jean-Marc then asked, taking his friend by the arm. "We have some very good Johnnie Walker."

Verlaque looked at Jean-Marc and was about to decline when the lawyer, who was also an old friend of Marine's, began to smile. "Just kidding," Jean-Marc said. "We have a bit of Ardbeg, if Julien and Fabrice haven't finished it yet."

"I hid the rest of it," Pierre said, appearing beside them.

"Good call," Verlaque said. He watched Pierre quickly put his arm through Jean-Marc's, but then draw it away. The couple had just moved in together and only very recently made their relationship public to the cigar club. "If you can sneak me some Ardbeg, that would be great," Verlaque whispered. "I was in court most of the morning, then spent the rest of my day having to eat galettes des rois."

Pierre looked at Jean-Marc.

"We're having more galettes tonight, aren't we?" Verlaque asked, following Jean-Marc and Pierre into the kitchen.

"Julien and Fabrice bought three at Michaud's," Jean-Marc said.

"For an insane amount of money," Pierre added.

"One's even decorated," Jean-Marc continued, his voice flat with sarcasm. "With a big cigar in brown icing. Julien and Fabrice charmed one of the salesgirls into asking the baker to add it."

Verlaque smiled at the thought of two overweight middle-aged men being able to charm a pretty young girl in her twenties. Jean-Marc opened a cupboard and reached his hand inside, pouring the hidden single malt into a crystal tumbler, then quickly closing the cupboard and handing Verlaque the glass.

"You can decline the galette," Pierre said.

Verlaque took a drink and smiled. "*Ah, la tourbe d'Islay.* I do like this heavy peaty taste," he said. "Thank you for managing to save me some." He sighed and leaned against the kitchen counter.

"Rough day?" Jean-Marc asked.

"It began terribly but was salvaged by hearing a ten-year-old sing Fauré, but then—" He closed his eyes and took another sip. "I'm not sure what happened after that. Something went wrong with Marine, but I have no idea what, or why. Do you two ever have those lapses of communication?"

"Never," Jean-Marc replied, while Pierre said, "All the time."

They laughed, and Verlaque added, "And I think I will decline on the dessert."

"What's this about dessert?" Julien asked, entering the kitchen. "When do we get our galettes?" He helped himself to a chocolate and Pierre slapped his hand.

"How can you still be hungry?" Pierre asked. "You had two helpings of Jean-Marc's daube."

"Don't worry, Julien," Jean-Marc said, flattered that his Provençal beef stew had gone over so well. "Antoine was just saying he might pass on dessert."

"What—?"

"Who's passing on galettes des rois?" Fabrice asked, forcing his way into the small kitchen.

"Antoine," Julien said, looking suspiciously at Verlaque's glass.

"Hey, guys!" Gaspard called out over the heads. Gaspard Baille was six foot four, almost a foot taller than Julien and Fabrice. "We want to start smoking the Hoyo de Monterrey. What are you all doing, gabbing in the kitchen like a bunch of old ladies?"

"*Merci, Gaspard!*" Jean-Marc hollered, ushering the men out with his hands. "I could use a little more room in the kitchen to load the dishwasher and start it running." Jean-Marc was never comfortable when he hosted a dinner party unless he had the kitchen cleaned and the dishwasher *en route*.

Pierre, knowing his boyfriend's quirks, followed the men out of the kitchen, taking Verlaque aside in the hallway. "When things have calmed down a bit, I have a favor to ask."

"No problem," Verlaque replied, trying to block out the noise of Julien and Fabrice squabbling over possession of an armchair. "Has your apartment sale gone through?"

"Yes, no hitches," Pierre said. "Cash buyer. My favor actually concerns the apartment. Well, not my apartment, but my neighbor's."

"The cranky old guy?"

Pierre laughed. "Yes, I quit the rue Boulegon for a more upscale street in Aix, only to end up with another cranky old guy as a neighbor."

"The well-off can be even more surly—"

"Antoine! Pierre! We're opening the cigar box!"

"*On arrive!*" Verlaque hollered back.

Verlaque walked into Jean-Marc and Pierre's small but elegant living room and saw Julien hovering over Fabrice—who had won the armchair fight—with his watch in his hands. "I'm timing Fabrice," Julien said, trying to pick at the small dial on his expensive Tag Heuer watch. His hands were too large, and Virginie, the club's sole female member, offered to help. Verlaque looked on, perplexed.

"Fabrice gets thirty minutes in the chair," Virginie explained, setting the watch's alarm with her slender fingers.

"Oh for heaven's sake," Verlaque replied, but he couldn't help laughing.

Gaspard passed around a small bundle of the evening's second cigar. Verlaque selected a bouncy, still-humid cigar, and took out his cutter. "There's no band," he remarked as he turned the dark brown torpedo-shaped cigar in his hand. He felt his cell phone vibrate in his jacket pocket and hoped that it was Marine.

"They're from our Cuba trip," Gaspard replied.

"*Bijou!*" Fabrice yelled.

"Jewel?" Verlaque asked, looking at Gaspard.

"That's my Cuban nickname," Gaspard earnestly explained. "We all get one, once we go to Cuba. You have to come on the next trip."

Julien added, "The welcome lady—a big, roly-poly Cuban— took one look at our handsome Gaspard and gave him that name on the spot."

"Bijou suits Gaspard perfectly. So what name did she give you two?" Verlaque asked, pointing to Julien and Fabrice.

Julien coughed and Fabrice changed the subject. "We bought these cigars at a private cigar roller's operation, in Centro Habana," Fabrice said.

Verlaque smiled at Fabrice's intentional use of the "b" in Havana.

Fabrice cut his cigar and began to light it. "It's a two-man show, in the back of this old hotel," he continued. "One guy rolls, the other guy, Emilio, is the patron. Brings you rum and coffee and sits down with you for a smoke. We bought tons. No cigar bands, either. Chic, eh?"

"There was a fashion designer who did that a few years ago," Virginie said. "Reverse marketing; hide the brand name. They just left four little white stitches of thread on the back of the dresses and shirts—"

"*Gracias*, Virginie," Fabrice said.

Virginie rolled her eyes. "Go ahead and tell everyone about this kid Alberto you met," she said.

Fabrice, the club's president, leaned forward. "We took two days and drove out to see the tobacco fields at Viñales," he said. "We had to show them to Bijou. And we stayed in this tiny village, in a bed-and-breakfast run by this nice old lady and her daughter."

"Neat as a pin," Julien said.

"You could have eaten off the floor," Fabrice added.

"And while we were having our mojitos on the terrace—" Julien continued.

"Naturally," Verlaque said.

"This Cuban kid, about twenty years old, comes over to us from the neighbor's patio and asks if he can speak French with us," Julien said. "And you should have heard his French."

"Parisian accent and everything," Fabrice cut in.

"Perfect slang, too," Gaspard added. "Like any law student here in Aix."

"Where did he learn it?" Jean-Marc asked. "I've heard the Cuban education is great—"

"Zero illiteracy in Cuba," Gaspard said.

"Bijou turned Commie on us over there," Julien explained.

Gaspard sighed. "There's just a lot that makes sense," he said, leaning back and puffing his cigar. "Free education up to the PhD level; zero illiteracy; free medical care."

"We have all that, too," Jean-Marc said.

"I'm not sure that France has one hundred percent literacy," Gaspard replied. "And I love the fact that they're not connected to cyberspace like we are—"

"Ha!" Julien snorted. "As if that's their choice!"

Gaspard tilted his head. "Well, I for one wouldn't miss not having Internet, or Facebook, or Twitter."

"I could handle no social media," Virginie said. "I wouldn't have to look at ten photos of my sister's kids everyday."

"This Alberto," Pierre said, refilling peoples' flutes with champagne, and trying to get back to the story. He hated political discussions at parties. And so far no one had remarked on his new flutes, bought at a consignment shop beside the Rotonde fountain. Each crystal glass was etched with a dragonfly—his favorite animal—and he was besotted with them. "So where did Alberto learn his French?"

"He fell in love with a French girl," Fabrice said.

"Classic!" Verlaque bellowed.

"She was studying music at the conservatory in Habana," Fabrice said. "Alberto explained that the best French music students often get sent to Cuba, whose conservatory is even more rigorous than ours."

"See," said Gaspard.

Verlaque thought of little Léa and tried to imagine her in Cuba in ten years' time.

"They're no longer together," Gaspard said. "But Alberto even visited her once. In Manosque!"

"Manosque!" Verlaque hollered again. Manosque was one of Provence's more authentic small towns, about an hour north of Aix.

Julien waved his hands in excitement. "Now this is the best part," he said. "So Alberto goes waxing on about Provence— how great the food and wine are, what a slow-paced life we have—"

"I don't," Jean-Marc said, who was a lawyer in a busy Aix firm.

"Yes you do," Pierre said. "Compared to lawyers in big cities."

"May I continue?" Julien asked.

"Sorry," Pierre whispered.

"So when Alberto excused himself to go to the bathroom, we three got our brilliant minds together—right, Bijou?"

"Yep," Gaspard said. "And we started scheming how we could get Alberto into France, to live."

"Get his working papers sussed, put up a collection for his plane tickets, etc.," Fabrice said.

"Great idea!" Virginie said. "I'm in!"

Fabrice held up his thick hand. "But it's not finished," he

said. "When Alberto came back from the john, we told him of our plan. And he was totally shocked."

"Of course," Pierre said. "Random acts of kindness—"

"No!" Fabrice said. "He didn't want to come!"

"He said that he could never leave Cuba," Julien added.

Gaspard sat back, smiling.

"Alberto said that he was a musician, and that his music was that of the island," Fabrice said. "Or something poetic to that effect. He said he loved France but would never want to live here. Can you imagine?"

"You never can tell what people are thinking," Julien said, puffing on his cigar. "It may be the opposite of what you've assumed, or what *you* would want."

"Nice philosophizing," Fabrice said, rolling his eyes.

Verlaque puffed on his cigar and thought of Marine. But the problem was, he couldn't even *guess* at what was wrong. He slipped his cell phone out of his pocket and looked at his message; it was from Sébastien, his real-estate-mogul younger brother. "So, Gaspard," he said, putting his phone away. "Now that you've seen some of the positive effects of Communism, are you going to do pro bono work when you finish law school? Community service, that sort of thing—"

"Are you kidding?" Gaspard asked.

Just then the alarm sounded on Julien's watch and he pulled at a reluctant Fabrice.

Verlaque took a sip of champagne and turned the flute around in his hand. "Nice glasses," he said.

Pierre leaned back, smoking, with his eyes closed. One thing that the Aix cigar club had taught Verlaque was that cigar lovers can come from all walks of life. He watched Pierre, who worked in a bookshop on the Cours Mirabeau, and probably made only slightly more than minimum wage, savor the last bit of his Hoyo de Monterrey.

"Ready to continue with your story?" Verlaque asked. "Now that everyone has left." Jean-Marc came in with three espressos on an antique tray, carefully setting it down on the coffee table.

"Yes, of course," Pierre said, sitting up.

"I didn't mean to disturb your last puffs," Verlaque said. "But I have to get to bed soon." He thought of walking home through the streets of Aix and trudging up the four flights of stairs to his apartment. However much he loved his apartment, with its view of Saint-Sauveur's spire and his small collection of paintings, he hated the thought of not sleeping next to Marine.

"*Oui, oui*," Pierre said, setting his cigar in an oversize pale-blue Havana Club ashtray. "Sorry, I had a long day that ended with a *réunion de copropriétaires*," he said.

"I loathe those meetings," Verlaque said.

"I'll say," Jean-Marc said. "Pierre came home in one awful mood."

Pierre gave Jean-Marc an angry look, which surprised Verlaque. Was everyone fighting today?

Pierre began, "So, my cranky neighbor, or now my ex-neighbor, is named René Rouquet. He came to the bookstore, asking for my help. I feel like I owe it to him to help, despite the fact that he was—"

"Cranky."

"Right."

"René helped Pierre buy his studio," Jean-Marc explained. "Almost fifteen years ago."

"Really?" Verlaque asked.

"Yes," Pierre answered. "He told me about a government scheme helping first-time buyers. I'm hopeless with money and never would have known about it if René hadn't told me. I inherited a couple thousand from my grandparents, and that was enough, with the government almost matching it, for the down payment."

"And of course prices in Aix were much less then," Verlaque added.

"Exactly," Pierre said. "Who would have thought I could sell a three-hundred-square-foot studio for so much money?"

"It *is* in the same building that Cézanne once lived in," Verlaque commented. "Just mention the famous painter's name and people's knees go weak, especially here, in his hometown. We all want a piece of Paul Cézanne."

Pierre shot Jean-Marc a look.

"How wise you are, Antoine," Jean-Marc said, sipping his coffee.

"What did I say?" Verlaque asked.

"Continue, Pierre," Jean-Marc said.

"René came into the bookstore yesterday," Pierre repeated. "More agitated than he usually is. He was going on and on about how sad it was that I moved away. It was very odd, as I used to be lucky to get a hello out of him. So, René finally manages to pull me away from a customer who was having way too much trouble deciding between the new John Grisham and the new John le Carré, and he asks if there's somewhere we can talk. But with good light."

"Bizarre," Verlaque said.

"It gets even better," Jean-Marc said. "Tell Antoine about René changing the locks."

"Yes, yes," Pierre said, waving his hands around in frustration. "I was trying to get to that."

"Sorry, Pierre," Jean-Marc said, getting up and taking the coffee tray into the kitchen.

Pierre shook his head back and forth, breathed in, and said, "René was as pale as a ghost and told me he wanted to have the locks on the front door changed."

"Was his apartment broken into?" Verlaque asked.

"No," Pierre answered. "I asked him that straightaway. But he seemed terrified and kept looking over his shoulder. So I led him into my boss's office and closed the door. It's only then that I noticed that René's carrying a plastic bag, gingerly, under his arm. Cradling it, actually. Then he asks me if I can lock the door."

Verlaque laughed but then noticed that Pierre's face was now also ashen.

Pierre went on, "I told him I couldn't lock the door so we'd have to take our chances, as by then I had guessed that he was going to show me what was in the plastic bag."

"Hence the good light," Verlaque offered.

"René sat down and then grabbed my arm so strongly it almost hurt," Pierre said. "And he said, 'You're one of the only people I can trust with this.'"

"Even though you rarely spoke," Verlaque suggested.

"Exactly. And then someone walked down the hall and René almost jumped into my arms."

"Wait, wait a minute," Verlaque stuttered, sitting forward and putting his index finger in the air. "You're not telling me that René was about to show you a Paul—"

"*Oui.*"

"I told you it was good!" Jean-Marc called from the kitchen.

*M*anon Solari lifted her black cotton skirt, trying not to get its hem wet, as she stepped past her mother cleaning their front stoop. "The bells haven't begun to ring yet, Maman," Manon said, giving her mother the *bise*. "You needn't rush." Manon hated to see Mme Solari, who would be turning sixty-five later in the year, working so hard. M. Solari, a stone-cutter, had died when he was fifty-seven, or fifty-eight; he had never been sure how old he was. His family had left Piedmont when he was a baby, and neither of his parents had ever learned to read or write in Italian, or French.

"The bells will ring soon enough," Mme Solari replied as she threw the last of the water out into the street. "And the police will be by any minute to check if we've washed. This is a task I'll never regret doing; you can't imagine how filthy the streets used to be, before you were born."

Manon glanced nervously toward the south. Mme Michaud would have her head if she wasn't in the shop by 8:15 a.m. And today was the 6th of January.

"The French are filthy," Mme Solari went on, now brushing water off their front step. She nodded to their neighbor, Mme Janot, who had just begun to wash down her front stoop as well. Manon winced, hoping that Mme Janot hadn't overheard her mother's assessment of French cleaning habits. Her mother, like her father, had come to Provence from Piedmont, as a young girl. "When I was your age the butchers would walk up and down these streets, carrying carcasses of pigs and lambs, trailing blood in their wake. Disgusting. Your father"—Mme Solari paused, making the sign of the cross—"always said that the law they passed in '50 was one of the few laws he ever agreed with."

As if on cue, the town hall clock began to chime. "There, you see," Mme Solari said, wiping her brow. "It's eight o'clock. You'll be late."

Manon smiled as she usually did when her mother warned her not to be late for work, and yet it was Mme Solari's chatter that caused Manon to have to almost run to Michaud's every morning. She said good-bye once more, promising to bring her mother back any bits of broken—unsellable—cake. How her mother had made it to such a ripe old age Manon had no idea, but one of her sisters—she had five—had joked that perhaps it was Mme Solari's sweet tooth.

Almost skipping down the rue des Guerriers, Manon looked up at the clear blue January sky. She was thankful to have been born in 1855, five years after the city fathers had ordered the citizens of Aix to stop throwing rubbish out of their windows. Her elder brother, Philippe, told her that almost anything could be found in the streets back then, especially near the tanneries. Even the nobles chucked garbage out of the windows of their grand mansions.

The Solaris were poor; Philippe, now a well-known sculptor, still had to sculpt in red clay. He couldn't afford marble. And so Manon knew she was lucky to work, even part-time, at Michaud's pâtisserie. Her sister Clara skinned rabbits to make hats; Catherine and Suzanne were *casseuses*: they each had four children so worked from home, cracking chestnuts that would be used in candy shops like Michaud's. Isabella had six children but made some money from tending her five mulberry trees that were used in silk farming. Maria—the lucky one, Mme Solari always said—was a nun.

Being the youngest of the seven Solari children, Manon had always been pampered. She was their red-haired baby. By the time she was ten, her parents were too tired to look after her, but it seemed that there had always been a sibling available to take her on walks. Their small house was at the north end of the rue des Guerriers, and from there it was a short walk, through the massive town gates, north along the rue Pasteur, out to the countryside. Collecting wild plants and flowers had been (and still was, when she managed it) Manon's favorite pastime. She couldn't wait for spring.

As she got closer to the place de l'Hôtel de Ville she could hear people chattering, horses braying, and water splashing from the square's fountain. The town hall was here, where her siblings had all been married by the mayor (except Maria, of course) before heading off to their church ceremonies. It was Manon's favorite spot in Aix, and if she had the money she would live here and not in the more fashionable Quartier Mazarin. She loved the colorful houses that surrounded the west side of the square—colors she knew, although she had never been outside of Aix, came from Italian buildings: ochre, red, orange, and yellow.

Manon smiled, remembering Philippe chattering on and on about the square's sculptures, most of them carved by Chastel. She walked up to the fountain and looked at a frowning, bearded stone man, spouting water from his mouth. Philippe was inspired by Chastel and used to run his fingers along the sculpture's wrinkled forehead whenever they passed by. "To think that Chastel was ruined by the revolution!" Philippe had cried to his younger sister. "He died in a poorhouse in 1793."

Manon, then eight, looked up at her big brother. "Did they kill him?"

"Not as such, no," he replied, looking up at Chastel's masterpiece above the Halles aux Grains and taking his sister's small hand in his. "They killed his clients."

Manon, now no longer a child but a woman of thirty, looked up at the grain hall and at Chastel's massive sculpture representing the Durance (a woman) and the Rhône (a man). She loved how the woman's leg dangled out over the pediment, like the Durance bursting its banks as it often did in spring. But Manon thought her too mannish—too muscular. She had tried to appreciate sculpture, and despite the fact that Philippe had studied sculpture in Paris and that her father had been *marrié à la pierre*, it was just not her preferred art. She loved color, and painting. Philippe had taken her, many times, to the Musée Granet to look at the paintings; he knew the museum's keeper from his days as an art student, and they never had to pay the entry fee. But now, with working and looking after her mother, Manon rarely had the time to go. And if she had to choose between the museum and the countryside, she would choose the latter.

Manon hummed as she picked up speed and continued walking toward the Cours; her father had refused to call Aix's grand main street by its new name—Mirabeau—and so she did, too. "It will always be the Cours à Carrosses for me," he used to say, as if the avenue's personality had been changed with the new name. Manon grinned, thinking of her father banging their aged wooden kitchen table with his massive fist, a fist that she would always remember being covered in a fine dusting of limestone powder.

When she was five years old, gaslights replaced the town's olive oil lights, and M. Solari railed against that, too. Manon imagined that her father had these opinions because it made him feel more Aixois and less an immigrant. As Philippe regularly reminded her, feeling like a real Aixois wasn't an easy thing. Even Philippe's friend Émile, now a famous writer living in Paris, and who had spent part of his youth in Aix, said he felt like an outcast in Aix because of his Parisian accent and an outcast in Paris because of his new Provençal twang. When Manon's fiancé, Jean-Auguste, died, M. Zola had come down from Paris and bought her not flowers, even though she loved them, but instead a book of the wild flowers of Provence. She would never forget that act of kindness. Manon secretly thought that the writer's lisp might have had more to do with his being ostracized as a young boy rather than with his accent, but of course she didn't say anything. And she liked his lisp, for she too had a blemish: a scarred face, the gift of a bout of measles.

After Jean-Auguste's death, Manon made a decision to

avoid courters—not that there were many in Aix—and stay at home to take care of her parents. She hadn't been looking forward to marriage—it was something she just sort of fell into; before she knew it, after having gone on a dozen or so walks with Jean-Auguste, they were engaged and everyone was celebrating. Jean-Auguste had been a nice man, a stonecutter like her father, and she felt awful that he had died so young. But she didn't miss him.

Whether it was grand or an imposter, as her father had called it—a street for those who just wanted to be seen—the Cours wasn't yet paved, even though her humble street in the Bourg Saint Sauveur was. Manon hated having to walk across the Cours, dodging who knows what, including horses and handcarts, to get to Michaud's at number 8. She sighed when she saw the queue and felt bad that she hadn't made an effort to come to the shop earlier than usual, even though she always started at 8:15. When she opened the door and squeezed by the crowd, she heard Mme Michaud's voice booming from the front counter, and she remembered why she hadn't come earlier: she wouldn't have been thanked, or paid. Mme Michaud's fat daughter Amandine was at her side, trying to disguise the fact that she had something sweet in her mouth and was slowly trying to chew. To give her credit, it had been Amandine who suggested that the shop bake the Parisian-style of galettes des rois, made from almond paste with a buttery, flaky pastry, as opposed to the Provençal version of a ring of brioche covered in *fruits confits*. The almond-paste cakes had become the better seller, and when Manon had told Philippe (who couldn't afford to eat either cake, unless his friends Émile or Paul bought one for him), he said that it was probably due more to fashion than taste. The Aixois always wanted to be Parisian.

Manon went into the back room and washed her hands in the basin and checked her hair—which she tied up in a bun for working at Michaud's—in a small cracked, cloudy mirror. "It's nice to see you, Manon," said Suzette, her best friend, who had just rushed in and squeezed Manon's hand.

"Suzette!" Mme Michaud cried from the front room. "Please hurry up with those boxes!"

Manon and Suzette exchanged looks; both, despite the fact that they were each among the eldest of the salesgirls, were terrified of Mme Michaud, who had the power, and capability, to fire anyone at a moment's notice. Both of Suzette's parents were dead, and she struggled to support her two younger brothers. Manon quickly tied her apron behind her back and walked out into the main room, taking her spot behind the glass-fronted counter, beside Amandine. Amandine, now with a different bonbon pressing against her left cheek, leaned into Manon and whispered, "What is the date today?"

Manon stood her ground and replied, "*La Fête des Rois. Le 6 janvier.*"

"Exactly," Amandine hissed. "You should have been here early."

"I'm paid to come in at 8:15, every day," Manon replied. "Hello, good sir," she continued, smiling at a customer and turning away from Amandine.

The customer asked for a traditional brioche-style galette, and she took the one he had pointed to and set it in a red box, tying it closed with Michaud's precious gold ribbon. They had been taught to use the silk ribbon sparingly; Manon sometimes gathered small pieces off the floor and slipped them into her pocket. She used those bits to give to her nieces, for their hair, or she sometimes used them to decorate homemade gifts she made for her mother and sisters. Once, she even found a long piece, discarded, on the paving stones outside the shop. That one she kept in her pocket all the time.

Carefully writing the price, 1.5 francs, on a slip of paper that would be turned over and reused, she gave it to the customer to take to the elaborately carved wooden front desk where Mme Michaud rang in the sales. Manon was grateful that she could read and write; Philippe and Émile had taught her. It had also been Philippe who bought her a black dress to wear to her interview with Mme Michaud; black cotton, along with a white smock that the pâtisserie provided, was the uniform. Suzette had borrowed a dress from an aunt and had worn it every day for almost a year until she had earned enough money to buy her own.

By 9:00 a.m. the bell attached to Michaud's front door rang incessantly. "Why don't they hang that bloody bell up, today of all days?" Suzette whispered in Manon's ear as she rushed by carrying three boxes of galettes for La Baronne de Montille.

"Because it reminds Madame of how much money she will make today," replied Clara, a fellow salesgirl, who had overheard.

Manon looked worriedly at Amandine, who was serving a well-known judge's wife. Amandine hadn't seemed to have heard. Manon would remind Clara on break—if they managed to get one today—not to speak so loudly. Manon didn't like the way the other girls gossiped or made fun of Mme Michaud, as hadn't her husband died of a heart attack, just as Manon's father had? Money didn't make grieving any easier.

Manon busied herself with wrapping two galettes and snuck a look at the judge's wife. The staff at Michaud's took pride in the fact that many women came to select and buy their own cakes instead of sending the maids to do so. Shopping at Michaud's was a pleasurable outing, one that the staff strived to uphold. The judge's wife was tall—rare in Provence—and she smiled naturally at Amandine. Her face was freckled, and her green eyes shone. She seemed to see that Manon was looking at her and she bowed slightly, and smiled even more. Flustered, Manon quickly wrapped ribbons around the boxes and wrote the prices down, handing them to her customer: Mme Frédéric, the very demanding priests' housekeeper at Saint Jean de Malte.

The bell rang again and Manon heard Clara groan.

"Your customer, Clara," Suzette said. "I'm busy with La Baronne de Montille's order for her ball next week."

"But I got here at seven o'clock," Clara said, rubbing the small of her back.

"Go and ask Mme Michaud for a break," Manon whispered. "I'll take the next customer."

"But Amandine will write it down in her little notebook," Clara complained.

"Don't worry about Amandine's notebooks. She's probably just writing down the sales figures," Manon said. "You go."

Clara thanked her and Manon looked up and saw a short man with receding hair and a thick beard. He wore a red cotton sash—a *taiolo*—around his waist, marking him as a true Provençaux, and carried a beaten leather satchel. "I'll have a galette des rois, please," he said. Before Manon could speak, he went on, "A brioche one. I have no time for those Parisian almond paste fancies."

Manon nodded. "Right away, sir."

"You're Philippe's kid sister, aren't you?" he asked.

Manon blushed to hear herself referred to as a kid. "Yes, I'm Manon."

"Give him my regards. I'm Paul. I've painted a few times with your brother."

Manon smiled. "You're also a friend of M. Zola's," she said, carefully placing his brioche in a box.

The client nodded then put his hand up. "Save the fancy box for someone else," he said. "Just put my cake in some paper."

"*Oui*, Monsieur—"

"Cézanne."

Chapter Four

❧

A Short Story, a Photograph,
and a Painting

Antoine Verlaque set his pen down and looked at what he had just written. Months ago he had begun writing short stories, a few paragraphs at a time. No one knew. He wrote in English; it wasn't his mother tongue, but he was bilingual and had been inspired after reading an essay about Samuel Beckett, who wrote his plays not in his native tongue but in French. The reason surprised, and delighted, the judge: Beckett claimed that writing in French gave his prose a roughness, an imperfection, which he liked. It suited his plays.

It was late and Verlaque knew he should be in bed. He looked at the framed photo on his desk: a black and white of Marine and him. Marine's best friend, Sylvie, had taken it while the three of them vacationed together on the Île Sordou. When Sylvie had thrust her small Leica into their faces, Verlaque had assumed she was using color film; it was summer and they were on a Mediterranean island—blues and greens abounded. But it had stormed the night before and the sky was—rare for summer—cloudy, and the sea choppy, and so Sylvie, who made a comfortable living as an art photographer, had wisely chosen black and white. The tops of their heads were cut off, which only made the portrait more intense; the viewer's gaze, instead of focused on their hair, or the background, was instead forced to examine Marine's and Verlaque's faces. They were both smiling, and laughing. As a child Antoine Verlaque had rarely smiled in photos, much to the chagrin of his beloved grandmother Emmeline. He now knew why he hadn't smiled in those photographs: to show his parents that he was not happy. M. and Mme Verlaque had failed to give their two sons the love and affection they so desperately needed. Whether they had noticed their son's expressionless face in family photos he didn't know. But Emmeline and Charles, his paternal grandparents, certainly had.

He stared at Marine's face in the photo and tried to read it. Was she unhappy? She was laughing, but then Marine always laughed around Sylvie. When they began dating, Sylvie's presence had been a thorn in Verlaque's side; he was jealous of the deep relationship and easiness the two women shared. It took him a year or more to realize that Marine needed Sylvie's craziness to balance her own calm, at times overly considerate, selflessness. Verlaque grew to appreciate—even love—Sylvie when he realized that they were alike: both bossy, and opinionated, and in some weird way both vying for Marine's love and attention. That week on Sordou taught him that Sylvie was not a threat; Marine was in fact stronger than the two of them, and it took both Sylvie Grassi and Antoine Verlaque to balance Marine Bonnet's steadfast and honest character.

He got up and closed the cover of his notebook and turned off the desk lamp. Tomorrow would be a new day, and he'd do anything to make things right again with Marine. She'd love, too, the story of old René and his supposed Cézanne painting. Verlaque walked into the bathroom to change and remembered that Marine's father, Dr. Anatole Bonnet, was somewhat of a Cézanne aficionado. Perhaps he would invite Marine and her parents over for dinner.

He began to unbutton his shirt as he stared at Pierre Soulages's large black textured painting; each time he did this he saw something new in it. Tonight, the artist's thick brushstrokes, reaching across the immense canvas vertically and then crisscrossing horizontally, reminded Verlaque of the bare branches of Provence's plane trees in winter. He stopped unbuttoning as he heard a ringing coming from the kitchen. Running down the hall, he grabbed his cell phone on the fourth and last ring.

"*Oui*," he said, buttoning his shirt back up as he balanced the phone between his cheek and shoulder. For some reason he knew that he would not be going straight to bed but would be heading out the door. He had hoped the caller was Marine.

"I'm so sorry, Antoine," Pierre whispered.

"What's wrong, Pierre?"

"I'm not sure. I didn't want to wake Jean-Marc—"

"And so you woke me."

Pierre took a breath and quickly continued, "Well, Jean-Marc has to be in court at eight tomorrow morning, and you had mentioned that you were taking the morning off."

"True," Verlaque answered. "And I was kidding about waking me. So what's wrong? You sound anxious."

"Just before going to bed I noticed that my cell phone was

blinking," Pierre explained. "I hadn't heard it ring during the club meeting. The message was from René—"

"The painting guy—"

"Right. He was frightened and whispering quickly into the phone. He was sure that he was followed down the rue Boulegon, and that someone was outside the hall, listening to him as he spoke."

"That's unsettling," Verlaque replied. "He didn't seem to be the kind of man to exaggerate or be paranoid."

"Exactly. I just tried calling him, and there's no answer. That's why I'm heading out the door. I've got to check on him. And I was wondering—"

"If I'd come with you," Verlaque said as he picked up his apartment keys off the kitchen counter and pulled his coat down from the coatrack.

"Twenty-three rue Boulegon," Pierre answered quickly. "Thanks!"

Verlaque ran down the four stories of winding red-tiled stairs as quickly as he could. He knew that he would reach the rue Boulegon before Pierre, and he hoped that Pierre still had a key for the street door. He also hoped, as he turned left onto the rue Campra, that René Rouquet had fallen asleep and could not hear his telephone.

It was almost 1:00 a.m. and Verlaque imagined—as he usually did when he walked late at night—that much of downtown Aix hadn't physically changed since Cézanne's time. The streetlights were now electric and the shop signs no longer painted *à la main*, but the buildings were the same, as were the narrow streets. People now slept, as they would have at 1:00 a.m. in the nineteenth century. Who had slept in his apartment? How many families had lived there before he bought the large seventeenth-century flat? When he took possession it was made up of four or five small, high-ceilinged rooms; Verlaque's architect had removed as many of the walls as permitted to make a large one-bedroom loft. What would those former tenants make of his stainless steel dishwasher? Or his glass-walled bathroom?

As he turned left onto Boulegon he heard footsteps running behind him. Pierre came up beside him and leaned over, gasping, with his hands on his knees.

"How did you get here so quickly?"

"I ran," Pierre said, coughing.

"You have the front door keys, I hope."

Pierre patted his back pocket. "I accidently kept them."

"Let's go, then," Verlaque said as they walked by the shuttered shops.

"I'm so worried," Pierre said, still out of breath.

"He'll be fine," Verlaque replied. "Is he a drinker?"

"Binge drinker," Pierre said. "Doesn't drink for weeks and then ties one on at the Bar Zola. Why do you ask?"

"Because he may have had a few drinks to calm his nerves and now is sound asleep."

Pierre mumbled something in acknowledgment.

Rue Boulegon was no longer a posh street that housed an eccentric artist, as it had been at the turn of the century; it was now a street of kebab stands, shops selling inexpensive clothing and jewelry from India and Africa, and other miscellaneous businesses whose owners couldn't afford the rent elsewhere.

"I've always liked Boulegon," Pierre said. "I miss it."

"I know what you mean," Verlaque answered, sensing that his friend, out of nervousness, wanted to talk of something neutral. "Every town should have a street like this, although I fear its time is running out."

Pierre was about to lament the increasing rents and globalization of Aix's shops but instead pulled the key out of his pocket that would let them into number 23. The urgency of René's message sounded once again in his head and he fumbled trying to open the door that he had passed through daily for years. He pushed the key in and turned for a third time; the heavy wood door finally opened and they entered the hallway. It had always smelled of dust to Pierre, and it did so this evening, but mixed with something odd, like wet woods.

Verlaque motioned for Pierre to leave the hall lights off. There was enough street light coming in through the transom window above the front door, and Verlaque pulled out his new cell phone and used its flashlight. Quickly they made their way up the stairs—much narrower than in Verlaque's more noble building—stopping when they reached René's door.

"Light," whispered Pierre, pointing to the strip of light shining under the front door. "And I can hear someone in there."

Verlaque held his finger to his lips. He held up his cell phone and made a dialing motion for Pierre to try René's phone.

Pierre pulled out his cell phone and called the old man's home phone. Within seconds they could hear the telephone ring. The shuffling noise in the apartment stopped.

Verlalque motioned toward the door, signaling what both men knew: there was an intruder in the apartment; otherwise René would have answered the phone. Verlaque thought that with luck the door might still be unlocked if the intruder hadn't thought to lock it behind them. He put his hand on the ancient brass doorknob and slowly turned. The door opened.

Before the judge could stop his friend, Pierre, panicked, ran in and called out to his former neighbor. "Pierre!" Verlaque called out. "Don't!"

The door across the hall to Pierre's former apartment opened, and a young man in pajamas rubbed his eyes and asked, "What's going on?"

"Police," Verlaque said. "Go back inside." He heard the man mumble something to a woman named Françoise as he quickly closed the door.

Verlaque looked back at René Rouquet's living room. An old man—he assumed Rouquet—was lying on the floor, near the fireplace. Verlaque saw blood on the threadbare carpet and noticed that the fireplace was made from Mont Sainte Victoire's orange-colored marble. Pierre was kneeling down, with his index and middle fingers on Rouquet's neck, immediately remembering the Red Cross lessons he had taken as a teen. Verlaque stood in the doorway and called an ambulance.

Pierre now smelled the woodsy scent that had permeated the entryway. It was cologne. He slowly turned around and stared, transfixed. Verlaque looked up from his cell phone and now saw the fourth person in the room, standing against a window.

"Please don't hurt me," the intruder said, in English.

Pierre looked quickly at his friend Antoine Verlaque.

"I didn't do it," the intruder said, pointing to René's body.

Verlaque held up his hands palms out and walked slowly toward her. She was one of the most beautiful women he had ever seen. Several inches taller than both he and Pierre, the slender black woman had the height, flawless skin, and high cheekbones of a runway model. Her eyes were almond-shaped and the color of honey, and she kept her hair in a large afro. She wore no jewelry, but she didn't need any. Her coat was a multicolored vintage Missoni that barked good taste, money, and bravado.

She slowly backed toward the kitchen, which both men could see was in a state of chaos, its cupboards and drawers open with contents spilling out.

"I speak English," Verlaque said. "My name is Antoine Verlaque; I'm the examining magistrate in Aix. This is my friend Pierre Millot—."

"He was like that when I came in," she interrupted, stuttering and pointing to the body. "The door was ajar and I walked right in."

"Who are you and what are you doing in René Rouquet's apartment?" Pierre cried out.

The Beauty—as Verlaque would later call her—stepped forward and held out a trembling hand. Antoine Verlaque reciprocated and shook her hand.

"You still haven't told us what you're doing here," Verlaque said.

"My name is Rebecca Schultz," she replied, switching to an almost-perfect French. "I teach art history at Yale University."

Chapter Five

The Neighbors Make Tea

René Rouquet's apartment, for the first time since he bought the flat in 1963, was full of people. Eric and Françoise Legendre had quickly dressed and were now passing around mismatched mugs of tea. The police arrived soon after the ambulance and began to mark off the apartment as a crime scene.

Dr. Agnès Cohen leaned over Rouquet's body, her hands on her hips.

"I thought Bouvet would have come at this late hour," Verlaque said to the coroner, who was slightly younger than himself, wore expensive bright-blue glasses, and wore her thick, prematurely white hair short and tidy.

Cohen smiled. "He has seniority," she replied. "I get the late-night calls." She glanced over at Rebecca Schultz, who was sitting in a corner, sipping tea, and staring at the wall. "Quite a suspect," the doctor whispered.

Verlaque shrugged, not wanting to respond. "How was M. Rouquet killed?"

Dr. Cohen kneeled down. "Head injury."

Verlaque looked at the marble fireplace, as did Dr. Cohen, who then said, "I'd say he hit the corner of the fireplace on his way down."

"So he was pushed," Verlaque said. "Or drunk?"

Cohen shook her head back and forth. "You have to be pushed with a lot of force to die from a fall like this," she said. "But he's old, and by the looks of it in poor health, which doesn't help."

"Time?" Verlaque asked.

She sat down on the floor, drew her knees up against her chest, and looked more closely. It seemed to Verlaque an odd position, more like she was at the beach than beside a dead body, but it *was* the middle of the night. "Very recent," she said. "No more than two or three hours ago."

"Thank you," he said. He reached out a hand to help the doctor up.

"I'll let you know if I can be more specific once I examine the body at the morgue," she said.

"Thank you," he said.

"You already said that," Dr. Cohen said, putting on her coat. "But I appreciate it. Bouvet never says thank you."

Verlaque walked over to Pierre, who was sitting on a wobbly wooden barstool, said good night, and told him to try to sleep. Pierre slowly slid off the stool, walked to the door, opened it, and, taking one last look at his former neighbor, walked out. Verlaque pulled a chair over to Rebecca Schultz's side. "If you answer all of my questions, you'll be able to go back to your hotel tonight and not sit in jail," he said.

Dr. Schultz did not hide her surprise. "You can't think I did *that*," she said, gesturing with her head toward the body.

"Then perhaps you should tell me what you were doing in an old man's apartment after midnight. And we'll speak in English, if you don't mind." He wanted to hear her side of the story in her native tongue. He immediately thought of Beckett.

"My French is fine."

"I know."

She sighed. "I'm an authority on Cézanne's works," she began. "And I've spent the past five years researching his life."

"His life?" Verlaque asked. "And not his work? You're an art historian."

"I'm interested in both, naturally," she replied. "But I've been commissioned to write his biography. Biographies are hot right now. They sell much better than art history books."

Verlaque smiled slightly, as he was a lover of biographies. "And so you know that twenty-three rue Boulegon was the artist's last residence."

She nodded and sipped some tea. "I booked into my hotel, on the rue Cardinale, at around five p.m. I showered, then walked around Aix, following those bronze Cs embedded into Aix's sidewalks. There are quite a few missing, by the way."

"They get stolen."

Rebecca Schultz sighed again. "Incredible."

"And you didn't come to Boulegon straightaway?" Verlaque asked. "Given that Cézanne died here."

"I was saving it for last," she replied. "Like the best candies, when you're a kid. Do you understand?"

Veralaque nodded.

She went on, "After strolling through Aix, I stopped for a Moroccan dinner on the rue Van Loo. It was just before eight p.m."

"Van Loo?" Verlaque asked. "That's off the beaten track,

isn't it?" He knew the restaurant and it wasn't one tourists could easily find, or would choose.

"Cézanne was married in the church on Sextius," she answered. "I wanted to go in, but it was locked, no doubt due to theft." She looked at Verlaque as if he were to blame for his countrymen's faults. "And then I spotted what looked like a very quaint North African restaurant. Small interior, handwritten menu, with beautiful Moroccan pottery on the tables. I've been in Aix enough times to know that it's hard to find a good restaurant here."

"Would the restaurant staff remember you?"

"Yes, certainly."

Verlaque stayed silent, waiting for her to explain why. They might remember her for her exotic beauty alone, which she was no doubt aware of.

"They'd remember, because the restaurant was run by a couple, and we spoke in some detail of the food, especially the desserts. There was one—I can't remember its name—made from dates. The woman—she was the one who cooked—was in the middle of making another batch in their tiny kitchen and led me back there to show me."

"What time did you leave?"

"I left just after nine p.m., then walked back to the hotel and collapsed on the bed. But I awoke around midnight—the people next door had just come back and were banging around in their room—and so I got dressed and went out for a walk. I naturally came up to Boulegon, as if my feet were leading me here. I knew that I should be seeing it in the daylight, but I couldn't stay away."

"Did you ring downstairs?" he asked.

Dr. Schultz raised her eyebrows. "No, of course not. I was

leaning against a shop opposite, staring up at the building, trying to imagine Cézanne's life on this street, in these rooms. I was about to go back to the hotel when I saw him."

"The deceased?"

"No. A guy—he was short and bald—running out of the building, carrying something, a painting, or a mirror, in his arms, wrapped up in a throw." Verlaque thought that the features "short" and "bald" described half the men in his cigar club. Schultz then pointed to the wall she had been staring at earlier. The dusty outline of a painting remained above the sofa. "I would imagine he was carrying the painting that had been hanging there."

"That sounds like a good guess," Verlaque said, looking at the bare spot. "But M. Rouquet wouldn't have had an expensive painting on his wall. He was a retired postman. Why would a thief steal some cheap painting owned by an old man living off his meager pension?"

"Do you know for sure that it was a cheap painting?" Dr. Schultz asked. "I've seen some strange art collectors in my day."

Verlaque gestured around the room. "Look around you," he said.

"Still—"

"You haven't told me why you came into the apartment."

"Curiosity. And because I had just witnessed a theft. I speak French—I come to France often—and I love this town, so I thought I might be able to help in some way."

Verlaque made a mental note to have Alain Flamant, one of his sergeants, check the dates of Dr. Schultz's previous trips to France.

"So you came in the apartment and didn't call the police or an ambulance when you saw M. Rouquet lying there."

"I was about to," she answered. "I didn't have my American cell phone with me, and it took me some time to find his home phone." She paused, and then said, "It was when the phone rang, just before you came in, that I was able to find it, buried under a heap of newspapers." She pointed across the room and Verlaque saw a small 1960s rattan table, indeed covered in newspapers, with the phone's black cord falling out and disappearing along the baseboards. Verlaque looked at the Beauty and knew that she could have been rehearsing her speech while he had been busy with the police and Dr. Cohen. The art historian, from where she had been sitting, sipping tea, would have had time to look around the living room and spot the table with its phone buried underneath the papers.

"That was us calling," Verlaque finally said. "From just outside the door. But my friend Pierre said he tried, too, before we came, and there was no answer."

"It must have been before I came in," she replied. "And I doubt the bald thug would have picked up the phone."

"And the apartment was in this state when you arrived," he suggested.

"Of course," she replied. "What would I want in an old man's apartment?"

"Perhaps you, too, were here to steal," Verlaque said. "Even in an old man's apartment. As you said, there are some strange art collectors."

Chapter Six

Paul

A s he walked into town he thought of how different his life would have been if he had followed his first dream of being a poet. Physically it would have been easier, no doubt; poets don't have to walk across the countryside, with an easel and paints strapped to their backs. They need only carry a quill and an empty book, and can work indoors, almost anywhere. The last time he saw Zola in Paris it was clear that his old friend didn't walk as much as he used to. Writers sit. And think.

He couldn't help walking. He loved it; it took him places where nature's shapes showed him what to put on the canvas. How could he get to the Trois Sautets bridge without walking? Or the Bibémus quarries? He would never paint in town, as some of his Parisian friends did. Buildings could be present in the scene, but only in their relation to the surrounding natural forms. They would never be the focus. The last time he was in Paris, Monet had showed him a series of canvases of the same scene in Bordighera, a fine house by the sea, painted at different times of day. He knew he had been rude when he had asked Claude how he managed to stay awake and not fall over from boredom when setting up his easel before the same building, day after day. He now sighed loudly, remembering with shame their argument, and Claude's gentle words in the face of his own loud and heavily accented ones.

He picked up his step, knowing that the sooner he made it to the druggist in the Hôtel du Poët, the longer he'd have to paint. He had that in common with Claude, and Auguste, and Camille, and even the intense Dutchman he had briefly met: the need to paint was relentless. If one was thinking of a scene, or planning out a composition in one's head, it was almost impossible to think of anything else. That's why he had offered to fetch his father's medicine—the usual boy who ran errands was off with his own family as his sister was ill—and at least while walking he could think over his next composition, with that bridge in Gardanne the focus. His father—now near death—had finally accepted his son's determination to be a painter. But he hadn't accepted Paul's relationship with Hortense; even after the birth of their son, Paul Jr., Hortense and Paul Jr.—now thirteen—were living in Marseille, in an apartment he rented for them, while he stayed at his father's house. He would paint Paul again, soon, but didn't want to see Hortense as yet. Every time they were together they argued. She missed her native Jura and its mountains, and her family, and although she would sit to be painted, she asked no questions of his work.

The sight of the Rotonde's new fountain did not make the painter happy. He thought it ostentatious. What was happening to his little town? Would the same thing happen one day to Gardanne? He couldn't imagine not seeing old Bauvé leading his sheep across Gardanne's Place Gambetta. Or the fields of beets, or olive trees. And the stacks of hay, so wonderful to paint.

He walked around a team of street sweepers who were taking a break, leaning on their brooms, and then a knife sharpener, yelling up his prices to a maid who was leaning out of an upper-story window. A woman's "bonjour" took Cézanne out of his reverie. He attempted a smile and returned her "bonjour" with a wave of the hand. He recognized her, as he did most Aixois; she was a judge's wife, who evidently did not think him mad for walking up the Cours with his collapsible easel and box of paints strapped to his back. Other women laughed, and children pointed. But he was used to that.

He walked by the Café Oriental, then the Deux Garçons. Both cafés made him miss Zola, who would be soon publishing yet another book, its subject a secret. He passed number 55, where he had lived as a young boy, the family crammed into an apartment above his father's hat shop. Before his father had reinvented his life as a banker. Before they were rich.

Finally he reached the top of the Cours where the druggist, a man who not only was aware of modern medicine and science but also knew much about Provençal herbal remedies, kept a shop in the Hôtel du Poët. The Cézanne family had been coming to M. Alphéron for decades. The bells chimed as he opened the door and walked in.

"*Mon cher Paul*," M. Alphéron said as he walked around the carved walnut counter and embraced the painter. His new assistant, a shy boy who had just finished his *license* in chemistry, turned slightly away. M. Alphéron was sixty-three, and here he was embracing a man who looked to be in his forties, or even older, who carried his paints on his back. This man, Paul, did not dress as one would have thought of a Cézanne, the owners of a bank and a beautiful house on the outskirts of town called the Jas de Bouffan.

"How is your father?" M. Alphéron asked, keeping his hand on Paul's back.

"He suffers," Paul said. "But, thankfully, in silence."

M. Alphéron smiled. He knew how difficult Cézanne Senior could be. Demanding, impatient, opinionated. "I have bad news," M. Alphéron went on. "I've mixed the first batch of medicine for your father. But the rest will have to wait until the end of the day; my shipment of morphine has been delayed."

"Just my luck!" Cézanne exclaimed. "I had planned on going to Gardanne to paint!"

"I'm sorry, Paul. Had we decided to extend the train lines to pass through Aix, as they did in Avignon—"

Cézanne raised his thick hand in protest. "I've heard enough of that. We were right to protect our town from the coming industrialization. Have you been to Paris lately? Trains and smoke everywhere! The whole city is black from coal soot."

"I've never been to Paris, Paul," M. Alphéron said, smiling.

Cézanne went on talking as if he hadn't heard. "And L'Estaque, where I painted in peace for years . . . now look at it! It may as well be a *quartier* of Marseille! Factories and chimneys are cropping up along the shore—"

"Ah, that I'm truly sorry to hear. The last time I visited your parents at the Jas, they showed me three of your L'Estaque paintings. All wonderful."

The assistant tried not to make noise as he dusted and rearranged the heavy ceramic jars that lined the shelves of M. Alphéron's pharmacy. He had been to L'Estaque twice and only saw a few fishing boats, some fishermen's shacks, and the sea. What in the world could one paint there? And as for Paris, he dreamed of going. He thought about it day and night.

"Ah," Cézanne said, grunting. He was thankful for the compliment but found it so hard to say so. "Well, there's nothing to be done. I'll be back later in the day."

"Why don't you walk north of Aix today?" M. Alphéron suggested. "Up past my house the garrigue is still bright and green, despite the cold weather. And the sky is blue."

Cézanne didn't like the suggestion of where to paint, or what to paint. He had been thinking of the bridge in Gardanne all the previous night. But if he had to be back at the pharmacy in the late afternoon, he didn't have much choice. *"Merci, mon ami,"* he replied, shaking M. Alphéron's hand. "I'll take your advice." He would walk north of Aix; it was a part of town he was less familiar with, but there were fine views of the mountain from the hills, and, as the druggist had observed, the sky was blue.

Although the family desperately needed money, Manon was thankful not to have to work today. She had packed a lunch— some dried bread, a slice of the wild boar sausage that one of her brothers-in-law had cured and given to Manon and Mme Solari, and two dried figs. She would head up north of Aix and walk until she tired. She had, along with her lunch in a cloth bag, her book of Provençal wild flowers that Émile Zola had given her. It was winter, but all year long some plants bloomed in her beloved countryside. She wished that her love of plants could give her work; she so desperately wanted a passion as Philippe had with his sculpting. Even her sister Isabella was obsessed with tending her mulberry trees.

Manon had spent more time at home that morning than she had wanted to; her mother needed her help making ravioli. Her sister Clara had come, too, to help, and Manon had overheard them whispering about her. What would become of Manon? Would she ever marry? Why did she not weep for Jean-Auguste?

She walked quickly uphill and out of town. She knew every fine house, and every small one, by heart. Her brother, Philippe, always told her that she had one foot in nature and one foot in town. He was the only one who didn't tease her when she tripped over her own feet as she gazed around and counted the cypress trees in front of each house, or noticed that the family at number 9 had painted their shutters a brighter blue. When she was younger she had worried that her curiosity of the natural and man-made world might make her mad. But the more she read—Philippe still took her to the public library in the Hôtel de Ville—she noticed that the poets and writers and artists she read about were concerned with the same things. So she stopped worrying. Besides, she was thirty years old now, and as Clara had pointed out to Mme Solari in a not-so-quiet whisper, Manon was "over the hill" and would never marry. So she was free. Free to go on walks, to examine flowers, to run her fingers over Aix's sculptures whenever she pleased. And if people thought she was mad, it didn't matter, because she was too old for any young man to care. And what Isabella told her about passing the age of twenty-five was true. "You'll see," Isabella had said, leaning over toward her youngest sister during one of their noisy family dinners. "No one looks at you after twenty-five. You become invisible."

Before she knew it, Manon was in the middle of the countryside, walking through a row of vines, looking up at the sky and Mont Sainte Victoire in the distance. She waved to the vineyard's owner, whom she often saw. He waved back and went on pruning. She smelled smoke and saw that he was burning vine branches in a neat pile at the end of one of the rows. She walked on, then, so as not to smell the smoke while she ate. She quickly walked through a small forest; she didn't like forests, even in the hot summer. They oppressed her, and there was no view. Only in the fall and early winter, when she looked for mushrooms with Philippe and her brothers-in-law, did she enjoy them. When she stepped through the forest, she stopped and squinted, putting her hand up to her forehead to see better, and then she saw him, only two meters away, painting furiously.

He turned quickly around and was about to complain when he saw Philippe's youngest sister.

"Monsieur Cézanne. I'm sorry to disturb you," Manon quickly said, turning to go.

"Perhaps I'm the one disturbing you," Cézanne replied.

Manon tried to smile but she was almost too nervous to reply. Here was Paul Cézanne, who had shown his pictures in Paris. And the Cézanne family was infamous; the father had begun his career selling hats and then had bought a bankrupt bank. Philippe told her that the Cézannes, despite their new wealth, would never be accepted by the Aixois nobility, but Manon was still in awe. And Paul Cézanne was almost as gruff as his father.

"I'm only out walking, M. Cézanne."

"But Mlle Solari, you walk with a book," Cézanne said, gesturing to her hand with his paintbrush.

Manon looked down at her wild flower guide; she had taken it out when walking through the vines to identify a small blue flower that grew in the rocky red soil. She was about to reply when she looked ahead and saw the view, and was mesmerized by it: Mont Sainte Victoire shimmered, surrounded by a clear bright-blue sky. A peasant's *cabanon*—built in rough stone, a red-tile roof, and perfectly proportioned—sat proudly in a field in the distance. But what so impressed her was the giant umbrella pine in the middle of the foreground. It was as majestic as the mountain itself.

"I can see why you're painting this," she said, almost in a whisper.

He stepped back from the canvas and Manon saw this as a cue that she could look at his painting. Philippe had described his friend's art to her, paintings that she knew only a few people liked. At first she saw only patches of color, but as she studied it more she saw the mountain, in gray and white and even pink shades, and the cabanon, and the sky that was nothing if not blue. "Monsieur, you don't sketch with charcoal first," she said, still staring at the painting.

"No," Cézanne replied. "I never have. I'm too impatient to get the shapes down."

"Before they disappear," Manon said.

Cézanne looked at her, perplexed. She spoke like someone who had studied art, like Claude's wife in Paris, not at all like a young Provençal woman who worked in a bakery. And certainly not like Hortense. But Manon Solari looked every bit a Provençale, from her layered skirts, the outer one in cotton with blue and white stripes, to her woolen cape and clogs. "*Ah, oui*," he finally said. With his hand he gestured around the vista before them. "Before all of this disappears."

Chapter Seven

❧

Cézanne's Apples and Pears

I f the apartment had once belonged to Paul Cézanne, today there was no sign of the painter. The high ceilings still had their carved moldings in place, and, thankfully, Bruno Paulik thought, the floor was still paved in hexagonally shaped tiles—*tomettes*—but someone with cheap and bad taste had outfitted the rest of the apartment. Each room was lined in a different wallpaper, usually a leaf pattern, except for the bedroom, whose walls had the bamboo effect popular in the seventies.

Paulik walked out of the bedroom, a mess like the rest of the apartment, and looked up to the living room ceiling where he imagined a small elegant chandelier may have once hung. In its place was a five-armed stainless steel light fixture whose lightbulbs were housed in yellow plastic globes. The commissioner of police liked old things—preferably from the seventeenth and eighteenth centuries—and although Paulik knew that 1950s and '60s design was all the rage in Paris, he knew that the stuff in this apartment would never make it into the galleries on the rue Bonaparte. But the apartment had good bones, and in a weekend he and his wife, Hélène, could turn an apartment like this into a showstopper: strip the wallpaper and paint the walls white, for now (Hélène, against his wishes, had just painted their dining room a "Wedgwood blue," and he loved it); buy used light fixtures off the Internet; and rummage around the architectural remnant shops on the Route de Célony that sold antique doorknobs, interior shutters, and nineteenth-century plumbing fixtures. He almost laughed out loud thinking of how different his life would have been had he not become a policeman but instead an interior designer.

"Come in, Pierre," Paulik's boss, Antoine Verlaque, said to a fair-haired, thin, and well-dressed man standing in the entryway.

"I hope I can be of some help," Pierre Millot said, stepping into the living room. Verlaque introduced the commissioner to his bookseller friend. "Up until a few months ago Pierre lived in the apartment next door," Verlaque explained. "And that apartment has the same floor plan as this one. Pierre was one of the last people to speak to René Rouquet. Have the officers questioned the other tenants?"

"Yes," Paulik answered. "We got their names and occupations from Mme Chazeau at L'Agence de la Ville, who runs their *syndicat*. That young couple next door didn't hear anything until you and Pierre arrived last night. They admitted that they had drunk a bottle of wine with dinner and were heavy sleepers. They heard you only because the husband had gotten up to go to the bathroom. There is a large apartment below, owned by an absentee owner who lives in Brussels. Below that are two small flats, both rented by students. The one student was visiting her parents in Nice this weekend, and the other was out clubbing until four a.m. They're owned by"—Paulik flipped through a small notebook—"Mme Philomène Joubert. She lives on the rue—"

"Cardinale," Verlaque said. "She sings in the choir at Saint Jean de Malte with Marine's mother. And the ground-floor flats?"

"A podiatrist has offices to the left of the front door," Paulik said.

"Dr. Pitavy," Pierre replied.

"And to the right of the door?" Verlaque asked.

"It's a big storage room," Paulik said. "Mme Chazeau told me that the clothing shop uses it for their extra stock. René Rouquet owned it."

Verlaque said, "Lucky him to have a débarras." Every inch of available space in downtown Aix was rented out. He had once almost made an offer on an apartment until he was told by the owners that the hundred-square-foot storage room in the basement wasn't part of the deal, unless he wanted to pay 60,000 euros for it.

"Pierre," Verlaque said, "does Mme Chazeau hold meetings of the apartment owners' association?"

"Um, yeah, she does," Pierre said.

Verlaque made a mental note to phone her; she was also the mother of a good friend who had just moved to Paris. "Right. We're looking for a rolled-up, or flat, painting of a woman. Pierre told me about it last night, after our cigar club."

"I thought that Yale professor saw a guy run out the door with it?" Paulik asked.

"She claims that he ran out carrying what looked like a framed painting," Verlaque answered. "Pierre saw the painting that Rouquet was so worried about, and it wasn't framed."

"If she was telling the truth," Paulik said. "Where is she now?"

"At her hotel," Verlaque said. "I've instructed her not to leave the country until we've told her that she may." Verlaque had walked Rebecca Schultz back to her hotel the previous evening, although two other policemen had also eagerly offered.

"Judging by the state of the apartment," Verlaque said, "the thief began looking for the painting, before pulling one off of the wall."

"Or the professor did," Paulik suggested.

Verlaque ignored the remark and went on. "Pierre, do you remember what hung there, in that bald spot above the sofa?"

Pierre rubbed his chin and then said, "Yes, I think so. It was an oil of Mont Sainte Victoire. A contemporary one—René won it during a Christmas lottery organized by the city. It wasn't bad; painted by a Dutch woman who lives in Provence part-time. She has some talent, but still—"

"Could a thief have mistaken it for the real thing?"

Pierre laughed. Neither Paulik or Verlaque said anything, and so Pierre finally said, "I suppose so. I guess some thieves wouldn't know the difference."

"Not ones around here," Verlaque said.

"Why take the painting off the wall and then still tear the apartment apart?" Paulik asked. "The thief—or murderer—would have seen the Mont Sainte Victoire painting right away. Another thing to ask Dr.—"

"Schultz. Rebecca Schultz."

"You should see her," Pierre said.

"That's neither here nor there," Verlaque said.

"Oh yeah?" Paulik asked, looking at Pierre.

"She's an African American beauty," Pierre said. "She looks like a runway model who's all of a sudden decided to be a pop singer. Very striking."

"Bruno listens only to opera," Verlaque said, smiling. "Okay, where do we start looking?" he asked, handing cotton gloves to the other men.

"Under the bed?" Pierre asked. "Behind the armoire? Sorry, I've never done this before and I'm trying to think of the obvious places."

"Safe-deposit box in a bank?" Paulik suggested.

"No," Pierre said. "René hated banks."

"Where did Rouquet find the painting?" Paulik asked.

Verlaque looked at Pierre, who replied, "He didn't tell me, and I didn't think to ask."

"It's very odd that Rouquet lived here for almost fifty years and came across it only now." Verlaque looked around the living room, at the clay floor and the baseboards, trying to see any loose tiles or boards. But the police had been through the apartment early that morning and hadn't reported anything odd.

"I thought the same thing," Pierre said. "But it's happened before, no? People finding Renoirs in their attics, Monets in the cellar."

"It could be a fake, too," Verlaque said. "Even painted by Rouquet. Did he paint?"

Pierre shrugged. "Not that I know of, but I didn't know him all that well."

"If he painted," Paulik said, "at least here, we'll find signs. Paint droppings and such."

"We'll each take a room, being careful not to disturb anything," Verlaque said. "The painting may be rolled up, or lying flat. It's not very big, right, Pierre?"

"Right," Pierre said. He held his hands about a foot apart.

Paulik walked over to a large bookcase, whose shelves sagged under their weight, and went immediately to the Z section.

"Émile Zola," Verlaque said. "Cézanne's best friend. Good thinking."

Paulik reached his hand in behind the Zola novels. Nothing. "They did having a falling out," he mumbled as he reached in behind the rest of the books. "Nothing here."

Verlaque walked into the kitchen and opened the cupboards. He and Marine had just watched the film *Good Bye Lenin!* and he remembered a poignant scene when the sister finds long-lost letters that had been slipped in behind the cupboard's cheap backboard. In fact, René Rouquet's cupboards were just as cheap looking as the Communist-era ones in the film. He carefully ran his gloved hand along each backboard, not finding any openings. He then opened the oven, the washing machine—Rouquet hadn't owned a dishwasher—and the fridge and freezer. Nothing. He could hear Paulik in the living room and Pierre in the bedroom.

"Is there a cellar in the building, Pierre?" Verlaque called out.

"No," Pierre called back. "I mean, yes there is one, but it's condemned. The water table is too high in this part of Aix."

"I'm not finding anything," Paulik said.

"Me neither," Pierre called from the bedroom. "I just tried the hatbox. You know, Cézanne's father—"

"Began with a hat shop," Verlaque answered. "Good try. Let's think about that for a minute," he went on. "I mean think about Cézanne clues. Bruno, what's the first thing that comes into your head when I say Paul Cézanne?"

"Mont Sainte Victoire. I see it every day and never tire of it."

Pierre suggested, "It may have been taped to the back of the Dutch woman's Victoire . . ."

"Maybe," Verlaque said. "Although that seems too obvious a place. Pierre, what's the first thing that pops into your head when I say Paul Cézanne?"

"Aix-en-Provence."

Verlaque looked around the kitchen. On the wall next to the fridge was a large firefighters' calendar, sold door to door just before Christmas to raise money for Aix's fire brigade. Verlaque quickly walked over to it and took it off the wall. "Nothing," he said, gently turning the pages.

"Nothing in the living room, either," Paulik said. "Someone else had cut open the underside of the sofa cushions for us. Again, it seems odd that the thief would have done that, given he left with the mountain painting."

"If that's the one he left with," Verlaque said.

"It was there last time I saw René, which was only a few days ago—Tuesday to be exact," Pierre said. "I came to hand over my last co-owners' check for the building maintenance."

"And if Professor Schultz is also looking for the portrait?" Paulik asked. "She could be the one who ransacked the apartment."

Verlaque nodded. He had thought the same thing when he found Rebecca Schultz in the apartment. But now—

"And you?" Pierre asked.

"I beg your pardon?" Verlaque asked, caught off guard.

"When I say Paul Cézanne, what do you think of?"

"Apples and pears."

"His still lifes," Paulik suggested.

"Exactly."

The men continued to search the apartment. After twenty minutes Verlaque walked over to the living room windows and looked out on to the busy rue Boulegon. "Pierre," he said, "who's that young guy across the street looking up at us?"

Pierre joined the judge at the window and looked down. "Oh, that's Momo. Mohammed's harmless. I told him this morning about René, and he's devastated."

"Look what he sells," Verlaque said.

Paulik walked over and looked out at Momo's shop. "It's a fruit stand."

Verlaque looked at Pierre. "Apples and pears."

"Momo is simple," Pierre said, touching the side of his head with his index finger. "Born that way. His uncle owns the shop. René was very kind to Momo."

"Trustworthy?"

"Completely," Pierre said.

Chapter Eight

❧

Dr. Anatole Bonnet Lends a Hand, and Eye

*L*et me do the talking," Pierre said as he locked the door to René Rouquet's apartment.

"Do we look like thugs or something?" Verlaque asked, winking at Paulik.

"More like cops," Pierre said, dropping the keys.

"Hurry up, Pierre!" Verlaque yelled.

The neighbor's door opened and the young man who had made them tea the previous evening asked if everything was alright.

"*Oui, oui, merci*," Verlaque said. "Sorry about the noise."

"It's all right," Eric Legendre said, rubbing his eyes. "I was just trying to catch up on lost sleep." He closed the door and the three made their way quickly down the stairs.

"Too bad that guy didn't hear people coming and going last night," Paulik commented as they were crossing rue Boulegon.

Verlaque nodded in agreement but then saw Momo. "There he is," he whispered to Pierre, giving him a gentle push between the shoulder blades.

Mohammed Dati was thirty-one years old but still looked like he was in his teens, partly due to his bright, shining eyes and rosy cheeks and partly due to his constant chatter and inquisitiveness. But the news of René's death had saddened him, and today Momo looked almost his age. Verlaque, Pierre, and Paulik watched as Momo helped an elderly man select fruit, carefully setting each piece on the store's balance. He took a large Pink Lady apple and slowly walked across the store, putting it back with the others, picking a smaller one. "The smaller apples are better, no?" Momo asked.

"Absolutely," the man said. "I can't eat a big apple anymore. Thank you, Momo."

Momo finished weighing the fruit. "That's 4.83 euros," he said.

The man opened a worn leather change purse and peered inside, moving the coins around with his crooked fingers. He turned it toward Momo, who took the purse and counted out the money. "Is everything all right today, Momo?" the man asked as he took his change purse back and picked up his woven market bag.

"I'm sad today," Momo answered. He began moving the clementines around, making it clear that he didn't want to speak.

"I'm sorry to hear that," the old man said. "Tomorrow I'll be back, and I bet you'll be better by then. *Au revoir.*"

"*Au revoir.*"

"Mohammed," Pierre quietly said as he approached the store's wooden counter. "Is your uncle here? Could we go in the back and talk? It's important."

"I don't feel like talking."

"I know that you're sad," Pierre said. "I am, too. But could you please ask your uncle to watch the shop while we talk in the back? Then when we're through I'll go buy you the new *Paris Match*. It just came out."

"Are there pictures?" Momo asked.

"Tons."

"I'll go and get my uncle."

"What was that all about?" Verlaque whispered once Momo had gone.

"You'll see," Pierre answered. "It's Momo's obsession."

Momo's uncle came out and gestured toward the back of the shop. If he did not look worried or even curious why three men, two of them strangers, would want to speak to his nephew, it was because he had just had a phone call from the owner of the building saying they were going to increase his rent by 40 percent.

"Momo," Pierre said to the young man as they stood among piles of empty crates. "These are my friends Bruno and Antoine. Bruno and Antoine are looking for the person who . . . hurt . . . René. We think that person may have been looking for something in his apartment. Did René give you something to take care of?"

Momo shook his head back and forth, biting his upper lip.

"Momo," Pierre pleaded, "it's really important that you tell us the truth."

Verlaque, looking around the room, said, "Momo. You sure have a lot of pictures of soccer players."

Momo nodded again.

Verlaque looked at the photographs, and flags, and posters, red and gold being the prominent colors. They were all of Manchester United.

"My grandmother was English," Verlaque said.

Momo's eyes lit up. "Where was she from?" he asked.

"London."

Momo's shoulders fell, and Verlaque quickly added, "But I go to England often and can bring you back more photographs of the team."

Momo waved his hands back and forth in the air. "With Wayne Rooney?"

"Of course." He looked at Momo's blue apron, identical to the one his uncle wore. "I'll bet they even have aprons with Rooney's photograph on them."

"Wow!" Pierre said. "Can you imagine?"

"Do you promise?" Momo asked.

"Yes," Verlaque said. He'd get on the Internet as soon as he got home and order one. There'd be no need to even go to London for it.

Momo then turned and bent down, opening the bottom drawer in his uncle's vintage metal desk. He stood up and handed Pierre a plastic bag.

Still wearing his cotton gloves, Verlaque flattened down the canvas as best he could. Pierre and Paulik pressed down on the other corners in their gloved hands and the three men looked at it in silence.

"You'll thank Momo again for us?" Verlaque asked, looking over at Pierre.

"Yes, I'll take him some comic books," Pierre said. "Although for a few seconds back there I thought that Momo wouldn't give us the painting. But his face gave everything away; I knew he had it."

"He was protecting it," Verlaque said. "It was very touching."

"Here we are talking as if it's a real Cézanne," Paulik said, looking down at the painting.

"It has to be," Pierre said. "At least it looks like one to me."

Verlaque looked at his friend with a raised eyebrow.

"Doesn't it to you?" Pierre asked. "Those blotches of color—"

"Blotches?"

"You know what I mean," Pierre said.

"Is it Mme Cézanne?" Paulik asked.

"It doesn't look like her," Verlaque said. "But he did paint his wife a lot. There, I'm talking about it as if I think it's the real thing, too."

"Who could identify the painting?" Paulik asked. "Other than Dr. Schultz, who's a murder suspect. Do we take it to Paris?"

"Let's start here, in Aix. We don't want to embarrass ourselves at the Musée d'Orsay cradling an obvious fake. Marine's father can help us," Verlaque offered.

"Dr. Bonnet?" Pierre asked. "Aix's favorite general practitioner knows a lot about Cézanne?"

"Yes, an incredible amount," Verlaque replied. "He's self-taught, but his knowledge is impressive all the same."

Paulik said, "The policemen who came early this morning to finish dusting found a name and phone number jotted down on a piece of paper. Edmund Lydgate—he's a retired Sotheby's auctioneer with a vacation house in the Luberon."

"You're kidding," Verlaque said. "Why didn't we find that last night?"

"That's a good question, and I gave the team a piece of my mind for missing it."

"Had René contacted him?"

"We tried calling his number but there was no answer," Paulik said. "Officer Schoelcher was going to keep trying."

Pierre looked at his watch. "I have to get back to the bookstore. Saturday is still, thankfully, a busy day for booksellers."

Verlaque said, *"Oui, bien sûr. Salut, Pierre."*

"À demain," Pierre said as he headed toward the door. He stopped and then asked, "If it's a real Cézanne, do you realize what it's worth?"

"Hundreds of millions," Verlaque said. "While drinking my coffee this morning I had a quick look on the Internet."

"I did the same," Paulik said. *"The Card Players* sold for $250 million."

"Who in the world—?" Pierre asked.

"The royal family of Qatar," Verlaque answered.

Anatole Bonnet had just been finishing lunch with his wife of forty-two years, Florence, when the phone rang. For a man of his age he was in good shape, as was Florence—they both biked to work and hiked on the weekends—so he was quick to get up and answer.

"Encore à table, Papa?" Marine asked, pacing back and forth in her own kitchen in downtown Aix.

"Just finished our yoghurts."

Marine smiled, glad she didn't have to eat with her parents—at least their food. The yoghurt would have been a supermarket brand, with zero fat, and lots of sickly fruit added to it. Her parents' weekly food budget was probably what she and Antoine spent in two days, something she felt no guilt about. Eating was something the Bonnet family did for fuel, not for pleasure, as Antoine, and even Sylvie, had taught her. Years ago Marine had shared office space, and frequently lunches, with a visiting law researcher from Seattle. While they explored Aix's restaurants, Susan described her childhood meals, which had consisted of their family of five racing through bland dinners. Marine had nodded in agreement. "What?" Susan had asked, staring in disbelief. "Your family ate like that, too? I thought it was an American thing."

"Nope," Marine had replied, stealing one of Susan's handcut french fries. "Lots of French families ate like that in the seventies. Our mothers were post–World War II babies and didn't learn to cook; they were out in the workforce, celebrating their independence from the farmhouse kitchen."

"As if a career can't go hand in hand with cooking decent food."

"And eating it."

"*Chérie?*" her father asked.

"Sorry, Papa," Marine answered. "I—well, Antoine and myself—have a favor to ask. It has something to do with a case he's working on—"

"Murder? Need a doc's opinion?"

"I'll fill you in later," Marine said. "But I can tell you it has something to do with Cézanne. That's why Antoine needs you to come to the Palais de Justice."

"I'm intrigued."

"I thought you would be. Can you meet us there in an hour? At three p.m.?"

"Does Antoine need a theologian, too?" her father asked.

"No, but thank you," Marine answered. Florence Bonnet and Antoine Verlaque weren't the best of friends, but Marine found it touching that her father would want her mother to come along. The Bonnets were inseparable.

Marine said good-bye and hung up the phone, thinking of her quick conversation a half hour earlier with Verlaque. He had immediately said that he was with Bruno Paulik, a hint that he couldn't speak intimately to Marine, but he did say, "I've been wanting to talk to you," before telling her about a supposed Cézanne portrait that he and Bruno were taking back to Verlaque's office. He had also suggested that she come for dinner that evening, promising to light a fire in his fireplace and cook his winter specialty, *choucroute*, which he picked up from an Alsatian deli around the corner from his apartment. She had agreed, intrigued by the Cézanne story and caught off guard by the call; but she was looking forward to the meal. Sauerkraut, sausage, and boiled red potatoes—accompanied by one of the stellar Rieslings that Antoine had in his cellar—were one of her big loves. She had become, despite her upbringing, *une gourmande*. "I'm also a pushover," Marine mumbled to herself as she made herself a coffee. She realized that she had overreacted on Friday evening, but she still had things she wanted to discuss with Antoine. It was time.

"Well, one thing I'm sure about," Anatole Bonnet said, looking down at the portrait and rubbing his chin, "it's not Hortense, Mme Cézanne."

"Is it even a Cézanne?" Verlaque asked, pacing back and forth in his office.

"I'd need to look at it longer, and have my books next to me," Dr. Bonnet said. "But I think so, yes."

"I have chicken skin," Paulik said, rubbing his muscular forearms. He adjusted the wool scarf that was twisted around his neck.

"It's not that cold in here," Verlaque said.

"Speak for yourself," Paulik replied. "The heat works every other day in this building."

"I'm freezing," Marine agreed. "Mme Cézanne always frowned, didn't she, Papa?"

"Almost without exception," Dr. Bonnet replied. "And this doesn't look like her. Mme Cézanne had straight brown hair—always tied back—a long, fine nose; a small mouth; and almond-shaped eyes. Hands clasped, like this." Dr. Bonnet nervously folded his hands together and Marine smiled, charmed by her father. His hands had more age spots than she remembered.

"There's a portrait of Mme Cézanne at the d'Orsay where she looks like she's ready to kill her husband," Dr. Bonnet said. "And it was painted the year of their marriage—1886. That always struck me as odd."

Marine felt Verlaque staring at her. She looked down at the portrait and said, "This woman, whoever she is, is radiant."

"Yes, she's having a good time," Verlaque said. "Which means that the painter was having a good time, too, *non*?"

"One would think that the two are related, yes," Dr. Bonnet answered.

"What makes you think that it's a real Cézanne?" Paulik asked.

"The colors, for one," Dr. Bonnet said. "It's full of color, even her face."

Marine bent down, getting as close to the canvas as possible without touching it. She said, "There are all kinds of color in her face: pink, of course, but look at those bits of green and blue. Even yellow." She pointed, her finger hovering about an inch above the canvas. "Yellow in her eyebrows, and at the tip of her mouth."

"Cézanne called them 'sensations of color,'" Anatole Bonnet said, "like planes of color falling on top of each other. It happens in the backgrounds, too; they were just as important to him as the face. Cézanne—I mean, the painter of this canvas—has given just as much attention to the green wall behind the sitter as he does her face. That's a Cézanne quality."

"You can see those Cézanne geometric forms here, too," Verlaque said, pointing to the canvas. "The ruffled collar of her dress is just a series of cylinders."

"*Exactement*," Marine's father replied. "But this has something else—"

"What?" Marine and Verlaque asked in unison.

"Personality," Dr. Bonnet replied. "Because Antoine's right—Cézanne was more interested in shape and color than in the sitter. But this young woman's personality shines through."

The foursome stood in silence, staring at the red-haired woman, who sat upright, laughing at the painter. She had full lips and large blue eyes, wore a simple blue blouse and skirt, and in her hands she played with a thin yellow ribbon. The chair was a wood-backed one of the sort still popular in Provence, and the wall was green with no paintings or other adornments.

"And Cézanne usually didn't reveal the sitter's personality?" Paulik asked.

"No," Dr. Bonnet replied. "He didn't. He never hired female models, either. Even his *Bathers* series he took from nude studies from the Académie Suisse in Paris, where he had studied as a young man. He was notoriously shy, especially around women."

"Hence all the portraits of Hortense," Marine suggested.

"Yes, he was married to Hortense, so there must have been an easiness between them, or a familiarity at least."

"Was it usual for him to sign his paintings?" Verlaque asked, pointing to the *P. Cézanne* written on the painting's right-hand bottom corner.

"No," Dr. Bonnet said. "He rarely signed, as he was frequently unhappy with his results. And he rarely dated his works, but this one is clearly dated, '85."

"As if he wanted to remember the date," Marine said. "Like dating the back of a photograph."

Anatole Bonnet mumbled to himself, took a clean handkerchief out of his pocket, and blew his nose. "His last portraits, painted in 1905 and '06, just before his death, were of his gardener, old Vallier," he said, folding up his hankie. "Those had more intimacy than the earlier portraits, at least for me, because you see in the old man's face the painter's own fear of dying, of growing old."

Marine looked at her father and tried to see if he felt the same fear. She had never spoken to her parents about growing old, probably because they never sat still.

"It's the gardener's aged, wrinkled hands that reveal Cézanne's old age," he went on. "And in those paintings the paint is layered on, very thickly, like in this portrait."

"It's very Rembrandtesque," Marine said.

"A very apt comparison," Dr. Bonnet said, smiling. "The paintings of Vallier are very moving, like Rembrandt's late self-portraits. But this one is joyous. And if we are to believe the date, it was painted a good twenty years before the Vallier portraits."

"So it's not in his later style?" Verlaque asked.

"Not at all," Dr. Bonnet answered. "But there's another mystery here, which is now giving me doubts as to the painting's authenticity."

This time Verlaque, Paulik, and Marine all blurted out, "What?"

"It's just that Cézanne rarely painted women," Anatole Bonnet said. "Especially young, pretty women. I can think of a portrait of a very old woman—she was probably a maid at the rue Boulegon—and the Mme Cézanne portraits, of course. And then maybe one or two others. But that's it. It would have been very out of character for Cézanne to do a painting such as this one. He's smitten."

Chapter Nine

❧

I Should Like to Astonish Paris with an Apple

*B*runo Paulik tore his brioche in two and took a bite. "You know what I don't understand?" he asked, still chewing. "Why are art experts always so intent on attaching dates and styles to a painting? 'This is his late style,' or, 'This is the blue period'—that kind of thing. How do they know? What if Cézanne just felt like slathering on the paint that day in 1885? It was a Tuesday, a sunny April day, and he *felt like* trying something new? What if, for once, he was in a jolly mood and just *felt like* having the sitter smile and laugh?"

"Or the sitter was so comfortable with him that she laughed naturally?" Verlaque said, looking over at the red-haired woman.

Paulik dipped a corner of his brioche into his coffee and Verlaque tried not to wince. Verlaque said, "But I think— although I get what you're saying—that an artist as serious as Cézanne didn't change his style on an April morning just for the fun of it. It was too risky; it took him so long to get there. Remember all those salon refusals, the bad reviews, the mocking—even in Aix?"

"Especially here in Aix."

"Right," Verlaque said, sipping his coffee.

Paulik chewed. "Yeah, I get it. I guess he wouldn't have had the interest, or the time, to start fooling around with another technique."

"By 1885 he had finally found his gift. He wouldn't take that lightly. But—"

"Who knows?"

"Right—"

"He was human," Paulik said, holding his arms out. "We change from day to day. We get giddy, or we're in a bad mood."

"Yes." Verlaque put his cup down and stared over at the painting.

Their musings were interrupted by a knock on the door. "Come in," Verlaque said.

Jules Schoelcher, a young policeman originally from Alsace, walked in and greeted his superiors with a stiff but sincere "Good afternoon." Seeing Paulik's half-eaten brioche, he added, "Bon appétit, sir."

"*C'est mon goûter*," Paulik replied. "It's five p.m., afternoon snack time all over the world."

"Any news on the Boulegon case?" Verlaque asked.

"The fingerprints we've found in the apartment are René Rouquet's, and a few of Dr. Schultz's. No others," Jules said.

"So the man she saw was wearing gloves," Verlaque said.

"Or she was lying," Paulik suggested.

"And I got ahold of Edmund Lydgate," Schoelcher said.

"The retired auctioneer?" Verlaque asked.

"Yes," Schoelcher replied. "René Rouquet did call him, but Lydgate claims he could hardly make sense of what Rouquet was saying. They hung up not having managed to make a rendezvous. Officer Flamant checked Lydgate's alibi; an old farmer named Elzéard Bois lives on the main road says he spoke with Lydgate Friday night. Besides, Lydgate told me he can't drive; he had his license suspended for impaired driving."

"Someone else could have driven him," Verlaque suggested. "But it seems unlikely that a retired auctioneer from a prestigious auction house would get caught up in this. What else have you got?"

"Officer Flamant and I are going over photos of art thieves who fit the description of the man Dr. Schultz saw," Schoelcher said.

"And?" Verlaque asked.

"Short, stocky, and bald fits more than half of them."

"As I figured," Verlaque replied, looking at his commissioner.

"Hey!" Paulik said as he wiped the crumbs off of the desk and put them gently into the palm of his hand.

"You're bald and stocky, but not short," Verlaque said, smiling. "Are any of those guys from Aix?"

"No," Schoelcher replied. "One lives outside of Paris; he's rehabilitated and has been working in trucking for years. The rest are still in jail. But—"

"Go on."

"It might not be an art thief, right? Just a thief who got lucky, who perhaps overheard Rouquet talking about the painting? Or found out about it somehow?"

"Good idea," Verlaque said. "I'll call Pierre and ask a few more questions about Rouquet's daily life."

Schoelcher turned to go and saw the canvas on Verlaque's spare desk. "Wow," he said, frozen. "She's—I mean it's—beautiful."

"We're having a hard time not looking at it," Verlaque said. "But it's going into the vault this evening."

" 'I will astonish Paris with an apple,' " Schoelcher said.

Paulik stared at the young officer and then looked at Verlaque.

"Pardon?" Verlaque asked.

"That's what Cézanne said," Schoelcher replied. " 'I will astonish Paris with an apple.' "

Verlaque walked down the north side of the Cours, happy he wasn't standing in the queue in front of Michaud's. He stopped once he was in front of the real estate agency's windows. Lacking much of a sweet tooth, he was more enticed by glossy real estate pictures than the beautiful chocolate desserts across the street. He played an imaginary game in his head as he looked at the photographs, eliminating each house until he found his favorite. He began with locations: the Drôme, too far; Saint-Tropez, too busy and phony. He wanted rough stone, so eliminated those covered in smooth stucco. He preferred asymmetrical to symmetrical, so eliminated houses that looked too boxy. His eyes finally rested on one with an enchanting, long lane leading up to the house that was lined with alternating plane and umbrella-pine trees. The more he looked at it the more familiar it became: it was the house of Jacob, a friend in the cigar club who had announced he was moving to London, where he worked most of the week anyway. A little bell sounded as the glass doors to the agency opened and a tall, slim woman in her early seventies stuck her head out the door, smiling at him. "It's a lovely house, isn't it?"

"I want it," Verlaque said, smiling. "Antoine Verlaque." He reached out and shook her hand.

"I know," she said. "Natalie Chazeau. I've seen you around Aix. Come in before you freeze to death; it's a good evening for German food."

"That's exactly what I'm getting for dinner."

"We'll go upstairs to the conference room," she said, ushering him inside. "I don't want an examining magistrate to see the mess in my office. Julie, take messages for me."

"*Oui*, madame."

"I've always admired your agency," Verlaque said as he walked up the stairs. "Very tasteful."

"Thank you," Mme Chazeau said, opening the conference room door. She liked the look of Verlaque and did not hide the fact that she was taking her time looking at him. It was, sometimes, a privilege to be old.

"How are sales since the crisis?" he asked.

"Slow," she answered, sitting down and motioning for Verlaque to do the same. "It's one thing to list exclusive properties, and another to sell them."

"Which is why you run the syndicat at number twenty-three rue Boulegon?"

"Exactly," she answered. "We had a meeting just before M. Rouquet's death."

"I know," Verlaque said, taking out a notebook and pen. "My commissioner told me. Was there anything peculiar or unusual about that meeting?"

"A few things," she said. "We had two new owners present, Eric and Françoise Legendre. They own an apartment on the fourth floor. They told me after the meeting that they both worked in restaurants in New York before moving back here.

They used their life savings to buy M. Millot's apartment, but to them it was a steal, compared to New York."

"I can imagine. I've briefly met them. What are they like, in your opinion?"

"He's a bully," she answered. "Françoise is sweet, but is under his thumb."

"Anything else?"

"Well, Pierre Millot came, even though he's already sold his apartment."

"That's odd," Verlaque said. "He didn't tell me he was at the last meeting."

"There was a quarrel about a storage space on the ground floor. Everyone wants to use it, but M. Rouquet didn't even seem to know it was his. He stormed out, and Pierre ran after him. I then saw them in the street, arguing."

"Thank you," Verlaque said as he finished writing. Another detail his friend Pierre left out.

"M. Rouquet definitely had something else on his mind that evening. Normally he argues about any raise in the monthly fees, but he just sat there, playing with his hat."

Verlaque put his notebook back in his jacket pocket. "You've been helpful, thank you. How is Christophe?"

"He's like anyone when they first move to Paris."

"He loves it?"

"Yes, and soon he'll hate it."

Verlaque laughed as he got up. He looked out at the plane trees just outside the office's windows and looked down into the street. Mme Chazeau said nothing, letting him watch the comings and goings of her fellow Aixois. "It's amazing, this view," he finally said. "You can see everything: people walking and chatting, a little kid having a meltdown in front of Michaud's, scooters racing up and down the Cours . . . but you can't hear anything. It's eerie."

"Triple-glazed windows," Mme Chazeau said. She liked the judge more and more.

"*Choucroute pour deux,*" Verlaque said. "*S'il vous plaît.*"

"With the usual sausages?" the deli's owner asked.

"*Oui, deux saucisses de Morteau,*" Verlaque said, pointing to the thin pink sausages. "And two Montbéliard, and a couple of frankfurters. And heaps of sauerkraut, please. Yours is proper sauerkraut, with juniper berries and peppercorns."

The owner scooped the cabbage into a large plastic container. "Thank you. It's my grandfather's recipe; he'd make it in the back shed with his brother every winter."

"One of my coworkers is from Alsace. He must come here. He's a good-looking guy, young, tall, and blond. Quite fit."

"Oh yes, I know him. Jules. Yes, he comes with his fiancée." The owner smiled. He knew that Verlaque was trying to be discreet about his profession, but he knew that Verlaque was a magistrate, and that Jules was a policeman.

"Oh, so they're getting married?" Verlaque asked. He knew that Jules was dating a cute brunette who worked at Aix's only coffee-roasting house, but he had no idea that they were engaged.

"He caught the bug," the owner replied, smiling.

"Disease, more like it," Verlaque said, thinking of his parents. He walked over to the small wine selection. "Jules is far too young."

The owner shrugged. "He must be about twenty-five," he said. "Maybe even close to thirty. I had two kids by then. Best thing I ever did."

"Some people do stay happily married, I suppose," Verlaque mumbled.

"Oh no, we divorced long ago," the owner said, laughing.

Verlaque laughed out loud.

"But I love my daughters," the owner went on. "That's what I meant."

"Enough talk about marriage, then. Do you have any new Rieslings?" Verlaque asked. "I have a few in my cellar, but I'm always open to new suggestions. I love Riesling; so does my girlfriend."

"Ah, the world's great undervalued wine," the owner replied. "Here, I just got six bottles of this one. Small family production, organic. Domaine Bott-Geyl."

"I like the modern label."

"Ah, never judge—"

"I know, I know," Verlaque said, excited to be on one of his favorite topics. "But I have a theory about winemakers who pay a graphic artist real money to design their labels."

"Go on."

"I figure that if they care that much about the label, and are willing to pay for it, then they must have put a lot of care and thought into their wine."

"I agree."

"I'll take two," Verlaque said. "Luckily I live around the corner."

"Luckily for me," the owner said. "Have a good evening."

Verlaque thanked him, paid the bill, and walked down the rue Gaston de Saporta, past the cathedral, turning left into the Place de l'Archevêché, which would take him to the tiny rue Adanson where he lived. Holding the food and wine in his right arm, he opened that building's elaborately carved wooden doors with his left. He saw his mail sitting on the marble console in the hallway but his hands were too occupied to pick it up; he'd do it later. Walking up to his fourth-floor flat he came across Arnaud—a young student who lived with his widowed mother on the first floor—coming down the stairs.

"Hey, Arnaud," Verlaque said.

Arnaud held up a drill. "*Bonsoir, Juge*," he said. "Just finished hanging the plate."

"Thank you. How does it look?"

"Funky."

"That means you don't like it."

Arnaud laughed. "It's not to my taste," he said. "That Soulages painting, on the other hand, I love."

"Me, too," Verlaque said. "Well, add your handiwork to my bill. And thanks."

"No problem. Have a nice night."

Verlaque opened his apartment door and set the bags on the kitchen counter. He quickly took out the wine and set the bottles in his wine fridge. He smiled, thinking of the conversation with the Alsatian shop owner, thankful that he could have interesting chats such as the one they had just had, with people he didn't know intimately.

He walked into his living room and pulled a thick Cézanne book off of his bookshelf. It had been a gift from his brother, Sébastien, when Verlaque had moved to Aix. He opened it to the first page and read Sébastien's inscription: *To my brother. Good luck in the South. You'll need it. Love, Séb.* Turning to the index, Verlaque scrolled down to look for Rebecca Schultz's name; it appeared a half-dozen times, on pages 6, 23, 25, 67, 218, and 219. He was glad that Paulik was paying Dr. Schultz a visit, and not him. He didn't have the time.

He quickly lit a fire in the fireplace and took a small Parta-gas out of his humidor and lit it, sitting down in a worn club chair with the book on his lap. He flipped through the book, looking at some of the color plates, then turned to a chapter entitled "Portraits and Figures." As Marine's father had said, there were few female portraits save of Mme Cézanne, and no young redhead. He read that the painter had complained that Mme Cézanne pined for her mountains and only liked "Swit-zerland and lemonade." Verlaque laughed, as he disliked both the drink and the country. He stared intently at the portraits, mesmerized by *Man with a Pipe*; the sitter's brown clothes, painted in vertical lines of color, disappeared into the brown background. The man's white pipe glowed, matching his bright-white shirt. The painting was in London, at the Courtauld, and Verlaque made a mental note to go and see it.

The author wrote that Cézanne was at ease with the workers of Aix—Verlaque could see that in the man smoking the pipe—and that the painter, especially toward the end of his life, be-came a recluse, speaking mostly to his maid and gardener. The author went on: *"These people had, for Cézanne, a bygone view of Time and Life."* Verlaque appreciated that the Time and Life were capitalized, and he sat back, smoking, thinking of his grandparents Emmeline and Charles, whom he had watched, despite their wealth and education, having remarkable conver-sations with their staff, and waiters, and shopkeepers. These sitters in the later portraits, the author wrote, were at harmony with nature and at peace with themselves. Much like Emme-line and Charles.

Verlaque looked at a portrait that Dr. Bonnet had men-tioned, of Vallier, the gardener, painted just before Cézanne died. The judge could see that here, despite having been a quarrelsome man his whole life, the painter was at peace. Verlaque's cell phone beeped and he looked at it; it was Marine texting that she was on her way. He flipped to the back of the book, where a timeline of the painter's life covered the last few pages. He turned to the year 1885: Cézanne had been in L'Estaque, near Marseille, in the spring. He visited Auguste Renoir with Hortense and Paul Jr. in the summer. Verlaque then let out a *"C'est pas vrai!"* and reread the passage out loud: *"June and July: with Hortense and Paul chez Renoir at La Roche-Guyon, regaining his composure after a mysterious affair with an Aix woman."*

Chapter Ten

❧

Manon and Cézanne

• JANUARY 15, 1885 •

Cézanne remembered Monet's gentle words, and the judge's wife's kind "bonjours," and so this time he forced himself to smile at Philippe's sister, Manon. It was their second meeting, and all week he had hoped he would see her again. But before he could say something, she spoke.

"Oh, M. Cézanne! Aix is changing so quickly," she said, throwing her arms up and then letting them fall against her thick striped skirt. "First they put an ugly eight-sided spire on the cathedral, then the same year they tear down our walls!"

He, too, had been saddened when the ancient walls that for centuries had surrounded and protected Aix were demolished. He was charmed that she referred to them as "our walls," for he also thought of Aix as "his" town. He said, "They took the walls down so that people could build homes in the countryside. Better for their health."

Manon nodded but didn't reply. Only rich families could move houses; her mother would always remain in her narrow four-room house on the rue des Guerriers. Her brother, Philippe, had always made fun of their street name, "the warriors." "That's the story of our parents' life," Philippe had recently told Manon. "They left Italy young to live; they came here and had to fight for survival; and then they die. The real life of a warrior."

"How long have you been painting outside, monsieur?" she finally asked.

"Since this morning."

"Oh, I see," Manon replied, biting her upper lip. He was as gruff as Philippe had said, but he hadn't understood her question. She tried again, "What I meant was, have you always painted like this, standing outside?" She remembered seeing a painting in the Musée Granet of a white-haired man painting, and he was clearly doing so *inside.* Her father had worked outside; some of her sisters worked outside; farmers and vintners worked outside; but here was a banker's son working outside. For there was one thing she knew: this was work for him, as it was for Philippe. It wasn't a hobby.

Cézanne found himself laughing. "Twenty years now. It's something they don't teach you in art school. I had to figure that out for myself. How long have *you* been walking *outside*?"

Manon laughed. "Since I was a little girl."

"You've always liked plants, Mlle Solari?" he asked,

"*Oui*," she answered. "*La nature.* There's more color here than in town."

"All the same, there is a lot of orange and yellow in Aix," he said. "Paris is gray."

"Philippe told me that about Paris, too. But out here," she said, looking at the scene before them, "there's green." She boldly walked toward his canvas and looked closely at it.

Cézanne said nothing. He couldn't help staring at her. Her curly red hair was tied back because of the wind, and her features were clear and strong. She had a long, thin nose, high cheekbones, and big blue eyes. Her face was scarred, but it didn't make her ugly, only distinctive. He realized he was being rude by staring, but she hadn't seemed to notice, so intently was she staring at the painting.

She said, "You've taken the blue from the sky and put in the needles of the pine."

Cézanne looked at his work. "Nature isn't just one flat color." He hadn't meant to mumble, but that was how it came out.

"No, monsieur," Manon replied. "It certainly isn't." She remembered as a young girl being fascinated by some dark purple flowers she had picked, later noticing that the same hue existed in the plants and the sky all around her. He thought like she did, this M. Cézanne, and she knew that he had been ridiculed in Paris, laughed at by the public, critics, and journalists. She, too, had been mocked, for her poverty, her scarred face, her enthusiasm for art.

She glanced at the painter—who was looking at his painting, arms folded—and wondered if under his felt hat he had any hair. He wore a patterned handkerchief around his neck, bright red with tiny yellow bees on it. It was the same kind of handkerchief her brothers-in-law wore, for fêtes. She tried to imagine Cézanne wearing it in Paris, as the girls at Michaud's gossiped he did, along with a bright-red flannel taiolo tied around his waist.

Philippe had told her of a disastrous weekend Cézanne had

spent at Zola's mansion in Médan, outside of Paris. Zola had tried, in vain, to introduce his old friend to the "wide world": successful writers, established painters, and wealthy collectors. There had even been a famous actress present. But Cézanne had stayed silent, fearful of being misunderstood, or ridiculed. Instead, Cézanne took Zola's boat—*Nana*—out across the river to a small island, and from there he painted the scene of Zola's bourgeois house and its neighbor, Médan's castle. Philippe had loved the painting—he had seen it on display at the art supplier Tanguy's—and another painter, Monsieur Gauguin, had purchased it. "That landscape shimmered," Philippe had told Manon, trying to sketch it out for her with his hands. "Greens and ochres so intense they gleam like silk!" She looked down at the half-finished painting before her and now understood Philippe's excitement. "When I saw your painting from the forest, it looked alive. As if it could jump off of the canvas," she said. She then added a word that Philippe had taught her: "three-dimensional."

For the first time since they had begun speaking, Cézanne found himself smiling. "And when you look at it up close?"

"It's more flat, but that isn't bad." She bent to get a closer look. "The way you put the paint down," she said, pausing, "it reminds me of Bibémus."

"The quarries?" Cézanne asked.

"Yes, the way the rocks are cut. My father was a stonemason. Those hatching marks in the rock are like your hatchings here." She pointed to the brushstrokes.

Cézanne couldn't wait to write down what she had just said. Here was someone who understood his art. Zola still thought Cézanne was trying to be an Impressionist; his mother and sister, no matter how smothering their attention, did not understand his art. And his father, he knew, hated it. He'd write to Zola when he got home and tell him of Mlle Solari's obeservations. Zola was furiously trying to finish a novel, so they hadn't been writing as much as they usually did. It was Zola who had taught him the value of never giving up and working until exhausted.

Manon looked at the bearded painter, who seemed to be lost in thought. She slapped her forehead and said, "I've interrupted your work. I'm so sorry, M. Cézanne."

"It's fine—" He had wanted to add "I'm glad you came again," but didn't. After two meetings they had shared so much.

"But the paint, it will dry, no?"

"I can take a break, mademoiselle," he said, trying to smile to put her at ease. "It's not as if I can finish one of these in a day. It sometimes takes me months or years to finish—or to be content with—a canvas."

"Then how do you know that a painting is finished?"

Cézanne looked at the scene before him, unable to meet her inquiring gaze. He finally said, still looking ahead at the giant green pine, "When I'm sure that I have conveyed not what I see, but what I believe in."

Chapter Eleven

La Sale Peinture

So you've done a bit of reading in a book on Cézanne and now you're an expert?" Marine asked, dipping a piece of frankfurter into mustard.

"Don't you see?" Velaque asked, opening a second bottle of Riesling. "A mysterious woman. 1885. In Aix."

"I get it, I get it," Marine said. "But the person who forged that painting may also have the same book." She winked.

"You're so cruel sometimes," Verlaque said, smiling. "I think that our portrait is the real thing. This evening I sat here, smoking, mesmerized by Cézanne's portraits, and by his life."

"Not you, too! I grew up traveling with my parents across Europe to see Cézanne's works."

"I thought you guys visited Romanesque churches."

"That was my mother's passion," Marine said. "Cézanne was Papa's."

"To think that he lived, worked, and walked here—" Verlaque gestured with his arm around the apartment.

Marine raised an eyebrow.

"Aix, I mean, not in my apartment."

"You never know," Marine said, holding out her empty glass. "Maybe their tryst was here, in your flat. Although I'm not convinced that he had an affair."

"Dr. Bonnet, are you challenging my thesis?"

"Not at all," Marine replied. "I agree with you that the girl in our painting may have been very special to Cézanne. But who says they slept together?"

Verlaque rolled his eyes and gave a suspicious grin. "Well, I've always thought that this apartment has good karma."

"I'll agree with you there. I love the new addition, by the way." She pointed to a large, colorful ceramic plate hanging on the wall above the door between the dining room and kitchen.

"Ah, Arnaud, my faithful handyman, hung that for me today," Verlaque said. "It was Emmeline's."

"I love those fat yellow lemons," Marine said. "They dance around the plate. Is it Tuscan?"

"Sicilian," Verlaque said, turning to look at it. "I remember her buying it, in a tiny shop in Ragusa." He poured Marine some wine and went on, "Poor Cézanne. How did those guys keep on painting?"

"You mean the Impressionists?"

"And Post-Impressionists," he said. "People hated their work, and they kept on painting."

"Luckily they were rich," Marine said.

"Not all of them," Verlaque replied. "Van Gogh didn't have a pot to piss in, as my grandfather would have said. And even if Cézanne *did* have family money, he still had no one buying his art. How do you go on? Do you know what Henri Dobler, the guy who owned the Pavillon de Vendôme in Cézanne's day, said about Cézanne's works? He called them *la sale peinture*. Dirty paintings! What an idiot!"

"You're using hindsight," Marine said, sitting back and rubbing her stomach, regretting eating the second saucisse de Morteau. "Perhaps *we* would have said the same thing. Can you imagine, seeing those weird hatchings, in the late nineteenth century? Then again, you did buy a Pierre Soulages painting long before he was fashionable."

"Thank you, my dear."

"Oh, before I forget to tell you, I picked up your mail downstairs," Marine said. "It's on the kitchen counter."

"Thanks," Verlaque said. "I saw it sitting in the entryway, but my hands were full. Anything interesting?"

"What looks like a personal letter from the director of the Pompidou in Paris," Marine said. "Do you owe membership dues?"

"Certainly not," Veralque answered. "I'm all paid up. That's the second letter Philippe has sent me."

"First-name basis with the director of France's most important contemporary art museum? Impressive."

"We went to boarding school together. He wants the Soulages painting for a retrospective they're organizing next year."

"Wow, Antoine," Marine said, lifting her glass for a toast. "That's incredible!"

"No, it isn't," Verlaque said. "And I told him so."

Marine shook her head back and forth. "Come again?"

"I can't let it leave here," Veralque said. "No way."

"I don't believe you," Marine said, setting her glass down. "You'd hog that gorgeous painting all to yourself? Not let anyone else have the pleasure of seeing it?"

"It would be a paperwork and insurance nightmare. They've got plenty of others."

"What if everyone said that? What if no one had ever donated, even for a few months, a painting to a world-class museum? You're selfish, do you know that?"

"I knew you'd pick a fight tonight," Verlaque said, throwing his napkin on the table. "Just like that tantrum after the Pauliks' galette des rois."

"And, guess what? It all has to do with the same thing!"

"Soulages?"

"No, you idiot," Marine said, getting up from the table. "Your ego!"

The Hôtel Fleurie was the kind of hotel that Bruno Paulik and his wife, Hélène, liked to stay in when traveling around France. Always downtown, these small one-star hotels were family owned, quaint on the verge of faded and sometimes run-down, and without the amenities that the Pauliks didn't care about anyway, such as televisions and minibars.

Paulik paced around the waiting room and then began flipping through the guest book, its passages written in a variety of languages that included French, English, German, and what looked to him like Dutch. The hotel's owner didn't seem fazed by having a policeman visit, and she sat behind the desk reading a novel, looking up now and then at the commissioner and smiling. He turned the guest book's pages, stopping at small drawings that guests had left, one of them a quite good sketch of the sitting room that he could see from the lobby, full of mismatched, not-very-precious antiques. Some of the entries were too long, or in languages he didn't understand, but toward the end of the book was a French entry written only a few days previously: *Room eleven, one evening, one woman, one man. Bliss.*

"Sorry to keep you waiting," a voice said from the doorway.

Paulik quickly closed the book, as if he had been caught looking at the lingerie pages of a La Redoute catalogue.

"I haven't been here long," Paulik answered.

"Perhaps we can meet in the sitting room," Rebecca Schultz said, turning to the hotel's owner for permission.

"*Oui, oui, oui,*" the owner said, gesturing to the sitting room. "*Allez-y.*"

"My room is the size of a postage stamp," Dr. Schultz said.

Paulik laughed, amazed by the American's perfect French. He looked at the professor's long legs, which were clothed in pink woolen tights under an orange leather miniskirt, and he wondered how someone with so much leg could fit into a small French hotel room, or bed for that matter. Blushing slightly, as he had while reading the guest book, he opened his small notebook as they sat down, and asked, "What exactly are you doing in Aix, Dr. Schultz?"

If the professor looked surprised, she didn't show it. "It should be perfectly obvious," she finally answered. "I'm here researching Cézanne, as I told Judge Verlaque."

"Were you researching Cézanne when you walked into René Rouquet's apartment?"

"I saw that there had been a robbery in the building—"

"So you went in to investigate?"

"To help," she answered, shrugging. "I was jet-lagged and not thinking straight. There I was, after spending years reading of Cézanne's last residence, able to go inside. Can't you imagine the temptation?"

"No," Paulik answered. "I would have stayed outside and called the police. Especially given your excellent French."

"I had forgotten my cell phone back at the hotel," she answered. "That I also told your boss."

If Dr. Schultz had attempted to belittle him by mentioning that he wasn't in command, Paulik thought, it hadn't worked. He was more than happy being commissioner and didn't have the law training to be an examining magistrate. But Dr. Schultz, despite her command of his language and expertise in art, obviously didn't understand how the French judicial system worked. He asked, "What did you do when you went into the apartment? What I don't understand is why you didn't call the police as soon as you saw M. Rouquet's body on the floor."

"I was in shock," Dr. Schultz replied. "Completely stunned."

"Didn't it frighten you?"

Dr. Schultz paused before saying, "No. Given my fatigue, and the astonishment of being in Cézanne's apartment, it all seemed unreal."

"Your fingerprints were found on a number of items in the flat," Paulik said. "The wardrobe in the bedroom, for example. Why in the world would you go into the bedroom when there was a dead man in the living room?"

Dr. Schultz began picking at what looked like imaginary lint on her tights. *Jesus, the lint trick*, Paulik thought to himself.

"The wardrobe was nineteenth century, and I imagined it being Cézanne's, given the rest of the cheap '60s furniture in the flat," she replied. "I opened it half out of curiosity, half from amazement." Before Paulik could continue questioning, she went on, "The same thing for the kitchen cupboards. I guess I had hoped to see those ceramic pitchers and plates from his still lifes in there. But what you must know is that I was only in there for a few minutes before I began looking for the phone to call the police. But then they came—"

"It took you a few minutes to decide?"

"Yes," she replied, staring at Paulik and then crossing her arms across her chest. "And if you were a black Jewish woman who had worked all her life to finally get a white Anglo-Saxon man's job, and you were caught trespassing and entering where there had just been a murder, you, too, would have thought twice before deciding to phone for help instead of running straight out the door."

Chapter Twelve

❧

Antoine Verlaque Invites Officer Schoelcher for a Beer

Marine stood under a streetlamp in the middle of the rue Adanson and texted Sylvie, who lived around the corner. "I'm still up," Sylvie texted back. "Come on over."

Marine walked quickly down the street, turning left on the rue Campra. At times living in Aix felt suffocating, especially when she ran into acquaintances from junior high or high school, people she hadn't liked when she was fifteen and whom she liked even less now. But tonight she was thankful that she lived in a town small enough to walk across in fifteen minutes. She buzzed three times in quick succession at Sylvie's door and it opened with a click.

Marine walked up to the third floor and smiled when she saw Sylvie standing in the doorway, wearing pink bunny slippers. Prada was Sylvie's preferred footwear.

"Hey, come on in," Sylvie said, giving Marine the *bise*.

"I hope it's not too late for you," Marine said, taking off her coat and hanging it on the overstuffed coatrack.

"For me, no," Sylvie answered. "But Charlotte's in bed. We were invited to the neighbor's for the Fête des Rois, even though it was officially yesterday."

"Oh, I'm so glad!" Marine said. "Did Charlotte go under the table?"

"*Non, grande drame!*" Sylvie said. "Charlotte's no longer the youngest. Their son Alex is now three, so he was able to call out everyone's name. Last year he was too young."

"Was Charlotte upset?"

"At first," Sylvie said. "I could see it in her eyes. But Alex was so cute calling out our names—he has a bit of a baby's lisp and can't say his s's, so my name becomes Tylvie—and after about two minutes Charlotte was laughing. A year ago I would have had to give her the 'not everything revolves around you' talk."

Marine smiled, thinking of Antoine.

"I put some tea on when I got your text message," Sylvie said, passing Marine a mug decorated with Man Ray's large black-and-white eye. "But I won't offer you any sweets."

"That's more than fine," Marine said. "I had two pieces of galette last night at the Pauliks'."

"You know," Sylvie said, pouring mint tea into their cups, "I hate almond paste."

"Yet another thing you have in common with Antoine Verlaque. He ate his to be polite."

"Well, I flat-out refused," Sylvie said. "But then again, I'm not as well bred as Antoine. So, what's up? Are you gonna whine into your tea like you did last week?"

Marine set her cup down and stared at her friend. "Did I do that?"

Sylvie nodded.

"I'm so sorry," Marine said. "I don't know what's wrong with me."

Sylvie blew on her tea, saying nothing.

Marine continued, "I have so much to be thankful for. But I can't shake this feeling of . . ."

"Disappointment?" Sylvie asked.

"Yes! It's as if my head is buzzing with obsessive thoughts about my failures."

Sylvie laughed. "You? Failures?"

"I teach in Aix, not Paris, not New York," Marine said. "I haven't published enough. It's a crazy panicked feeling I get—especially in the morning—that I've let life pass me by. And it makes me feel so ungrateful."

Sylvie set her her mug down and went into the living room, picked up a magazine, and came back, throwing it on the kitchen table.

Marine looked at the cover and said, "Sylvie, not *Psychology Today*—again."

"It's called the U-curve," Sylvie said, sitting down. "And you're not alone. Research being done at a few English and American universities has uncovered a recurrent pattern in various countries around the world: that life satisfaction declines with age the first couple of decades of adulthood, bottoming out right now—in our early forties."

"Interesting."

"I know," Sylvie answered. "And it has nothing to do with whether you're from a rich or poor country, married or divorced, employed or unemployed, with or without children. The common denominator is the age—our forties—when we experience this feeling of discontentment."

"There's just one little problem."

"Yeah," Sylvie said, "you're not in your forties yet."

Marine smiled.

"But," Sylvie went on, pointing in the air, "you've always been ahead. You skipped a grade, right?"

Marine laughed. "Yes. And I'll be forty soon enough. So where does the U-curve come in?"

"It gets better," Sylvie said. "That's the good news. All of a sudden, somewhere in our early to midfifties, the nagging feeling that we're losers disappears. And apparently sixty is awesome."

"Hurrah," Marine said flatly.

"Yeah, well, the research indicates that people in their seventh decade are at their emotional peak of happiness. It's like they're on a high."

"My parents," Marine said. "I can hardly keep up with them."

"There you go."

"There's an obvious explanation," Marine said, tapping the table.

"Spoken like a true lawyer," Sylvie said as she opened the window to allow the smoke from her cigarette to billow outside.

"Time horizons grow shorter as we age. People concentrate on what is most important," Marine said.

"Meaningful relationships."

"For example. They focus on the present."

"Walks in the countryside and that kind of crap."

Marine laughed. "Are you suffering from these forties blues?"

"A little bit," Sylvie said. "Especially in the morning, like you said. But having Charlotte to look after keeps my inner demons at bay."

"Charlotte is the same age as Léa Paulik," Marine said. "And when I see Léa with Antoine, and he laughs like he's a kid, I get this knot in my stomach. Am I jealous?"

"Hmm," Sylvie said, finishing her cigarette and setting the ashtray in the flower box, closing the window. "No, I don't think you're jealous of Léa. You see moody Antoine all happy at the Pauliks', and you don't understand why he isn't like that all the time. Do you want his attention all the time?"

"No, that would be suffocating."

"Do you want him to be happy only when he's with you?"

"No," Marine answered. "I want him to be happy all the time. He deserves it."

"What do you think makes Antoine so happy at the Pauliks'? What do they have that you don't have?"

Marine looked at Sylvie.

"I think I just answered my own question," Sylvie said after a pause.

"So maybe I'm not in this forties blues thing yet."

"No, I don't think you are," Sylvie said. "There's a very specific reason for your feelings of disappointment. You want to have what the Pauliks have, with Antoine Verlaque."

Verlaque was surprised to see someone he knew looking up at the sculptures on the Halles aux Grains pediment. It was late and the streets were full of tipsy students on their way to and from Aix's many bars and cheap restaurants.

"Good evening, Officer Schoelcher," he said.

"Oh!" Jules Schoelcher replied. "Judge Verlaque. I wasn't expecting to see you here."

"I live around the corner."

"So do I." Jules quickly stubbed out his cigarette on the pavement.

"You should smoke these," Verlaque said, holding up his half-smoked Churchill short. "No chemicals, handmade."

"I don't even smoke," Schoelcher replied. "I bought these out of desperation. I had a fight with my girlfriend—"

"The coffee shop girl?" Verlaque asked. "Sorry, news travels fast at the Palais de Justice."

"Yeah, I know," Jules replied.

"That makes two of us."

"Excuse me?"

"This evening I had a good row with Marine, my girlfriend. Care for a walk?"

Being that Antoine Verlaque was about a mile ahead of him in the chain of command, Jules didn't feel like he could refuse. But he felt some kind of connection with the judge: Jules was known at the precinct, this he knew, as an uptight, by-the-book policeman from Alsace, and Verlaque was known as a rich Parisian. They were both outsiders in Aix. "Sure," he said.

"The strange thing is," Verlaque said as they walked through the square, "I don't even know why Marine's angry with me."

"Oh, I know what's bugging Magali," Jules said. "And it's always the same argument we have. She hated being with my folks at Christmas and I hated being with hers at New Year's."

"Oddball families?" Verlaque asked. "Sounds familiar. I sometimes think that Marine's mother wants to drive a dagger through my chest."

Jules laughed. "Magali sees my family as uptight Germanic Catholics. But you should see hers! I hate to say this, but . . . *ils sont ploucs!*"

"Low-class?"

"Oh my God," Jules went on. "Marseillais but not the fun-loving Marseillais that you see in old Pagnol movies, or see in restaurants having a great, loud time. Her brother has been in prison for theft, her father drinks too much and is a domineering lout, and her mother just sits there chain-smoking, wringing her hands . . ."

"That sounds awful."

"Yeah, and I have so much respect for Magali, that she got out of that family and is here in Aix. She loves her job, and she paints these amazing still lifes—"

" 'I will astonish Paris with an apple,' " Verlaque said. "Was it Magali who taught you that?"

"Of course," Jules said. "Magali's still lifes are more a cross between Cézanne's and Frida Kahlo's—but still, they're amazing."

Verlaque tried to imagine what a Cézanne/Frida Kahlo still life would look like.

"It was such a stupid fight—" Schoelcher stopped there, thinking maybe he was talking too much about his own problems. But he figured that the judge would speak up if he wanted to divulge information on his fight with Marine Bonnet, whom Schoelcher knew—thanks to blabbermouth officer Roger Caromb—was a well-known law professor whose classes were year after year full, not because of her beauty but because of her fascinating lectures. Two of his fellow policeman had even snuck into one of her classes when it was found out that she was dating Verlaque. "Riveting," one had said, while the other had made a sweeping motion with his hand over his head. That had been Roger.

Verlaque stopped in front of the Bar Zola, which he realized he had wanted to go to all along, with or without company. "Care for a Guinness?"

"A decent beer sounds perfect."

"I have an ulterior motive for coming here," Verlaque explained, opening the door to allow wafts of smoke and loud Rolling Stones music to pour out. "This was René Rouquet's favorite spot to come and tie one on."

"After you."

Chapter Thirteen

❧

Commissioner Paulik, Charmed

Jules led the way, pushing through the crowd. He looked over his shoulder and Verlaque signaled to the bar. The tall blond policeman gently excused himself as he squeezed through the patrons, finally finding a spot at the bar big enough for the two men to stand. *"Deux Guinness, s'il vous plaît,"* Jules told the barman as Verlaque arrived beside him.

The barman, who wore a long beard and a Harley-Davidson T-shirt, looked twice at Verlaque before saying, in a mock posh accent, *"Bonsoir, Monsieur le juge."*

"Hey, you got your hair cut," Verlaque said, his hand motioning a chop just below his ear.

Jules Schoelcher tried not to look surprised.

"It looks really good," Verlaque said, giving the barman a thumbs-up.

The barman rolled his eyes but finally smiled. "Wife's orders," he said while slowly pouring out the Guinness. "Apparently classical music concerts and long hair don't jibe."

"Bruno told me that your son plays piano wonderfully," Verlaque said. He looked at Jules and said, "Léa and—"

"Matthieu," the barman said.

"Léa Paulik and Matthieu are at the conservatoire together," Verlaque explained. Schoelcher took a sip of his beer, looking from his boss to the barman, trying to block out the noise from the music and the bar's patrons to understand just how these two very different people seemed to know each other.

"Patrick," the barman said, reaching across the bar.

"Antoine," Verlaque said, taking the barman's hand that was adorned with three or four skull rings. "And this is my colleague Jules." Verlaque took a sip of beer, smiled, gave the barman another thumbs-up, and said, "Have you heard Léa sing Fauré's 'In Prayer'?"

Patrick pretended to wipe tears from his eyes.

"I have the same reaction," Verlaque said. He took another sip, then looked around him and said, "Zola gets a young crowd in, no?"

Patrick shrugged his shoulders. "Mostly," he said. "Except at the bar," he added, winking.

Jules said, "Don't look at me."

Verlaque laughed. "Thanks, Jules." He then leaned across the bar and asked, "But older guys do come here, don't they? Did you know a retired postman named René?"

Patrick leaned his muscular forearms on the bar. "Why the past tense?"

"He's dead," Verlaque said.

"Why is it every time you come in here," Patrick asked, "I lose a valued customer?"

Verlaque shrugged. "When was the last time he came in?"

"That's easy," Patrick said as he wiped down the counter with a small towel. "Last night."

"Did he chat with anyone?" Schoelcher asked.

"Yeah, me," Patrick said.

"That's all?"

A girl bumped into Jules and they both said "*Pardon*" in unison.

"But you can see that if you're standing at the bar—" Patrick said.

"Anyone can hear," Jules said, looking over at the girl and smiling.

Verlaque sipped more of the Guinness and asked, "What did you talk about?"

"It was René doing the talking," Patrick said. "He got more and more incoherent as the evening went on. I finally cut him off around ten o'clock."

Verlaque said nothing and waited for the barman to go on.

"It's a little weird," Patrick said. "Okay, he's bragged before that he lives in Cézanne's old apartment, but this time he was saying that he found something in the apartment. Something that was once Cézanne's."

"*Pauvre gars*," Verlaque said. "He should have kept his mouth shut. Was he specific?"

"Well, I took it to be a painting," Patrick said, "because he was talking how valuable it must be." Patrick laughed and then said, "He was going on about Christie's and Sotheby's. Did he really find a Cézanne painting?"

Verlaque looked around him and closed his eyes slowly, then opened them. "We're not sure what it is," he said. "But if it is—"

Patrick whistled. "So I see what direction you're going with these questions," he said. "Should we step outside?"

Verlaque and Jules put their coats back on and made their

way through the crowd carrying their half-finished beers. Patrick followed, having poured himself a whiskey. "Let's walk around the square," he said, closing the bar's door behind him.

Verlaque relit his Churchill and they strolled toward a statue of a wild boar that sat in the middle of the square. "Was René murdered?" Patrick asked as they stopped beside the statue.

"Yes, last night or early this morning," Verlaque said. "He called a former neighbor, worried that he had been followed home."

"*Oh merde*," Patrick said. "I feel like it's my fault. I should have cut him off earlier."

"It could have been a break and enter," Jules said. "Unrelated to your conversation in the bar."

"But it is important that you remember who was standing at the bar next to M. Rouquet," Verlaque said. "Any short, thick, bald men?"

Patrick took out a cigarette and lit it. "One or two," he said. "But of all the students, riffraff, and lonely hearts in here last night, that's not who I remember best."

"Oh really?" Verlaque asked.

"There was this Amazon," Patrick said, shaking his head back and forth. "One of the most gorgeous women I've ever seen."

Verlaque and Schoelcher exchanged looks. "What did she look like?" Jules asked.

"Tall, black, striking in an original way," Patrick said. "Like she had just walked off the fashion runway, but circa 1972."

Bruno Paulik sipped his *vin chaud*, watching people walk up and down the Cours. The more he tried to think of his wife,

Hélène, the more the image of Rebecca Schultz popped into his head. He hadn't meant to stay so long at the Hôtel Fleurie, but the hotel owner had put on an opera CD and he and Rebecca— as she had insisted he call her—chatted about the music for longer than he realized. It was Bizet's *Pearl Fishers*, an old recording sung by Enrico Caruso and Giuseppe De Luca, the men's voices in perfect harmony.

"Have you seen the film *Gallipoli*?" Rebecca asked.

"Only about a million times," Paulik replied.

"This is the song that the officer is listening to," Rebecca said.

"Yeah. He knows that the next morning his soldiers will be going over the top," Paulik said. "And he with them."

"He's drinking champagne—"

"It's his wedding anniversary. It kills me to watch that scene," Paulik said. "It proves that there's no need for violence and gore in a war movie."

"I agree," Rebecca said. "Just some opera and a man staring at his wife's photograph."

Paulik was brought out of his reverie by his cell phone ringing. "Bruno? Verlaque here."

"Yes?"

"Am I interrupting?"

"No," Paulik answered, embarrassed that he had been thinking of Dr. Schultz.

"Schultz has been bullshitting us," Verlaque said. "She was in the Bar Zola last night."

"You're kidding." Paulik quickly finished his hot wine and motioned for the bill.

"Beauty is a complex subject."

"I'm not following," Paulik said.

"Cézanne said that," Verlaque said. "But it fits our Yale professor. Listen, I'm going to try to get some sleep now, and then I'll go into the Palais de Justice tomorrow and also speak to Dr. Schultz. I don't expect to see you because tomorrow's Sunday. Okay?"

"Right," Paulik said.

"You're extra chatty tonight, Bruno. Is everything all right?"

"Sorry, the fatigue seems to be catching up with me," Paulik said. "I'll see you Monday. Feel free to call me with any updates." He hung up and set some coins down on the table.

On the way to get his car out of the underground parking garage under the Palais de Justice, Bruno Paulik found himself looking into the windows of some of Aix's finest clothing stores. He had never bought clothes for his wife; besides, Hélène's daily work gear was blue jeans or coveralls and a wool sweater if she was working in the cellar. She looked fantastic dressed up—Bruno loved a short, sparkly gold dress she wore for wine-tasting and publicity events—and he couldn't remember her ever talking about fashion. She certainly didn't read fashion magazines; she subscribed to *La Revue du Vin* and *Vinum*. And so why, he asked himself, when five minutes earlier he had so desperately wanted to see his wife, was he wasting his time looking at a two-thousand-euro Sonia Rykiel dress? Research, he answered. He was trying to understand what kind of money their top suspect, Rebecca Schultz, spent on clothing. *No, Bruno, stop trying to imagine what Rebecca Schultz would look like in the Rykiel pink knit dress.* But even with his untrained eye, Bruno Paulik knew that Dr. Schultz wore a lot of money on her back. *And on her long legs.*

Paulik sighed and moved on to another shop, this one full of designer shoes. Did university professors make that much

money in the States? He knew in France that professors, as civil
servants, made about the same salary as he did, and that wasn't
much. How could Dr. Schultz afford such clothes? Perhaps
Marine Bonnet, who had colleagues who worked for American
universities, could fill him in? He pressed his nose up against
the glass. The January sales hadn't yet started, but the shiny
black Prada shoes, with their transparent, glass-like heels,
would be still be more than three-hundred euros on sale.

His phone rang.

"Are you busy, sir?" Alain Flamant asked.

"No," Paulik said, staring at a pair of knee-high green and
purple Italian leather boots, fascinated by the intricate stitching
running up their sides. "Not really."

"If you're still in Aix, sir, I think you should come in to the
precinct. A body has been found," Flamant went on. "Shot.
We've identified him as Guy Maneval, small-time crook twice
jailed for burglary. But he was found with—"

"Yes?"

"Well, a landscape around his neck. I mean, someone
slammed a painting over his head."

"Seriously?"

"Um, yeah. But probably after he was killed."

Paulik was suddenly desperate to get home and see Hélène,
who at five foot two would never make a fashion model but who
was the most beautiful woman in the world to Bruno. But instead of walking underground to fetch his car out of the Palais
de Justice's parking lot, he walked through the front door, nodded to the policeman on guard, and walked upstairs to see what
Alain Flamant had to tell him.

Chapter Fourteen

❧

A Family of Three

*H*e's been shot through the head, once, clean," said Dr. Cohen as she looked down at the lifeless body that laid in Aix's morgue. "Killed late last night or early this morning, so he's been dead for ten hours or so. The killer, by the looks of it a professional, used a .22 caliber revolver. Head shot, up close; the bullet's still in there. It spun and spun around," she said, motioning with her hands, "inside the curved interior of the dead man's skull, causing instant death."

Paulik looked down at the dead man and took a deep breath, wishing the doctor would keep her narrative more scientific. "A .22 revolver makes noise," Paulik said.

"Not the Russian ones," Flamant said.

"Where was he found?" Paulik asked as he continued to look at the body.

"Down by Pont de l'Arc," Flamant said.

"And if the killer didn't have a Russian revolver?" Paulik asked. "Pont de l'Arc is quiet."

"There's a disco by the river," Flamant said. "It would have been loud on Friday night."

"You're right," Paulik answered, nodding. "At any rate, get some officers down to the river to ask joggers and the gypsies if they saw or heard anything. Are the gypsies still camped down there?"

"Yes," Flamant said. "They were watching as we cordoned off the scene of the crime. Whoever shot Maneval didn't care that he would be identified. But I recognized him anyway. Small-time thug. I think he's a bouncer at La Fantasie."

"I recognize him, too," Paulik said. He thought of a six-month-old Guy Maneval, cradled by his mother; a nine-year-old Guy, chasing some kid in the school yard; then a fifteen-year-old Guy, smoking and already getting into trouble; and downhill from there.

"Do you still need me?" Dr. Cohen asked, covering the body with a sheet. "I got called away from a dinner party."

No," Paulik said. "I'm sorry about the dinner. Maybe you can still make the dessert."

"I hate sweets," the doctor answered. "Good evening."

"Good-bye, and thanks," Paulik said. He turned to Flamant and asked, "And this painting?"

Flamant pointed to a table behind the commissioner.

"There's not much left of the painting," Flamant said, "as it was pushed over the victim's head. A warning?"

"If it's the same painting that's missing out of René Rouquet's apartment, then it's a clue intentionally left by the killer, linking Guy Maneval to René Rouquet."

"And the Cézanne mystery."

"Did the same person kill the two men?" Paulik asked. "Or did Maneval kill Rouquet and then did someone kill Maneval? Maneval was killed by a professional."

"And Rouquet wasn't," Flamant said. "Or that's the way it appeared."

"Well," Paulik said, looking down at the painting, "it looks like there's enough left in the corners for Pierre Millot to identify it as the painting that hung above his neighbor's sofa. Let's put it in a bag and take it to the Palais de Justice. There's no reason to bring Pierre here."

Marine sat in her childhood kitchen, holding her head in her hands as her father passed her a Kleenex. She looked around at the kitchen—vintage 1973—and although it was ugly and not functional, she knew that her parents would never change it. Her parents hated change, and loved routine. Since she had become a full-time professor in Aix, Marine made it a habit of having breakfast with her parents every Sunday morning, before they headed off to Mass at Saint Jean de Malte. It got her out of bed, and she enjoyed the early-morning walk when Aix's streets were still empty. Both she and Antoine had been raised to be early risers, and she had recently read an interview with a three-star Michelin chef who, when asked to what he owed his success, answered, "My parents never letting me sleep in as a teenager."

"This must be about something other than Pierre Soulages and the Pompidou," Anatole Bonnet said, setting down his coffee. "Although I enjoyed that story."

"I'm a law professor," Marine said, blowing her nose. "I've published law articles, I pay my mortgage on time, my students and colleagues respect me. But—" She sighed and her father waited for her to finish her sentence. "It's just that sometimes Antoine Verlaque makes me so damn mad," she said.

"Me, too!" Marine's mother said from the living room.

"Florence, you're not helping," Anatole Bonnet called to his wife.

"So . . . ," Anatole Bonnet said, "you think that Antoine should loan the Pompidou the Soulages."

"Papa," Marine said. "This has nothing to do with Soulages!"

"Right, sorry."

"No, I'm sorry," Marine said, taking her father's hands in hers and looking again at the age spots. "Look at the state of me," she said. "I'm being irrational for the first time in my life and it's killing me. I can't stand myself. He brings out the best and worst in me."

Anatole smiled and motioned with a nod of the head toward the living room, where Florence was simultaneously finishing the *Le Monde* crossword, listening to a play on the radio, and eavesdropping on their conversation.

Marine smiled and dried her eyes.

"Do you want to tell me what's bothering you?" Anatole asked his daughter. "I'm not sure I understand."

Marine sighed and said, "I'm not even sure myself, but the other night, we were at the Pauliks' house—"

"The commissioner who looks like a thug?"

"Right," Marine said. "He's a teddy bear, actually. Well, there we all are, laughing our heads off as Léa—she's their ten-year-old—sits under the table and calls out who gets which piece of galette. And I see that Antoine is having the time of his life. He adores that kid—" She stopped and took a breath. "And I got jealous, not of Léa, but of the Pauliks and their cute family of three." She stopped speaking and looked at her father.

"I always loved our cute family of three," Anatole said quietly, not wanting Florence to hear. Their son, born a few years earlier than Marine, had died of infant crib death. He and Florence, in their seventies, were only now speaking to a therapist about it. He hadn't told Marine about the therapy sessions, twice weekly on the Cours Mirabeau.

"I realized that evening that I want to have a family," Marine said. She then loudly added for her mother's benefit, "Yes, with Antoine Verlaque."

"Shouldn't you be speaking to Antoine about this?" Anatole asked, with a puzzled look on his face.

"Of course I should," Marine said. "If I can stay Zen long enough. Why is this subject making me so crazy?" She slapped the wooden table. "Why am I embarrassed about this wish?"

"Because you've always thought out your life so rationally," Anatole said. "At age six you reorganized our kitchen, and at age nine you were campaigning for Mitterrand for president." Dr. Bonnet smiled and added, "I'm sure the Verlaques were not looking forward to having a Socialist run the country."

"No, they weren't," Marine said. "They took one of their only trips together as a family just before the elections, to Montréal, to see about getting Canadian passports in the event of Mitterrand winning. Which he did, so they just hid their money in Luxembourg."

Anatole Bonnet tried not to frown. "So it seems to you that now, at age thirty-five, you're acting instinctively, following your heart, and that scares you."

Marine looked at her father and smiled.

"And it shouldn't," Anatole went on. "Your mother and I drew up a list of pros and cons before deciding to have children. It seems stupid now, but back in the early '70s all of our friends were reproducing like rabbits without giving it a thought. Or that's how it seemed to us. And then when it happened it seemed like the most natural thing in the world. We were over the moon."

"But Antoine had such a lousy childhood."

"All the more reason to talk to him about your feelings," Anatole said.

"Goddamn crossword!" Florence Bonnet yelled. "Who cares about movie stars? Nine letters. Who played Cyrano—"

"*Depardieu!*" Marine and her father answered in unison.

"You're not being fair to Antoine, Marine," Anatole said. "He's being selfish about the Soulages, I agree. But his opinions about children and marriage may surprise you." He wasn't sure why Marine had come to him with these questions, but he was glad. He wished that he could have spoken to his own parents about life's big decisions. No doubt Sylvie had given Marine advice, and although he liked Sylvie, he would never wish his daughter to have a child without a partner as Sylvie had done.

Florence Bonnet came into the kitchen and set her coffee cup in the sink. "I couldn't help but overhear."

Marine and her father laughed. "Whatever you do, chérie," Florence said, kissing her daughter on the forehead, "we support you one hundred percent. And now I'm off for choir practice before Mass starts. Philomène will have my head if I'm late. I'll see you there, Anatole."

"*Oui, oui,*" Anatole Bonnet mumbled.

They heard Florence put on her coat and hat and rush out the front door. Marine reached up and touched her forehead where her mother had uncharacteristically kissed it. "Well, I should be going, too," Marine said.

"Will you go to Antoine's?"

"Yes, I think so. At least to tell him that he should loan the Soulages. Should we walk into town together?"

Anatole shrugged.

"What's wrong, Papa?"

"I'm not going to Mass."

"Aren't you feeling well?" Marine asked.

He paused. "I'm not sure I believe in it anymore."

"*Oh mon dieu!*"

"You can say that again," Anatole said, trying to smile.

"How long have you been feeling this way?" Marine asked, reaching once again for her father's hands.

Anatole thought about her question. He wasn't sure, but his doubts began surfacing after their first few appointments with the therapist on the Cours Mirabeau. As a medical man he had never questioned the death of their baby boy. Thomas had stopped breathing in his crib, for whatever reasons. "A few months now," he answered.

"And Maman doesn't know."

Anatole laughed. "It's not like I'm afraid of your mother—"

"But you don't want the conflict," Marine said. "I'm a bit like that with Antoine. We have to be sure, you and I, before we start tipping the bottle and letting out all our fears and questions and demands."

"Exactly."

Marine's cell phone rang and she saw that the caller was Antoine. "Do you mind if I pick up the phone, Papa? It's Antoine."

"Go right ahead. I'll make more coffee."

"Hello, Marine the Magnificent," Verlaque said. "Don't say anything until I say this: I love you, and I'm going to loan the Soulages to the Pompidou. I'll even take you to the opening night."

"I'd love that," Marine said.

"And we'll stay in one of the many spare bedrooms at my parents' place. It's around the corner from the Pompidou. It's time you got to know them."

Marine held out the phone in disbelief. "Okay."

"I just had a call from my father this morning," Verlaque went on. "He was being his usual vague self, but finally managed to tell me that my mother is sick, and in a hospital."

"Antoine! That's awful! What's wrong?"

Anatole Bonnet turned around from making coffee.

"I think it's the eating disorder she's had all her life," Verlaque said. "I'm going to go up to Paris in the next few days."

"As you should," Marine said.

"In the meantime," Verlaque continued, "I was wondering if you, and your father, would be available for a lunch date today, in the Luberon."

"Just a second and I'll ask him. Lunch in the Luberon, Papa?" Marine asked her father.

"Since I'm not going to Mass, I guess I'm available," Anatole answered. "Your mother is having lunch with Philomène Joubert and some other people from the choir."

"Yes," Marine said to Verlaque. "What's going on?"

"There's a retired art auctioneer, a Cézanne expert, who lives up there. I just called him and he invited us up for lunch. It's a bit weird, I know, but he lost his license driving drunk so can't come to us. René Rouquet had also called him; we found the phone number written down on a piece of paper in Rouquet's flat."

"We'll pick you up," Marine said. "This is exciting. We may get some answers about the painting. What's this man's name?"

"Lydgate. Edmund Lydgate," Verlaque said. "You can ask your father if he's heard of him. He's English but I think he must speak French."

"We'll be ready," Marine said.

"I'd invite your mother but I know she hates me."

"She's at Saint Jean de Malte," Marine said, smiling. "And she doesn't hate you. She has a hard time with the cigars."

"And my family money."

"And the antique Porsche," Marine said, laughing.

"The list goes on and on!"

"She'll eventually come around. But we do need to talk. I want to explain what happened the other night, after the Pauliks'."

"Okay," Verlaque said. "But first, we eat."

Chapter Fifteen

୬

Beauty Is a Complex Subject

• JANUARY 23, 1885 •

*I*t's so beautiful here, even in winter," Manon said, looking at the vista before them. "Don't you think so, M. Cézanne?" She passed him a dried fig. They had already passed the time speaking of the weather (warm and sunny, with no wind) and the painter had suggested they sit and share their lunches. He was every bit as awkward as her brother, Philippe, had described him, and yet she liked his company, and she was intrigued by his art.

"Beauty is a complex subject," he answered, carefully tearing the fig in two and slowly eating half. "It's the hills and mountains of Provence, fields in sun, pine forests, villages clinging to craggy slopes, the sea . . . But I'm not interested in the specific features of the landscape."

Manon looked over at his half-finished painting and said, "You're making it complicated, monsieur," she said, smiling. Philippe had told her that a peasant once saw Cézanne throw a rock into the middle of a landscape he had been working on. "So, what *is* beauty for you?"

Cézanne looked at her, surprised and slightly annoyed by her audacity. He shrugged. "A better painter can show you the detail of the pine tree, or the petals of a flower."

She pressed on, having been taught by her brother to question art. "*Mais pour vous, monsieur—*"

Cézanne looked at her. "Mlle Solari, you can be very . . . persistent." He looked straight ahead, but he could feel her eyes on him. Why not answer her questions? Isn't that what was missing with Hortense? "*Bon, mademoiselle,*" he began. "Beauty for me is in the form, and color, of a natural object. That other painter, the traditional one, he's painting reality for you. I'm questioning it. At least I'm trying to. There, you've made me answer your question. Thank you for the fig." He reached over and patted Manon's shoulder, then quickly drew his hand away.

"Figs are a treat," Manon said, as if she hadn't even noticed his touch. "We eat a lot of soup at home."

"Soup is one of the best things we can put in our bodies."

"Well, M. Cézanne," Manon said, laughing, "ours is mostly broth, with a little bread. You're still hungry after you've had a bowl."

Cézanne drew his legs up to his chest, embarrassed by his family's wealth. "How do you find working at Michaud's?" he asked, coughing. "Is Mme Michaud kind to you girls?"

"Oh yes," Manon answered, feeling the painter's awkwardness, so answering with a half lie. "She lets us take home leftover desserts. Not at all good for Maman's sweet tooth."

Cézanne laughed. "Your brother, Philippe, and I once met a woman in Paris—a rich woman who is a patron of the arts. She ate only sweets. You should have seen her!" He held out his hand in front of him, imitating a giant stomach, and blew out his cheeks. Manon laughed and he spoke on, encouraged. "She never walked. Anywhere! Walking, and eating soup every day, like a Provençal, that's a good life."

"But *Paris*," Manon said. "To be able to buy art, and live in Paris."

"I'm surprised you're interested in Paris, Manon. May I call you that?"

"Yes, of course," she replied. He hadn't given her the permission to call him Paul, but she didn't think she could ever call him that. He was much older than she, came from a wealthy family, and as a painter had traveled in circles she could only dream about. She said, "But who isn't interested in the capital, especially if you've never been there?"

Cézanne laughed. "Yes, you've never heard the trains blasting through the night, or the drunk men and women in Montmartre—"

"Women, too?"

"Yes, sadly," he said. "And so many of the old neighborhoods are gone now, just like your old wall in Aix. Baron Haussmann tore them down to build grand boulevards; they're vast and straight, all right, but for the rich, lined with luxury shops and cafés."

Manon smiled. "Your rich patron must waddle to them."

Cézanne laughed and slapped his knee. He had been intrigued by Manon's sensitivity, but she was funny, too. Her southern accent was charming, and it reminded him of his own life in Paris, of things he wouldn't tell her. He just said, "And

Parisians can be unkind." He thought of the laughter that rang through the Salon des Refusés in 1870 when he had been barely thirty years old and terrified of Paris. Fifteen years had already passed since that night, and yet he still cringed when remembering the art critic Monsieur Stock's words: "*Such a shocking Southern accent!*" Monet had tried to cheer him up. "Chin up, Paul. Stock said that I painted with a spatula, or a scrubbing brush—"

"And I with a broom," Edouard Manet had chimed in, patting Cézanne on the back.

"A spatula works quite well, actually," Cézanne had said quite seriously, and his friends broke into laughter.

Manon saw that Cézanne was smiling and she said, "There must be some good things about Paris, M. Cézanne."

"Yes," he answered. "There are your fellow painters in Paris, your comrades, and that's a good thing."

"And M. Zola."

"*Oui, lui aussi.* But I prefer Provence and its countryside and villages. What do you do out here, anyway? Besides walking."

"I collect plants," Manon said, lifting up her cloth bag.

"To use in cooking?"

"Of course," she answered. "I gather everything we need for a *bouquet garni* . . . thyme, rosemary—"

"I know, I know," Cézanne said, getting impatient. Even if his family now had a cook, he did know what went into a bouquet garni. "Bay leaf, marjoram—"

"Finding marjoram is the hardest part."

"Ah, what I wouldn't give for a good ratatouille right now," Cézanne said. "But of course it's not the season."

"We call it caponata *chez nous*," Manon said. "It's better than Provençal ratatouille."

"Oh, indeed?"

Manon laughed at the painter's sarcasm. "Yes, indeed. We add capers and vinegar. It's a special dish for us, of course. We made it when my sisters were married."

Cézanne tried to think back on his childhood and remember a day when eggplants and red peppers were considered a luxury. He looked down at his pants and played with a loose wool thread. Manon remembered Philippe telling her that Cézanne had a child and a mistress but his family didn't approve of her, and so they were never married. "I not only collect plants for cooking," she said, trying to cheer him up.

"Really?" he asked, turning toward her. "Are you a medicine woman, too?"

"Maman and my sister Clara are the *guérisseurs* in the family. I use plants to make scents."

"Really? Do you mean lavender oil?"

"That's just one of the scents that I love. Verbena is one of my favorites."

Cézanne said, "We have some large ones at the Jas de Bouffan." He stopped there, doubtful that he could ever invite her to the family home to pick verbena blossoms. Besides, his sisters guarded it for their tea. "Do you make the oils for yourself?"

"It started that way," Manon said. "And then I made them for my sisters and friends, as gifts, and now, at Michaud's, I sell a few to the girls, and Madame and her daughter."

Cézanne smiled. "*Quelle entrepreneuse!*"

"But that's not all," Manon said, her voice excited. "I'd like to make other products."

"Like what?"

"Creams."

"I don't understand."

Manon rubbed her face and arms with her hands.

"Beauty creams?" Cézanne asked.

"I'm not sure they make you more beautiful," Manon replied, laughing. "But they certainly would make your skin feel softer. More fresh."

Cézanne had seen fancy creams in glass and porcelain pots at the druggist's. Did his sisters Rose and Marie use these creams? They certainly had the money to buy them. "Why on earth would you want to rub some concoction over your face?" he asked.

Manon smiled, unperturbed, as if she had already thought out her answer. "Look up at our sun," she said. "Even in January it shines. You've seen what it does to grass, or to the paint on a house's shutters. Imagine what it does to your skin."

Cézanne looked up to the sun, shielding his eyes.

She went on, "And in Provence, to top things off, we have—"

"*Le Mistral.*"

"Exactly. The wind."

"But to make these creams," he said, "what would you use? Actual cream?"

Manon laughed. "No, but I think it should feel like cream. I've been reading about it in the library. I can use my oils for the scent, but I need shea butter, and cocoa butter. They're from Africa. And I'll need what they call an emulsifier."

"Something to blend it all together?"

"Yes, like what mustard does in our salad dressing. You need it so that the other ingredients don't separate over time. I'd like to find something here, in nature, that I can use. But not mustard."

Cézanne laughed. "Would you mind if I wrote to some of my Parisian friends?" he asked. "A few of them have been to

Africa, to paint, and they frequent trading companies in Paris where products from our African colonies are sold. We may be able to find those butters."

"That's so kind of you," Manon said.

"You can owe me," Cézanne said, seeing a frown of worry develop on his new friend's face. "Make your creams, Mlle Solari, and we'll figure out how to sell them here in Aix, and you can pay me after the orders start pouring in."

"I don't know what to say, M. Cézanne."

"Well," Cézanne said, looking ahead at the giant pine and then turning to her, "we began the conversation talking about beauty. Now perhaps you can tell me what beauty is for you."

"We cannot look away from something we think is beautiful, no matter how much we try," she said. "We can't take our eyes off of it."

Chapter Sixteen

❧

Anatole Bonnet Drives— Very Slowly—to the Luberon

*B*runo Paulik stood in front of his closet, whose door had a full-length mirror, and put a white shirt in front of his torso with his right hand, and then a pale-blue one with his left. He repeated this for five minutes, switching back and forth between the two.

Hélène Paulik walked in, putting on her coat. "Bruno, what are you doing? We'll be late."

"I think I should vamp up my wardrobe," he answered, quickly hanging the white shirt back up and putting on the blue one.

"Vamp up? Is that my husband speaking?"

"Well, I work in Aix, which is a pretty fashion-conscious place," he said. "Even Verlaque wears pink shirts sometimes, with bow ties."

Hélène snorted. "My weird uncle Geoffroy wore bow ties. Besides, Antoine can get away with it."

"What do you mean?" Paulik said, buttoning up his shirt while he followed his wife out of their bedroom.

"He has pizzazz," she said, twirling her hand in the air. "I don't know if it's because he's Parisian, or part English, or wealthy . . ." Her voice trailed off as she hollered for Léa.

Léa, who had been waiting at the bottom of the stairs, already dressed for the cold but clear January day, looked up at her parents and sighed. "I'm roasting in my coat, you two."

"Sorry. Your father thinks he's George Clooney," Hélène said.

"I don't have his hair," Paulik said. "Or any hair, for that matter. What about Jean Reno?"

Léa laughed and he went on, encouraged. "As a matter of fact, I saw him in a commerical the other day, for cashmere sweaters."

"Reno, the beloved thug and gangster of our nation's cinema, selling cashmere?" Hélène threw up her hands in disgust and grabbed her purse. "You can drop us off at the cinema and then we'll meet you at the Mazarin when our film is over," she said to Bruno as she gently pushed him and Léa out the door. "Although I don't know why you have to work today."

"Verlaque has a last-minute lunch meeting, in the Luberon. He's meeting a retired art dealer who lost his license and can't drive. It has to do with the Céz—" He looked over at his daughter, pursing his lips.

"I know about the Cézanne painting," Léa said, getting into the car.

Paulik turned around and looked at Léa. "It's a secret, okay, chérie?" he said. "We're not even sure if it a real Cézanne."

"Is it pretty?" Léa asked. "Or ugly?"

"It's pretty," Paulik said, putting the car in gear. He drove past their vineyard, brought back to life by Hélène, one of

Provence's star winemakers. "It's of a girl; she's about twice your age—"

"Twenty."

"Right," Paulik said, smiling. "Or maybe three times your age."

"Thirty."

"Right again," he said, turning onto the Route Nationale 7 that would take them into Aix. "She has red hair, and a blue blouse, and she looks very happy."

"Smiling?" Hélène asked. "Doesn't sound like a Cézanne portrait."

"Why is it so important that you have to work and can't come to the movie?" Léa asked. "It's just a painting."

"That's a good question, sweetie," Paulik said. "Well, we think that someone got hurt because he found this painting in his apartment, the very apartment that Cézanne lived in."

"Did someone steal the painting?" Léa asked.

"No, but they tried to."

"Why?"

Paulik said, "Cézanne has been dead for more than one hundred years, and so his paintings are now worth a lot of money."

"More than our car?"

"More than our house," Paulik said.

"With the vineyard," Hélène added.

"That's stupid," Léa said. She let out a little moan and added, "My tummy hurts."

"Look straight ahead at the road," Hélène said, rubbing her own stomach. "We'll be on the highway soon." They drove on in silence, Paulik wondering if Dr. Schultz would notice the effort he took that morning with his wardrobe, Hélène wondering why her husband had been in the bedroom for so long, and Léa trying to work out how many zeros the price of the

Cézanne painting would have. She thought it would be well over a hundred euros, as her friend Julie's mother had spent more than that on a purse and after that Julie's maman and papa had had a big fight. She had no idea what their own car cost. She knew that their house and the vineyard had been bought by Judge Verlaque, but that her parents were somehow partners with him, because of the wine her maman made.

Paulik dropped off his girls at the Cinema Mazarin to see a documentary about migrating birds, then parked the car in the underground parking below the Palais de Justice. He would have liked to watch the film with them, but he was anxious to get to the Hôtel Fleurie and hear Dr. Schultz's side of the story. Why had she been at the Bar Zola? By chance? He hardly thought so, given the bar's location on a tiny street in the middle of Aix. The rough clientele, with the cigarette smoke and loud music, were sure to eliminate any chance of the bar making it into a guidebook used by Americans. But Rebecca Schultz wasn't an ordinary tourist. No ordinary woman. He felt the same pang in his stomach as he had while trying to choose a shirt.

Passing the Quatre Dauphins fountain in the Quartier Mazarin, Paulik popped a mint into his mouth. He turned up the rue Cardinale, where, despite Saint Jean de Malte's doors being closed, he swore he could hear Mass finishing with a flourish of organ and choir. Walking into the lobby of the hotel, he was surprised to see the same receptionist, still reading her book. He thought for a moment that she had stayed up all night, but she had must have gone home—somewhere—to sleep. "Hallo!" Paulik said, waving.

The receptionist looked up, surprised. "Back again, commissioner?"

"I forgot to ask Dr. Schultz a few questions last night," he said. "Would you mind ringing her room?"

"I don't mind," she said. "But it won't do any good."

"Sorry?"

"The professor checked out this morning."

"How's the mileage in this Kangoo?" Verlaque asked, leaning his elbows on the front seat ahead of him. Marine turned around and smiled.

"Top notch," Anatole Bonnet replied as he drove. "It only takes five point five liters of diesel fuel to go one hundred kilometers. It's the most practical car I've ever had."

"It's neat being so high up," Verlaque said, smiling and trying to catch Marine's eye in the rearview mirror.

Marine covered her mouth with her hand and tried not to laugh. Not a specialist in makes of cars, even she knew that her parent's Renault Kangoo was one of the ugliest minivans on the market.

"What can you tell us about Edmund Lydgate before we get to Gordes?" Verlaque asked. "Have you ever met him?"

"No. But I know that he's very knowledgeable," Dr. Bonnet replied. "He worked at Sotheby's in London and New York for years. Quite funny, which I'm told makes him a popular speaker at conferences. I've never heard him lecture, but friends have."

"Does he speak French?" Marine asked.

"Yes, I'm told with a charming accent. I heard that something happened, and he quit the auction house very suddenly."

"Did it have to do with his drinking?" Marine asked.

"I'm not sure," her father answered, taking a corner at about half the speed as Verlaque did in his Porsche.

"Papa," Marine said, trying to be patient, "just to remind you, our appointment is at noon."

"I'll get us there on time, don't worry."

"Just enjoy the view, Marine," Verlaque said, smiling, sitting back with his hands behind his head.

"I have been, Antoine, thank you very much," she answered, looking out of the window at the dormant vineyards. "Even in the winter, Provence is beautiful."

"Especially the Luberon," her father said. "When you were young, we thought about buying a weekend house up here. One of my patients, who was elderly and a childless widower, was selling the family home."

Marine looked at her father. "Really?"

"A nice old stone house," Dr. Bonnet went on.

"Papa," Marine said, "it would be worth a fortune now."

"I know," he answered. "But it was a lot of money for us at the time, and your mother couldn't imagine going every weekend. It seemed like a long way from Aix."

Verlaque tried not to laugh, as they had only been on the road for less than forty minutes and were almost at Edmund Lydgate's house. He had driven farther for a good cup of coffee. At that moment his cell phone rang and, excusing himself, he answered it, listening to Bruno Paulik's news of Rebecca Schultz's disappearance. "*Merde*," he said, hanging up. "Dr. Schultz has gone missing."

"I told you so," Marine said, turning around to face Verlaque. "I didn't trust her."

"You never met her."

"Just the sound of her was enough," Marine said. "Being an Ivy League professor and top model don't mix."

"Oh, I don't know, chérie," her father said. "You could be a model."

"*Merci, Papa.*"

"If you straightened your hair," he went on, slowing down the Kangoo to almost a full stop. "I've heard the nurses talk about hair straighteners you can buy—"

"Marine's hair is lovely," Verlaque cut in.

"More to the point," Marine said, "I teach at the University of Aix-Marseille. Far in prestige from Yale University."

"And a whole lot cheaper," Dr. Bonnet said. "Education for all, rich or poor."

"I stayed up late looking at the photos we took of the painting," Marine said, to change the subject. She despaired over her colleagues' petty internal wars, their constant comparing of French schools against international ones on the Shanghai rating scales, and the general lack of supplies and disrepair of the Aix *faculté*. "And I read about Cézanne until about three a.m. Look at our picture," she said, pulling a Polaroid of the painting out of her purse. "Who is the sitter? Antoine, you said that Cézanne had an affair in 1885. Whether or not they actually consummated their relationship, if we can date this painting to that year, we'd be surer of its authenticity."

"What do you think, Dr. Bonnet?" Verlaque asked.

"I think it *could* be the mysterious Aixoise of 1885. Look at what she's wearing," Anatole Bonnet said, nervously glancing at the Polaroid while trying to drive. "Is she wealthy? Upper class?"

"Certainly not," Verlaque said. "It's not a shiny silk dress, for one."

"Exactly," Anatole said. "So she's poor, but happy. And Cézanne liked to spend time with workers and peasants. The wealthy made him angry, and intellectuals made him nervous."

Marine nodded. "Last night I read about a party at Monet's in Giverny; Monet complimented Cézanne, who then flew into a rage. He was so awkward he couldn't even accept a compliment from a friend."

"There's something else that bothers me, other than her smile, which you said, Dr. Bonnet, was rare for a Cézanne portrait," Verlaque said, taking the photograph in his hands. "Ah, I know now. It's the bright colors of her dress. They seem too bright for a poor girl at the end of the nineteenth century."

"That bothered me, too," Marine said.

"But the clothes in Provence were much more colorful than in other parts of France," Anatole said. "Even one hundred years ago, Provençal fabrics were full of color, especially in Arles."

"True," Verlaque said. "But this girl's wearing an orange skirt and a bright-blue blouse. Provençal clothes were colorful, but not that bright. Her clothes, if she was poor, would have been faded after repeated wearing, and the sun. No?"

"Think about what Cézanne was interested in," Anatole said, slowing the car down.

"Um, he didn't care about reproducing reality," Verlaque suggested.

"I get it, Papa!" Marine said. "He dressed his sitter here—with whom he was in love, or very infatuated—in the most classic Provençal colors he could find. *He made it up.* It's the blue of our sky, and orange, its complement. She may not have even been a redhead."

"Yes, you're right," Verlaque said. "As the red he's used in her hair is the same red as the earth out at Bibémus and Mont Sainte Victoire."

"That may be stretching it a bit, Antoine," Anatole said.

"Really?" Verlaque asked, looking disappointed. "I thought that I was on to something."

"Well, hopefully Edmund Lydgate will be able to give us

an expert opinion on the paint and brushwork," Marine said. "Papa. You've stopped the car."

"There it is," Dr. Bonnet said, looking out the windshield. "Gordes. I always pull over here to look at the view."

"It's so much lovelier from afar than when you're in the middle of it," Marine said, sitting back and gazing upon the medieval village clinging to the cliffs. "It's too busy now."

"So, good thing we didn't buy that house," her father said, smiling.

Verlaque looked ahead, trying to count how many of the coveted village houses had swimming pools.

Chapter Seventeen

❧

Le Mas des Lilas

*M*arine looked at the directions from Edmund Lydgate that she had printed out. "I think we're here," she said, folding the paper in half. Her father slowed the car down and pulled into a drive. "The *borie* must be on Lydgate's property," she continued. "I've never seen such a perfectly rounded one. To think that someone spent weeks, many decades ago, building that with fieldstones and no mortar. Just to store grain or hay in. It's so beautifully built and so well proportioned that it becomes a work of art."

"*Mas des Lilas*," Anatole Bonnet muttered as he strained to read the wooden sign above the mailbox. "I don't believe it. This was the house, Marine."

"What do you mean?" Verlaque asked. "Is this the place you almost bought?" He refrained from saying "should have," for he could see the stone house at the end of the drive. It was a rambling two-story eighteenth-century house, built in the white stone that made Gordes famous—and unbearably busy in summer—and its multipaned windows were framed by pale-green shutters. Ivy crept up half of the building, and the wooden front door was crowned by a thick, twisting trunk that wrapped its way around the door and spread out in both directions above it. No plant expert, especially during the winter months, Verlaque thought it was wisteria.

"Yes, this is it," Dr. Bonnet said. "Even the name is the same. Your mother loved the *borie*, Marine."

"I can see why," Marine said.

Dr. Bonnet drove cautiously up the stony drive and Verlaque was tempted to swing open his sliding door and jump out.

"See those lilac trees? That's where the house gets its name from," Dr. Bonnet said, pointing to his right. "Although they're dormant now. They were in full bloom when we visited the house. There were white ones, too."

"And there's M. Lydgate," Marine said. "With a full head of white hair to match the lilacs."

Edmund Lydgate had heard the Kangoo on the drive and was thankful his guests were on time. He had a chicken from Bresse in the oven and didn't want to serve a dry, overcooked *poulet*. He gestured for them to park beside his battered Clio, which he could no longer drive. "Welcome!" he cried, hoping he wasn't putting it on too thick. He didn't like visitors.

He held out his hand and firmly shook Anatole Bonnet's hand, then Marine's, and finally Verlaque's. Marine smiled at Verlaque and winked; she liked the look of Edmund Lydgate. He wasn't tall, thin, and distinguished as she had imagined a retired English art auctioneer to be; he was instead short and portly, with thick white hair and a white handlebar moustache. He wore a loudly colored jacket of thick yellow, red, and blue stripes, and navy wool pants. His bow tie was crooked—pink with light blue polka dots.

"*Allez, allez,*" he called out, waving his arms in the air. "We'll positively *freeze* out here."

"We almost bought this house, Monsieur Lydgate," Dr. Bonnet said while Lydgate hurriedly hung their coats up in the hallway.

"Really?" Lydgate said. "How extraordinary. I've owned it for more than a half century. And lucky thing, too. I couldn't afford it now. Come into the salon."

Verlaque looked at Marine and raised an eyebrow; Lydgate didn't seem the bit interested in the odd coincidence that Marine's father knew the house. But if M. Lydgate did not physically resemble what Marine thought an English auctioneer should look like, his furnishings fit the bill. Every spare inch of the living and dining rooms was filled with art and antiques, from Napoleon-era writing desks and commodes to 1950s Italian lighting. The walls were covered in framed paintings, and, like the furniture, they seemed to be from various eras.

"Please sit," Lydgate instructed, again flapping his arms. "I'll serve some sherry, and then I'll look at your treasure. Unless you'd care for something stronger. Single-malt whiskey, perhaps?"

"Yes, thank you," Verlaque said as he looked around the room.

"Oh good," Lydgate said. "I'll join you in one."

As Lydgate busied himself with the drinks, Marine said, "Your paintings, M. Lydgate. They're all portraits."

"Yes, indeed," he answered, handing Marine and her father a glass each of sherry. "I'm a sucker for them. I think it's because I like being alone. They keep me company."

"Then I'm glad you agreed to meet us," Verlaque said. "Thank you."

"Of course your commissioner didn't give me much of a choice, seeing as someone was killed over this piece of canvas."

"When did M. Rouquet call you?" Verlaque asked.

Lydgate raised his eyes to the ceiling. "Hmm, a few days ago. Wednesday? Thursday? It was hard to understand him, and I'm proud of my French. He was very excited."

"Do you know how he got your phone number?" Verlaque asked.

"That's a good question," Lydgate replied. "No, I don't know. My license has been temporarily suspended, so I couldn't drive to Aix, and it seems he couldn't drive up here. He blathered on about an old scooter."

Verlaque nodded; Pierre had told him that René got around on an old, disused post office scooter, still yellow but missing one of the panniers. "Did Rouquet sound frigthened?"

Lydgate thought for a moment with his hand on his chin. "No," he replied. "Just excited."

"And he didn't mention any names? Anyone who might be following him?"

"No. The only name he mentioned was Cézanne's. Well, now that we've all been served drinks, how about a peek at this canvas?" Lydgate asked.

Verlaque stood up, took the canvas out of its bag, and un-raveled the bath towel that he had brought from his apartment to protect it.

"Oh dear," Lydgate said, pointing to the towel.

"What?" Verlaque asked.

"Fibers, dear boy, fibers. Never mind; lay it over there," Lydgate said, motioning to a polished mahogany table. "I say, how did you manage to sneak the painting away from the Palais de Justice?"

"Authority," Verlaque said. "Plus, I didn't tell anyone. But I did bring gloves," he went on, taking a pair out of his tweed jacket.

"You can wear those," Lydgate said, also pulling a pair out of his jacket pocket. "I'll wear my own."

Verlaque unrolled the canvas and Lydgate immediately put a hand to his mouth, gasping, "Oh my! It's a beauty." He quickly put on the gloves and looked at the painting for some minutes, humming quietly to himself. Anatole Bonnet paced the room; Marine stayed quietly sitting, watching Lydgate; and Verlaque stood beside him, his hands folded behind his back. The only sound, when Lydgate wasn't humming, was the ticking of a clock.

"Fine blues and greens," Lydgate finally said.

"Are they Cézanne blues and greens?" Verlaque asked, smiling.

"Oh yes. And they're repeated throughout the painting, just as he would have done."

"But other painters did that, too, right?" Marine asked. "Repeated the colors, I mean. Put the green from the grass also in the sky, that kind of thing."

"Quite so, like Vermeer," Lydgate replied. "But Cézanne did more than repeat color. He didn't just delineate shapes—cubes, cylinders—by outlines; he did it by meticulous use of color changes." Lydgate pointed to the girl's large buttons on her blue blouse. "Look," he said. "Here, a series of color gradations determined the roundness of this button. Normally it's easiest to see with fruit in his still lifes. But he did it with flat shapes, too—like the back of her chair. They are not uniformly colored, as we imagine that this classic cane-seated chair was—a dreary kind of brown oak." Lydgate shook his shoulders. "Oh, how I detest oak!"

"I agree," Verlaque said. Anatole Bonnet looked at his daughter with a puzzled look. Some people had preferences for different kinds of wood? He and Florence had bought most of their furniture from the Camif catalogue.

Dr. Bonnet said, "To Cézanne the chair is a series of planes, not just an object to sit on. The chair is subject to the same kinds of color variations as clouds and water."

"As is the wall behind the girl," Verlaque said.

"Ah yes," Lydgate quickly answered. "Again, so many color variations. All painstakingly done by small parallel brush-strokes. No wonder Cézanne was always in a bad mood!"

"There's something that amazes me when I look at a Cézanne," Dr. Bonnet said. "Not one element stands out. A mountain, a cabanon, a pine tree: all equally important."

"Normally yes," Lydgate said. "Harmony."

"The poet Rilke wrote, 'It's as if every place were aware of all the other places,'" Dr. Bonnet said. "Cézanne called it 'joining hands.'"

"That's lovely," Marine said. She leaned over the painting and looked at it. "But this painting—" she said. "The girl is more important than the other elements, isn't she? I see her first, more than the wall, or the chair. She shimmers."

"Ah yes," Lydgate said. "*Quel dommage.*"

"What do you mean? Are you saying because of the girl it's not a real Cézanne?" Verlaque asked.

"I don't think it is, no," Lydgate said. "But it's a master copy."

"Are you sure?" Marine asked. Lydgate had seemed taken with it.

"It's awfully well done. I'll need more time with it. But first, we must eat. I had the butcher in Apt deliver this *poulet de Bresse*." Lydgate ushered them into the adjoining dining room.

Verlaque smiled at the thought of buying meat a few towns away, liking Lydgate more and more. The table had been set with much polished silver and pressed white linens, and Marine followed their host into the kitchen to help serve. "You can take the *gratin dauphinois*, dear," Lydgate said, handing Marine a pair of oven mitts and gesturing to the oven. "I swear there's no cream in it!" he said. "Just oodles of butter!"

Much admiration of the golden *poulet* was expressed as Lydgate proudly opened a 1989 Domaine Leroy. "You're being very generous, Mr. Lydgate," Verlaque said in English. "I've never had Lalou Bize-Leroy's wines; only read about them."

Lydgate looked at the bottle as if confused. He then said, "Working in an auction house for so many years did have its advantages," as he poured a little wine into Verlaque's glass to taste.

"It's delicious," Verlaque said.

Lydgate smiled and filled the rest of the glasses. "Velour," Marine said after tasting it. "Silky, but thicker, like velour."

"So, Mr. Lydgate," Verlaque said after they had begun eating, "have you ever come across the fact that Cézanne had a mistress—an Aixoise—in 1885?"

"No," Lydgate said—almost too quickly, Marine thought. "But I'm not an expert in the biographies of artists."

"Who is?"

"Well," Lydgate said, setting down his fork, "Rebecca Schultz from Yale, for one."

"Unfortunately she has disappeared from her hotel," Anatole Bonnet said, helping himself to more gratin.

"What say you?" Lydgate asked. "What hotel? Is the eminent professor here? In Provence?"

Verlaque glared at Anatole, who shrunk down in his chair.

"Yes, she is," Verlaque answered. "She was the one who found M. Rouquet's body, in Cézanne's old flat."

"Oooh, suspect number one, and now she's flown the coop," Lydgate said, pressing his two hands together, the tips of his fingers meeting. "Of course she has her own motives."

"Pardon me?" Marine asked.

"The Schultz collection," Lydgate said, carving more chicken. "I'm surprised you haven't heard of it."

"That's why her name rang a bell!" Dr. Bonnet said, slapping his forehead. "I knew she was a historian, but there was something about her past that I kept trying to remember."

"Would you two care to fill us in?" Marine asked.

Lydgate opened another bottle of Leroy and poured it out. "Imagine this: 1961. A young Jewish couple—she's a high school teacher and he runs his family's fruit and vegetable delivery company in lower Manhattan. They live in a rent-controlled apartment and cannot have children. One evening he—Isaac Schultz—sees a small Cézanne in a gallery window on his way home from work. It costs five thousand dollars. More than two years' rent. He goes home and talks to his wife—Judy—and they decide to buy it. In installments. It takes them two years. Five years on, they own four Cézannes, two Picassos, and a Duchamp sculpture that they put in the middle of the living room. The fruit company flourishes when people in Montana and Kansas insist on having clementines and avocados all year round, and Isaac's brother Irv turns out to be a whiz at trucking and logistics. They become comfortably well-off, but never billionaires, like today's collectors. Everything

the Schultzes earn from then on is spent on buying art. They
seldom go to Europe, never dine out. She doesn't wear furs or
jewels; he patches his broken eyeglasses with masking tape.
They never buy a car. Yet by the early '70s they own almost
thirty Cézannes of Mont Sainte Victoire alone. Only one thing
is missing."

"A child," Verlaque said.

Chapter Eighteen

✍

Edmund Lydgate's Prognosis

What an inspirational story," Marine said. "I remember Gertrude Stein telling a young Hemingway to buy art and nothing else. The Schultzes took her rule to heart. Are they still alive?"

"Isaac Schultz died three years ago," Lydgate said. "And Judy in September."

"And the art collection?" Verlaque asked. "Rebecca will inherit, no?"

"Yes, poor girl."

"I'm not following, Mr. Lydgate," Verlaque said.

"Nasty American inheritance taxes. There's no way Rebecca can keep the art, as she'll have to pay tax on the current market value of the paintings."

"That's insane!" Marine said. "Her parents obviously had no idea when they bought the art how overblown art prices would become."

Lydgate said, "And knowing the trade like I do, she's been hounded by Christie's, Sotheby's, the Japanese, and the Russians."

"Perhaps this young woman may not want the stigma attached with owning such a spectacular art collection. That requires a certain kind of person, one who likes being in the limelight, for instance," Dr. Bonnet said.

Oh, I think she'd enjoy that, thought Verlaque. Rebecca Schultz was now hardly a chief suspect; why kill for a Cézanne if you grew up with them hanging in your kitchen?

"Do you have any idea what the Schultz collection will sell for?" Marine asked.

Lydgate got up and began clearing the dishes. "To give you a rough idea, a small watercolor study of Cézanne's card players recently sold at Christie's for almost twenty million dollars. And the Schultzes owned major paintings, not watercolors."

"So even if she can't afford to keep the collection," Marine said, "Dr. Schultz will be a wealthy woman after the sale."

"Yes, indeed," Lydgate said.

"Let me help you clear the dishes," Anatole Bonnet said, jumping up.

"Thank you," Lydgate said. "I'll give you some dessert plates to set out for the cake you so kindly brought. I see it's from Michaud's; I'd recognize that red box anywhere."

With Lydgate and her father in the kitchen, Marine turned to Verlaque and whispered, "So that clears Rebecca Schultz, doesn't it? Why would she kill for a Cézanne?"

"I was just thinking the same thing," he answered. "And according to our host, it's a fake."

"But Schultz doesn't know that," Marine said. "She hasn't seen it. Perhaps she desperately wants it as a personal vendetta— against whom, I don't know."

"And she'd know about Cézanne's Aix lover," Verlaque said, "as his eminent biographer. That fact was easy enough for even me to find out." He reached into his jacket pocket and checked his cell phone. "No messages," he said.

"She can't have disappeared into thin air," Marine said. She then raised an eyebrow and added, "Being such a beauty."

Lydgate and Dr. Bonnet returned with a *tropézienne* proudly displayed on a crystal cake plate. "Who needs chocolate when there's Chantilly?" Lydgate asked.

"Mr. Lydgate," Verlaque said as the cake was cut and served, "there's something I've never understood about art."

"Go on," Lydgate said, putting a piece of cake in his mouth and sitting back in his chair with a look of bliss.

"How do you, or any expert for that matter, know that Cézanne didn't just feel like changing his style for this particular painting?" He had been thinking more and more about his conversation with Bruno Paulik, and was now less confident of his argument.

Edmund Lydgate looked perplexed.

Verlaque went on: "How he felt on that particular Tuesday morning, for example."

Lydgate smiled and Verlaque could see that Marine's father had a look of concern on his face.

"Stop looking at me like I'm a half-wit," Verlaque said, trying to joke.

"My dear fellow," Lydgate said in English, "an artist as serious as Paul Cézanne didn't just change his style one morning for the fun of it."

"Why not?" Verlaque asked, crossing his arms and waiting for more detail.

"It took him so long to get to that point," Anatole Bonnet said, switching the conversation back into French. "He had been an outcast, but by 1885 he had finally found his gift. Think of all the teasing he got in Paris. Even the Aixois didn't understand him."

Lydgate said, "He wouldn't have had the time, nor the interest, to start fooling around with another technique. It's how people like me—"

"Experts."

"Yes," Lydgate said, smiling. "It's how experts can be so sure of what we're looking at. Although—"

"Yes?" Marine asked, leaning in.

Lydgate glanced in the direction of the canvas and got up from the table. He walked over to it, hands held behind his back, and bent down. He picked up a loupe and began looking at details in the painting, humming once more. He looked over at Verlaque and said, "There's a bottle of *eau-de-vie* in the kitchen, dear fellow. Would you mind serving us some? You'll see the small glasses set out beside it."

Verlaque did as he was told. Anatole Bonnet set his hand over his glass; even if he hadn't been the driver, he never drank anything stronger than wine. Marine got up and walked over to Lydgate's side. "What do you see, or not see?" she asked.

"Very astute," he answered. Dr. Bonnet and Verlaque joined them. "I see the preliminary sketch on the canvas, and Cézanne always did that in brush with a watery blue paint, never with charcoal." He pointed those parts out. "And I don't see black coffee."

His guests looked at him, perplexed, until Marine said, "As an ager?"

"Yes. Black coffee poured over a canvas will get into the teeth of the material. Rubbed in by hand, the coffee dries, and in four and a half minutes you've aged the painting a hundred years."

"There must be other ways to fake the age," Verlaque said.

"Vacuum cleaner dust does a great job, too," Lydgate answered.

"You've got to be joking."

"Not at all," Lydgate said. "A master forger in northern England even painted with cheap house paints for years until being caught." Lydgate took a large gulp of the eau-de-vie and continued looking at the canvas with the loupe. "This painting hasn't been fiddled with," he said. "I don't see any signs of artificial aging. But I would need more time, and better equipment to look at it with. You don't suppose—"

"You can look at it all you want at the Palais de Justice in Aix," Verlaque said. "But I can't let it out of my sight."

"May I take a few photographs?" Lydgate asked.

"Five," Verlaque replied, smiling.

Lydgate handed Marine a small camera. "Would you mind, dear? We need more eau-de-vie." Lydgate picked up his glass and held it out. Verlaque poured and Lydgate drank his fiery drink as he paced the room. Marine watched the expert, wondering if he had been steering them into believing that painting was a fake. Lydgate was, after all, passionate about portraits. But now he seemed to be undecided.

"You gasped when you saw the painting," Marine said. "Your first instinct was that it was the real thing."

Lydgate looked at her. "You're right." He walked back over to the canvas, set his empty glass down on a table, and looked at the painting, his hands held behind his back.

Verlaque looked at Marine and smiled; Lydgate was now standing on the opposite end of the table, looking at the canvas upside down. *Shouldn't have had that second eau-de-vie*, thought Verlaque.

"It's the subject matter that's bothering me," Lydgate finally said, turning to face Marine, Verlaque, and Dr. Bonnet. "An unknown woman, wearing too-bright clothes, and smiling at the painter. Manet, possible. Monet, too. But not our Paul Cézanne. I'm sorry."

"We don't own it," Verlaque said. He kept to himself the thought that perhaps two people were killed over a fake Cézanne. Why? "So we're not desperate for it to be a genuine Cézanne. But I thank you for your time."

Edmund Lydgate could hear Dr. Bonnet's ugly car slowly make its way down the drive, stopping at the end to make sure the road was clear, and then driving off. He poured himself a little more eau-de-vie while he cleared up the table, stopping to sigh; the sight of the painting had made his heart race.

A door opened and closed upstairs, and he walked into the hallway and waited at the bottom of the stairs, his hand resting on the brass ball at the end of the wrought-iron balustrade. As he saw the elegant black high heels and green tweed pants, he thought of his dear wife, Hazel. She had been dead almost ten years, but a day didn't go by when he didn't think of her, especially when in the garden. Hazel, who, unlike him, had exercised. Hazel, who, unlike him, had refrained from alcohol and watched what she ate. But the cancer didn't seem to have cared about all that.

"I hope you left me something to eat," the woman said, now at the bottom of the stairs, holding out her thin hand for him to take.

"Yes, indeed, Beauty," Lydgate said, taking her by the hand and leading her into the kitchen.

"Great; I thought they would never leave," Rebecca said, going to the sink and washing her hands. "You know, Edmund," she said, turning to him as he lifted a plate of leftovers from the oven that he had been keeping warm for her, "I never thought of myself as beautiful. More a freak. Too tall; crazy, unruly hair. The little petite blond girls, they were the beautiful ones. Never me."

Lydgate smiled. "Oh, where are they now?" he asked. "Their blond hair now dyed with frosty tips, and their figures gone plump."

"I highly doubt it, given where I grew up," she answered. "But thanks." She followed him into the dining room as he quickly made a spot for her. She lifted a fork and began eating with much eagerness. "Edmund, your gratin is . . . awesome!"

"You need to put in check how many times you use the word 'awesome,'" he said.

Rebecca smiled and wiped the corners of her mouth with the linen napkin he had given her. "So, my dear man," she said, "what's your verdict? Did you do the upside-down trick like I told you?"

"Yes, my dear," he answered. "I'm sorry to disappoint you, but it was a mess. A fake, but a good one."

Chapter Nineteen

❧

Dedans/Dehors

*B*runo," Verlaque said, getting up from behind his desk, "sometimes I think you use me for my espresso maker."

Paulik smiled, shaking his boss's hand. "Only on Monday mornings, sir. Besides, it will warm us up."

Verlaque turned the machine on and both men stood facing it, waiting for the little red light to blink, signaling that it was warm enough to make coffee. "We'd better not watch it," Verlaque said.

"You're right," Paulik said, turning his back to the small red machine. "Flamant was here all day yesterday researching Guy Maneval."

"And?"

"He worked as a bouncer at La Fantasie, for one thing."

"Mafia connections?" Verlaque asked, as the club was known to be owned by the Corsican Mafia.

"Yes," Paulik replied. "And one of his colleagues is in jail right now, so Flamant and Caromb paid him a visit. Guess who? Kévin Malongo. Malongo was more than happy to cooperate. From what we can piece together—including what you gained from the barman at the Zola—Maneval must have overheard René Rouquet brag about the painting, followed him home, and then in a scuffle killed Rouquet, taking the only painting he could find that looked vaguely like a Cézanne."

"What was he hoping to do with it?" Verlaque asked. "It's not as if it's easy to sell something like that. If he had taken the right painting, that is."

"Malongo says that Maneval had screwed up a drug deal and was hoping to make things right with Fabrizio Orsani."

"He was going to give the painting to the godfather?" Verlaque asked. He turned around to face the machine. "The light's flashing."

Paulik rubbed his hands together. "I'll have a ristretto."

"Me, too," Verlaque said. "Then a second."

"Ditto."

"How did Maneval screw up a drug deal?" Verlaque asked. "Was someone killed?"

"No," Paulik said. "Apparently Caromb and Flamant shared a good laugh with Malongo over this. Maneval was transporting bags of heroin from Marseille to Paris, and he lost them."

Verlaque handed Paulik a coffee. "Poor guy," he said. "How does one lose heroin?"

Paulik sat down, sipping his coffee. "That's the best part," he said, laughing. "He lost it on the TGV."

Verlaque sat in the back of the unmarked car, happy to have Roger Caromb drive. In all his years as a magistrate, this was the only time he had butterflies in his stomach. That he had managed to get an appointment with Fabrizio Orsani so soon was beyond belief; calls had been made throughout the morning, and after lunch Paulik had poked his head in the door of his office, informing Verlaque of his four o'clock appointment.

Verlaque pretended to look through files, wishing he could just sit back and enjoy the view, but he didn't want to have to talk with Caromb. They sped down the A52, a winding highway usually free of traffic thanks to its tolls. This was also the shortest way to get to Orsani's, as he did not live in Marseille but near the charming seaside village of Cassis. Verlaque knew, without ever having been there, that the Orsani spread would not be in the village itself but on Giens, a peninsula in west Cassis surrounded by the sea and home to a few estates. The luxurious hotel Les Roches Blanches was also there; it had been a favorite hotel of Verlaque's grandparents. Winston Churchill had also been a guest, painting watercolors from its terrace.

Caromb signaled to exit the highway at Carnoux; Verlaque leaned forward and said, "Get off at the next exit, Roger, if you don't mind. There's another toll, but we'll drive down through Cassis vineyards."

Caromb shrugged and mumbled, "Yes, sir," and continued driving. He always took the Carnoux exit drove to Cassis on his days off; it saved on the extra 1.20-euro toll, and there was a tabac in Carnoux where he usually pulled over to buy extra ciggies, or a few beers to take down to the beach.

They took the next exit, and the car wound its way down through the vineyards—mostly white grapes—of Cassis, one of France's smallest appellations. At the village's first roundabout they turned right and drove up a hill, passing small, expensive hotels. Verlaque laughed out loud at one called the Royal Cottages; how could a cottage be royal? Once at the top of the village they turned left onto Giens peninsula, Caromb following the instructions given to him by another officer. "So," Caromb said as they slowed down before a set of black gates, "this is the godfather's place, eh?"

"Nothing of the sort," Verlaque said, perturbed as he usually was with Caromb. "Fabrizio Orsani owns a small shipping company, and a few hotels, restaurants, and nightclubs." Who knows? Verlaque mused. Perhaps Orsani wasn't connected with the Mafia. Perhaps the Corsican godfather really was untouchable, hiding out somewhere in the hills behind Marseille, or Ajaccio.

"Yeah, I heard he imports olive oil, too," Caromb said, laughing. The reference to Mario Puzo's award-winning book-turned-movie-trilogy was not lost on the judge and he decided to play along.

" 'Leave the gun, take the cannoli,' " Verlaque said, quoting his favorite line from the first film as a security guard approached their car.

Caromb held back his laugh as he rolled down his window and announced, "Officer Roger Caromb, and Judge Antoine Verlaque. We have a four o'clock appointment with M. Orsani."

No, we don't, Verlaque thought. *I do*.

"ID," the guard said, peering at them.

Caromb handed him their badges and the guard looked at the photos and then long and hard at both men. "Go on up," he finally said, handing back their IDs. "Just park at the top of the hill by the stone wall, next to the motorcycle. Then follow the path beside the wall to the front door."

The drive snaked its way up a hill, with views of Cassis, the sea, and Cap Canaille to the east and the open sea to the west. Caromb parked the car and they got out, Verlaque pointing to a stone bench. "I don't think I'll be too long," he said.

"Yes, sir," Caromb said, stretching and then sitting down.

Verlaque followed a narrow path that curved as the drive-way had, following a stone wall that was about seven feet high. He was immediately impressed, and surprised, by the house. It wasn't a faux-Italianate mansion with loggias and statues. Nor was it an ultramodern white minimalist creation, which he had also thought possible. It was a single-story brick and stone house with a red-tile roof; had the roof been shingled, the house would have been at home in the American Midwest. It was at peace—not competing—with its natural surroundings. The building materials were natural. A long pergola whose ceiling was made of polished wood beams protected the visi-tor from wind, rain, and sun. The pergola's ceiling was punc-tured every so often with holes to allow mature trees to sprout through. Here, along the covered walk, the plants were luxu-rious, and spoke of constant watering and attention. Thick palms lined the walk, along with vigorous ferns and, he imag-ined, colorful tropical flowers in summer. As he got closer to the front door, the house's true character shone. Giant plate-glass windows from floor to ceiling let the visitor peek inside rooms, while the occupant inside must feel as if he or she were outside, in a tropical garden. Verlaque tried not to gawk into the rooms, but from a sideways glance he could see white curved walls, books, and statues.

The front doors, massive and made of pale wood, opened before he reached them. A small, white-haired man who wore a black Nehru-collared coat and round tortoiseshell eyeglasses held open one of the doors. "Good afternoon, Judge Verlaque," he said, stepping aside.

Verlaque shook his hand and said hello.

The man smiled. "I'm Fabrizio Orsani. Please come in."

"Thank you for the invitation on such short notice," Verlaque said, stepping inside the large foyer.

"*C'est normale,*" Orsani said. "I was distressed by the violent death of one of our employees. Please follow me into the living room."

They walked along red terra-cotta floor tiles, so polished Verlaque was afraid he would slip, into the living room resplendent with light thanks to the plate-glass windows. The smooth walls here were painted the color of rich cream, giving warmth to the room whose ceiling was rough gray concrete.

"This is a beautiful home," Verlaque said. He had hesitated to speak of frivolities but wanted Orsani to know that he was here with good intentions, whether the old man was the godfather or not.

Much to Verlaque's surprise, Orsani beamed. "Thank you. It's a small house, as you can see. We bought it twenty years ago for the site. The existing house was a dark and drab 1950s building. My architect simply smashed open every window, replacing them with floor-to-ceiling glass, letting the sea, and garden, come inside. He calls it *dedans/dehors*. He wrote a book about it."

Verlaque took another look at the living room. Orsani was right; it wasn't much bigger than his own salon, but the plate-glass windows—allowing the outside to come in—made the room look three times as large. He immediately regretted his apartment with its narrow eighteenth-century windows that he would never be able to change.

"Coffee?" Orsani asked. "Sparkling water? Both?"

"Both, if I may," Verlaque answered.

Orsani didn't snap his fingers, as Verlaque had fantasized, but half turned his body when, as if his nose had been pressed against the living room door, a young man appeared.

"Jean-Louis, two espressos and two sparkling waters, please," Orsani said. He motioned to a restored 1950s leather sofa. "Please, sit down, Judge."

"Thank you," Verlaque said. "Did you know Guy Maneval?"

"No, not at all," Orsani said without having to reflect. "I have a big operation, with many outlets and employees. I'm told that he worked off and on as a doorman at one of our clubs in Aix."

Verlaque tried to get the image of this cultured elderly man owning a disco. "Yes," he said. "And the night before Maneval was murdered he broke into an apartment in downtown Aix, may have killed the apartment's owner, and ran off with what he thought was a Cézanne painting. Did you know about that?"

Orsani shook his head and shrugged. Jean-Louis returned carrying a tray, served the men their drinks, and quietly left, leaving, Verlaque noted, the door open about an inch.

Verlaque said, "Maneval was found shot, with the faux Cézanne shoved over his head. Is there any meaning in this?"

"Not for me, no."

"You're not collecting Cézannes?"

Orsani made a sweeping gesture with his hand. "Have a look around, and I think you'll see that contemporary art, along with African sculptures, is where my art interest lies."

Verlaque did as he was told and got up and walked around the room, taking in the large, colorful canvases.

"Besides," Orsani said, still sitting, "the price of a Cézanne is, even for me, out of range. One must be royalty these days to buy Impressionists and Post-Impressionists. And not impoverished European royalty, either."

But this one was being stolen for you, Verlaque thought. *You didn't have to pay for it.*

Verlaque looked into the dining room, located up three steps and surprisingly small and intimate. He stood with his hands on his hips, looking at the all-black painting on the dining room's far wall.

"Are you a fan?" Orsani asked.

"Yes, a rather fanatical one," Verlaque said. "There's going to be a Soulages retrospective at the Pompidou."

"Yes, and that painting is going to be a part of the show."

Veralque refrained from saying that his was, too, and that they would see each other at the *avant-première*. If Orsani went to such events.

"I hesitated when they asked me to loan the painting," Orsani went on. "But Elena, my dear wife, said that I was being selfish."

Verlaque smiled. "You have quite a collection of art," he said, looking around the room. He remembered an article in a law journal, written by a Commandante Barrès, France's leading expert in art theft. In the article, which the police officer had comically titled "To Catch a Thief," she cited the importance of stolen art in the organized crime world: art used as payoffs, bribes, and debt repayments. In the Mafia, art was used as money.

Orsani looked at the judge, and as if he could read his mind, said, "Well, if there's nothing else? I'm afraid I have another appointment." Before Verlaque could reply, the living room door suddenly opened, and Jean-Louis reappeared.

"Jean-Louis will see you out. By the way, Judge, in case you're wondering, I buy from a reputable gallery in Zurich, and one in Paris."

Chapter Twenty

❧

Granet's Bright Clouds

• FEBRUARY 26, 1885 •

Manon watched as the young Countess Émilie de Saporta sat in the sedan chair, fanning herself although it was a cold February day. The countess was carried by two young men, one in front and one behind, each holding on to wooden rails that passed through brackets attached to either side of the covered chair. They stared straight ahead, either proud of their task or horrified by it. The sedan chair itself showed its age and the crumbling fortune of the Saportas: the wood was weathered, and the gold-painted details needed touching up.

Émilie de Saporta was sickly and, at thirty years of age, was beyond marriage material. It was rumored at Michaud's that the countess's parents had all but given up on marrying off Émilie when a colleague of her father's, a rich notary from

Lyon, lost his wife to illness. The notary—as Amandine Michaud had eagerly reported to Manon and her fellow coworkers—was over fifty years of age, fat, with a bulbous red nose and tiny almost-pink eyes. Manon stood on the Cours, remembering the Michaud salesgirls laughing and Amandine's almost-look of yearning, and she thought, *At least that will never happen to me.* She coughed and wrapped her shawl around her to keep warm. *I'd rather be poor.*

"Un jour son palanquin va être dans un musée," a voice said behind Manon's shoulder.

Manon slowly turned around. "Do you think so?" she asked, smiling.

"Certainly, Mlle Solari," Cézanne said. "Soon the day will come when the rich will stop being carried around like handicapped royalty, and their silly sedan chairs will be displayed in quaint little country museums."

"And the label will read: A one-person sedan chair, carried by two porters, used up until 1900 throughout Europe."

Cézanne laughed. "Very good! Our turn of the century will bring about so many changes."

"But we have fifteen years to wait," Manon said. Fifteen years was a long time. So many illnesses could creep up on you in that amount of time. Even the rich notary's wife in Lyon could not escape it.

"Well, until then, how about a walk?" Cézanne asked. He refrained from putting out his arm, as they were on the Cours Mirabeau. "I have good news, mademoiselle," he added.

"I'll meet you somewhere," Manon said, feeling the eyes of Amandine Michaud on her back. Clara was right to worry; what did Amandine keep track of in her little notebooks?

"Damn these social rules. I don't care if people—"

"I do," Manon said firmly. "By the pine tree. Where we first met." She shook his hand and walked off.

Cézanne took out his pocket watch; it was almost noon. He would buy some cheese, bread, salami, and wine and take it to their meeting spot. It was cold out; how he wished he could take her somewhere warm. He walked off in the direction of the cathedral, and as he walked he tried to figure out just how much of his allowance could be spent on renting a small caba-non or apartment somewhere. Gardanne, perhaps? They were not known there and he could give Mlle Solari train money. But he was already paying for Hortense and Paul's apartment in Marseille. Mademoiselle was such a sensible girl; would she even agree to seeing him behind closed doors? *What are your intentions, Paul Cézanne?* he thought. He put his hand on the doorknob of his favorite boulangerie and realized that his intentions were pure: all he wanted, at that moment anyway, was to paint Manon Solari.

"Did you come by way of Le Tholonet?" Manon asked. "The long route?"

Cézanne found himself laughing. So many times he had been teased, especially in Paris, only to leave the dinner party, or café, in a rage. But Mlle Solari could tease him lovingly, warmly. Innocently.

"I bought us lunch," he said. He sat down on the cold grass and reached into his cloth bag. "Look," he said, unwrapping two small rounds of goat's cheese. "Rocamadour."

Manon beamed. "I've had that cheese only once before."

Cézanne's back stiffened with pride. His father's bank-ing money was at least making this young woman happy, and filling her stomach. *And when it comes to that*, he thought, *I put*

in many long days at the bank, too. He thought back to an afternoon sometime in the early 1860s when his father had been
interrupted by a fellow clerk, and an annoying one at that—
what was that fellow's name?—who knocked hesitantly on M.
Cézanne's office door, carrying a bank ledger that he set gingerly on the old man's desk, all the while not hiding the slight
smirk that appeared at the corners of his mouth. The ledger's
last page glared up at the banker: it was a poem, written in his
son Paul's obvious hand: *Alarmed and damaged, old Banker
Cézanne / Finds his place taken by a painter man.* It wasn't long
after that incident that Louis-Auguste gave his son permission
to leave the bank to return to Paris to chase his artistic dream.
The old man didn't like the idea of Paris, or of his son living in
that dirty, and probably dangerous, neighborhood in the 6th
arrondissement near the Jardin du Luxembourg. At least Émile
Zola was there, and the old man knew of Zola's furious work
ethic. He would be a good influence on Paul.

Léopold, thought Cézanne as he unwrapped the salami.
That was that rascal clerk's name.

"Is it beef or pork?" Manon asked, sniffing the salami and
rubbing her hands together.

"Both," Cézanne said. "It's a blend. The butcher gets it once
a week from Arles."

"I'm spoiled, M. Cézanne," she said. She then drew a handkerchief up to her mouth and coughed.

"We should find somewhere else to meet," Cézanne said.
"It's too cold here."

Manon shrugged. "I'd be happy anywhere," she said. "I love
watching you paint."

"I could paint indoors," he answered, ripping off a piece of
baguette and handing it to her.

"Philippe told me of your still lifes. Apples and pears that fall off the kitchen table!" She poked him in the ribs and smiled. "Philippe said that they're gorgeous, and avant-garde. He said that someday critics will look at those paintings and finally see what you were trying to do."

"But not in my lifetime." He realized he was being morose, and tried to change the subject. Mlle Solari was always so happy. "Did Philippe teach you about art? You know as much as any of us in Paris."

Manon blushed. "Once a week Philippe took me to the Musée Granet. He said that most of the works are second rate—"

"Except Granet's own paintings."

"Exactly!" Manon said, putting down her bread and cheese in order to gesture as she talked. It was one of the things Cézanne liked about her. "Those bright clouds!"

"And his relaxed, loose brushstrokes!" Cézanne said excitedly, pouring Manon wine into a small metal cup he always carried in his backpack.

Manon thanked him for the wine and she watched as he concentrated on cutting the salami with his penknife. How he had changed in the few weeks they had been meeting in this field on the edge of the forest! At times he could be the gruff painter whom the girls at Michaud's gossiped about, but those times were fewer and fewer. She almost felt like she could tell him anything now. But she would not ask about his mistress and son, nor did he speak of them.

"You said you had news, M. Cézanne," Manon ventured. Could it be about his mistress and son? Or was he returning to Paris, and she wouldn't see him anymore?

Cézanne smiled and reached into his backpack. "My friends

in Paris came through for me," he said. "These arrived in this morning's post."

"The shea and cocoa butters?"

"Two jars of each," Cézanne said, handing them to her. "With your scented oils you're almost on your way."

Manon reached over and wrapped her arms around his neck. "Thank you!"

He tried not to recoil from her touch. It had surprised him, but it was what he had been dreaming of. "Now you just need your emulsifier."

Manon's brow furrowed. "That's going to be the tricky part," she said, taking a piece of salami and putting it in her mouth. She smiled. "So good," she said after she had swallowed.

"Well," Cézanne said, reaching over to pour her more wine and, as he did, smelling the lavender scent she always wore. That she *created*. "I had a talk with old Vallier."

"Who is that?"

"The gardener at Jas de Bouffan. I told him that I have a . . . friend . . . who needs a blending agent for a face cream they're hoping to make. And do you know what he did?"

"Tell me, monsieur," Manon said, enjoying the game.

"He took me out onto the back of the property, behind Maman's rose garden. *Vers les ruches.*"

"Ah! Beehives!"

Cézanne smiled. "Vallier is saving some of the wax for you, mademoiselle. I think it may work."

Chapter Twenty-one

↣

A Game of Xs and Os

As Rebecca Schultz gazed out the window, she let her mind wander. There wasn't a day that went by when she didn't think of her parents. She had been orphaned shortly after her birth, and now she was, at thirty-four years of age, once again an orphan. Her parents' friends had rallied around her, as had her Uncle Irv and his ditzy wife, Deborah. But it wasn't the same as having Isaac and Judy (when she had turned eighteen she suddenly began calling her parents by their first names) around all the time. Even when she had moved across the country to attend the University of California Santa Cruz—then to Berkeley for an MA, then Harvard for a PhD—they had always been in her head, little voices that encouraged her. Big, shiny faces that smiled and watched her bloom. The elderly woman sitting beside her was reading a collection of Alice Munro stories translated into French; it was just the kind of thing Judy would have read.

She was a baby when they brought her home; the Schultzes

had already both turned gray. But their energy was vast—vast enough to care for an energetic but well-behaved little girl. The apartment, as Rebecca remembered, was often full of visiting—usually hungry—artists, or gallery owners who had come to pick the brains of her parents, who as amateurs had developed an uncanny eye for modern and contemporary art. One of her earliest memories was being caught playing ball in the living room. "Rebecca!" Judy had called out. "Watch out for the Duchamp! Remember our rule! No ball in the living or dining room, but down the hallway is fine." The Duchamp had been sold to pay for her Harvard tuition; Rebecca didn't miss it and Judy once confided in her that the bronze-and-glass sculpture had been "Isaac's choice, not mine."

At parties, Judy Schultz liked to retell the story of her daughter's first sleepover. Rebecca had just turned seven, and returned at ten the next morning tired but happy. Judy had tried not to ask too many questions—she hadn't slept well—and finally Rebecca had looked up at her and said, "Karen's family is very nice, but where do they put all their Cézannes?"

Rebecca still owned her parents' apartment in the East Village, a neighborhood that Irv and Deborah had said, until it recently turned chic and expensive, that Isaac and Judy had been crazy to live in. But Deborah, bless her, had helped Rebecca pack and donate many of her parents' belongings she wouldn't be keeping: her father's simple, well-cut suits and garish ties; her mother's well-worn wool skirts and tiny silk blouses, both of which were much too small for Rebecca. She did keep most of her mother's purses, which were the one splurge, besides art, that Mrs. Schultz had allowed herself. Rebecca gave an elegant crocodile-skin clutch bag to Deborah, who immediately started crying.

Rebecca shifted in her seat, trying to get comfortable. She

looked down at her pale-green 1960s Dior purse, and whispered, *Judy, I need you.*

It had been a race to catch the 7:05 p.m. train. Roger Caromb earned his salary by getting Verlaque to the Aix TGV station four minutes before the train was about to leave. Caromb had double-parked the car on the square below Verlaque's apartment as the judge ran up the stairs and quickly packed an overnight bag, at the last minute throwing in an extra shirt, as he was already sweating. He would change shirts on the train. Caromb then wheeled the car around the corner to the Palais de Justice and parked in front, lights flashing, while Verlaque went inside to get the painting, running up the stairs to the second floor and down a hallway that led to the vault rooms. Verlaque opened the first room with his key and stopped, surprised to see someone in it. "What are you doing in here?" he asked.

A young woman turned around, surprised. She put her hand to her heart and said, "I'm so sorry. I came in here to have my tea."

Verlaque looked at her, perplexed. "What on earth?"

She gestured to a teapot that sat on top of a low filing cabinet. "We all have tea in here, Judge Verlaque. It's the warmest room in the building."

He stood there and could indeed feel the warm forced air streaming in through a series of vents along the top of the walls. He looked ahead and saw that the second door, this one gated, which led to a smaller room where evidence was kept, was securely locked. "I know you from somewhere, don't I?" he asked.

The woman stepped forward and held out her hand. "My name is Françoise," she said. "I'm a maid here, hoping to get promoted to secretary someday." She smiled. "We also met the other night on the rue Boulegon. I am . . . was . . . René Rouquet's neighbor."

Verlaque said, "Ah yes, that's where I met you; Aix is so small. I'm sorry, but you'll have to drink your tea somewhere else; I need to get evidence out of the next room."

"Of course!" Françoise said, grabbing her mug off a table. "I'll make tea in the kitchen. Good evening!"

Verlaque watched her go and opened the second door with another key and took the painting. He left, locking both doors behind him, and ran into Paulik in the hall.

"I have your train ticket," Paulik said, handing it to Verlaque. "I went down to the car and Caromb said you were up here."

"Since when do the staff use the vault rooms to stay warm?"

"Since the heating went on the blink," Paulik replied, readjusting his wool scarf. "But they shouldn't be in there. I'll have Mme Gérard send a memo around."

"Yes, please do that," Verlaque said, stuffing the train ticket in his pocket. They ran down the stairs together. "Did you know that Rouquet's neighbor works here, as a cleaner? I thought that Mme Chazeau gave you a list of the occupations of rue Boulegon's tenants."

"She did," Paulik said. "But the cleaners don't work for us."

"Pardon?"

"It's a subcontractor," Paulik said. "Called Netoyage-Aix. That's probably why it didn't register with me; they have contracts all over Provence. You see their vans everywhere."

"Is it a coincidence? Check into it," Verlaque said. "And tell them to stay out of the vault!"

"Yes, sir." They got to the car and Paulik opened the passenger door.

"I'll call you after I meet with Hippolyte Thébaud and Commandante Barrès," Verlaque said as he got into the car.

Paulik saluted and waved as the car sped off. He knew that the traffic between Aix and its TGV station would be heavy, but Caromb could use the blue flashing light if need be. Paulik had never met Hippolyte Thébaud, but Antoine Verlaque had once given him a detailed—and somewhat humorous—description of him over lunch months previously. "A dandy" was how Verlaque had described him, and in Paulik's limited experience, dandy meant that Thébaud was of a slight build, paid careful attention to what he wore, spoke softly, and probably favored old-fashioned accessories like a carved walking cane, or a rose in his jacket lapel, or even a top hat. Bruno Paulik had been born and raised on a farm in the Luberon and had never seen a dandy, although his wife, Hélène, had once introduced him to a famous wine critic from England who Paulik imagined fit that definition. Or *his* definition of dandy, at any rate.

Hippolyte Thébaud was one of France's most sought-after wine theft experts, if not *the* expert. What set him apart from other consultants was not only his photographic memory when it came to wines but the fact that he learned everything he knew while in jail. Both the judge and the commissioner immediately thought of using Thébaud's connections in the fraud world to help them determine the origins and authenticity of the canvas. "A legitimate art expert is one thing," Verlaque had said, "but an art expert who has painted copies, or sold them, will be able to look at this portrait in a different way." Mme Gérard had managed to book an appointment with Commandante Barrès, who had penned the article "To Catch a Thief," which was icing on the cake.

Verlaque realized that he had been lucky to catch the train, as his appointment with Hippolyte—they were, thanks to a prior case involving stolen wines, on a first-name basis—and with Hippolyte's art fraud buddy Hervé was the next morning at 9:00 a.m. But buying a train ticket at the last minute always came with conditions; most of all, the coveted solo seats in the first-class cars would all be taken. He pulled in his legs as the small boy facing him fidgeted and squirmed. The boy's mother was playing—or texting, he couldn't tell—on her iPhone as the child tried to occupy himself. Verlaque dreaded the *carées* on the TGV: four seats, two side by side that faced two others, a narrow table in between. The old man to Verlaque's left had already fallen asleep by the time the train got to Avignon, and his gentle snoring seemed to be in perfect rhythm with the train itself. The train crossed over the Rhône and Verlaque squinted, trying to see the center of Avignon. Despite the dark, he could see it lit up, and was amazed, as he always was, at just how much, especially at a distance, Avignon's medieval Palais des Papes loomed over—dwarfed, even—the much-newer buildings that surrounded it.

He opened his Moleskine notebook and considered ripping a page out and giving it to the kid across from him, with a pencil, so he'd have something to do. The mother was still playing with her cell phone. Verlaque sighed and began to look through his notes on the case. He drew a blank. Two murders, one lost American professor; all of this over a painting that Edmund Lydgate had said was a forgery. Was Lydgate lying? Why? If the painting was a fake, as he claimed, it would be kept as evidence at the Palais de Justice and later be destroyed. It's not as if Lydgate would be able to get his hands on it, months or even years later, and sell it.

A waiter came by and passed out menus. The old man woke up and quickly ordered a pasta salad and a ham sandwich. Verlaque looked at the menu and asked for the risotto.

"Sorry," the waiter apologized. "We can't deliver hot food anymore, only cold meals. For hot meals you need to go to the bar car."

"I'll get something in Paris, then," Verlaque said, handing the menu back. He hated cold dinners and didn't feel like making his way to the bar car. Besides, from here he could see the edge of his leather bag, sitting on the luggage rack at the front of the car.

The woman and child began to eat sandwiches and cheese, and Verlaque was relieved when she pulled out fruit and water instead of giving the kid a soda and sweets.

Verlaque pulled out a book about Cézanne and began reading. He had always enjoyed looking at Cézanne's paintings but had never before realized the Aixois's importance to modern art. It was Cézanne who first used his imaginative powers to paint, something that almost every artist of the twentieth century would follow. Nature was almost a spiritual matter for Cézanne: the cosmos, where everything was interrelated. Verlaque set the book down and thought of someone he had met on a past case, Jean-Claude Auvieux, a gardener who tended the grounds of a château outside of Aix that was now a small luxury hotel. Jean-Claude was the closest thing he could imagine to being a contemporary Cézanne; he made a vow to soon visit the gardener. He picked the book back up and looked at one of the early paintings, of Cézanne's father, painted in 1866 when Cézanne was twenty-seven. The old man wears a small black cap and sits in an armchair, his thick hands reading a newspaper, *L'Evénement*. Verlaque grinned, enjoying the painter's joke: Cézanne's banker father reading a nineteenth-century left-wing newspaper. It would be as if his own father read *Libération*. The author suggested that Cézanne was mocking his father. Verlaque looked out at the darkness and then again at the painting. Perhaps Cézanne wasn't being mean-spirited. Perhaps he was pleading for understanding, trying to communicate with his father.

Verlaque saw that the old man's meal had been delivered, and he ate with gusto, smacking his lips. He had finished all of his Bordeaux and was now digging into the chocolate mousse, which he ate with even more enthusiasm than he had the sandwich. The little boy watched, fascinated.

Verlaque's stomach began to growl. The old man—slowly, this time—sipped a Cognac, pulled out his newspaper, and began to read. It was almost 8:30 p.m. They still had an hour and a half until Paris, and Verlaque decided that a hot meal, red wine, and a Cognac would help to sedate him in preparation for his arrival *chez les parents*. His brother, Sébastien, was away, at some resort in Morocco, so when Verlaque's father had told him of his mother's illness, it seemed appropriate that he stay at their house. M. Verlaque Senior had made the tiniest hesitation before saying, "Yes, do come. I suppose you'll eat on the train?" With that comment, or hint, in mind, Verlaque made his way to the bar car.

By the time Verlaque got back to his seat, carrying a miniature Cognac bottle and a plastic cup, the boy was fidgeting even more. His mother hissed, *"Arrêt-toi!"* Verlaque reached into his briefcase, which was in the compartment over the seat, and fished through it until he found an extra pen and some paper. He put the paper on the table between him and the boy and drew the horizontal and vertical lines for a game of Xs and Os. The boy slowly picked up the pen and looked curiously at Verlaque. "You go first," Verlaque said.

"If you don't mind," the boy's mother said, giving him a half smile, "I'll take this opportunity to visit the toilets."

"Go right ahead," Verlaque said. He smiled and poured himself a glass of Cognac.

They were playing their twelfth game as the train rolled into the Gare de Lyon and stopped on the quay. The boy smiled as Verlaque put away the paper and pens. His mother had jumped up and was fussing with their bags. "*Voilà, Mamy et Papy,*" she said, motioning to an elderly couple who stood outside their window, frantically waving. The boy clapped his hands and pressed his nose against the window. The scene immediately reminded Verlaque of Emmeline and Charles, his grandparents, and he became the young boy.

"Enjoy Paris," Verlaque said.

"*Merci, monsieur,*" the mother said as she tugged at her son. "Hurry up!"

Verlaque put on his coat and pulled his briefcase down from the rack above, letting the other passengers shuffle past him. He wanted to be the last person to disembark. He could no longer see his leather bag on the luggage racks by the door and assumed that someone's big suitcase was blocking it. As if played out in slow motion, he watched in dismay as each passenger tugged at his or her suitcase, pulling it off the rack, and with each suitcase gone his was nowhere in sight. His mouth became dry and his heart began to beat faster and faster. And all for a mediocre hot meal. The next-to-last person to get off was a tall blond businesswoman. He had seen her get on in Avignon, and she grabbed a small silver overnight bag and almost skipped off, revealing an empty luggage rack.

Chapter Twenty-two

✕

At Home, on the Rue des Petits Pères

*Y*ou *what?*" Marine yelled down the phone. "*Ce n'est pas vrai!*"

"You don't have to yell," Verlaque whispered. He wanted to say, "It happens all the time," but Marine knew that. They had both heard a report on the radio of a Chinese businessman on his way to Geneva who left a priceless Ming vase on the train. They had both made fun of the poor man, too. Verlaque felt more sympathetic now. He sat in his boxer shorts on the edge of the twin bed, looking down at his bare knees. His mother, now in the hospital, would normally be asleep in the next room, and his father's room, he thought, was across the hall. Or at least Verlaque assumed his father was there; surely at seventy years of age his father had stopped his philandering. Or perhaps at seventy it would be at its worst?

"And you saw no one who could be—"

"A Mafia thug?" Verlaque asked. "Or an art thief? No."

What was I supposed to be looking for? Verlaque almost asked. *Grace Kelly dressed in black, wearing a cute little mask?*

"But you could see the luggage rack from your seat, right?"

"Yes."

"So you would have seen someone grab your bag."

"Well—"

Marine sighed. "Unless you got up from your seat without taking your suitcase with you."

"You have to go to the bar car now if you want a hot meal—" He stopped explaining, realizing how pathetic he sounded. What he didn't tell Marine was that he had been distracted by the young boy, and the thought of seeing his parents, and so had forgotten to take the leather bag with him to the bar car.

Marine couldn't help from snickering and Verlaque held the phone away from his ear. "The old man beside me was drinking a Cognac," he went on. "It smelled so good—"

She said, "You lost what might be a Cézanne painting, worth millions, because you wanted a cheap miniature bottle of Cognac? You don't even like Cognac!"

"It's true that, given the choice, I prefer Armagnac."

"Antoine! Be serious!"

Verlaque began to laugh.

"The bloody thing's probably a fake anyway," Verlaque said, taking a Kleenex and blowing his nose.

"That's not what my father thinks," Marine said. "And if it's a fake, why are people so desperate to get it?"

"I feel numb, really, which is very odd. I should be worried, or angry at myself, but I just feel numb. Here I am sleeping in my parents' house, after all these years. You know, the last time I was here I spent an hour with them, in one of their stuffy drawing rooms, and I don't think they said one word to each other.

They asked me a few perfunctory questions, I answered them but without giving them too much information, and then we all yawned, as if on cue, and went to bed. Tonight I saw my father just long enough to say hello. And he loaned me some clothes."

"I'm sorry, Antoine."

"You know, there was a little boy on the train," he said. Marine could hear the urgency in his voice. "And his mother didn't say one word to him, except to tell him to shut up and stop moving. The poor kid didn't have any games or activities to do. And then when we pulled in to Paris, his grandparents were there, waiting for him. I watched him jump off the train and fly into their arms."

Marine saw the parallel to Verlaque's own grandparents. "Will you be able to visit your mother tomorrow?"

"I hope so," Verlaque said.

"Go to bed, sleep well, and in the morning you'll be able to start looking for the painting. It can't have disappeared into thin air." She paused and then added, "There's something that's bothering me—"

"Me, too," Verlaque said. "I was followed onto the train."

"Yes," Marine answered. "It's as if you've been followed all around Aix. I wonder if we were even followed into the Luberon."

Verlaque got up and looked out the window down onto the rue des Petits Pères. He watched a young couple walking arm-in-arm, and in the opposite direction, an old man walked a tiny dog. He pulled the drapes shut.

He said, "But the officer who drove me to the TGV station drives like a total maniac. No one could have kept up with us."

Marine thought for a moment, sipping her herbal tea. "A motorcycle could have."

"*Merde!*" Verlaque said, getting into bed and pulling up the down-filled quilt. He was suddenly cold, and he missed Marine. "You're good, Professor Bonnet."

"Plus, motorcycles have primo parking at the station, don't they?"

"Yep. Right in front of the doors."

Verlaque awoke the next morning refreshed but with a knot in his stomach. He had twice taken the canvas away from its safe room at the Palais de Justice and now it was lost. He showered, thankful that someone, probably a staff member, kept the guest bath well stocked with expensive soaps and shampoos.

His father had laid out a clean shirt for him to wear—they were roughly the same size, although with age his father had lost the middle-age paunch that Verlaque was now growing. On the twin bed opposite was also an unopened pack of boxer shorts . . . a gift? Or his father didn't care for the striped pattern? "You can keep the socks if you like," his father had said, handing Verlaque a pair of colorful, silk-knit Missoni socks that probably cost more than the shirt. "I've only worn them once and they're a little too big," his father said. "They were a gift—" *From an Italian mistress?* Verlaque pulled on the socks—they fit—and he thought of Rebecca Schultz's Missoni coat.

He finished dressing and made his way downstairs, taking in for the first time in years the medieval- and Renaissance-inspired furnishings that his mother had installed throughout their Parisian home. The colors, he realized, weren't displeasing—reds, gold, and greens—but were probably out of fashion. The wooden staircase had been restored at great expense; that he remembered. The wood was elaborately carved with gothic-style arches, and the apartment's original owner—an opera singer—

used to perform at the top of the balcony while her dinner guests watched down below.

His breakfast was laid out in the dining room and a maid appeared with a pot of coffee and freshly squeezed orange juice. He smiled at her—a not-quite-elderly kind-looking woman with bright eyes and rosy cheeks. "Thank you—"

"Hortense," she answered.

"I don't come here often. Have we met before?"

"Yes, Judge Verlaque," she answered. "A few times."

Verlaque was embarrassed. He should have remembered her. He knew, now, that before he met Marine he had been a self-obsessed egomaniac. Hortense would have served him, and he wouldn't have paid her the time of day. He took a sip of coffee—it was hot, and strong—and said, *"Le café est délicieux. Merci, Hortense."*

She smiled, did a slight bow, and left, leaving him alone in the dining room, where he ate a fresh, buttery croissant beneath a colossal Louis XIV crystal chandelier. Had Hortense remembered that he preferred croissants to pains au chocolat? Probably.

He finished eating, wiped his hands off on a large green linen napkin—he only liked white linens, perhaps a direct result of his mother's taste—and picked up his cell phone. He was relieved when Hippolyte Thébaud answered on the first ring. Thébaud sounded disappointed when Verlaque canceled their meeting—he didn't tell Thébaud that he had lost the painting—but instead suggested that they reschedule. That would buy him some time. The next call was to Bruno Paulik, who listened patiently while Verlaque went over the TGV story.

"Bon," Paulik finally said. "It's just after eight a.m., so who-

ever followed you to Paris isn't back in Aix yet; the first morning train leaves Paris at six nineteen a.m. and arrives in Aix at nine nineteen a.m.—I know because I've taken it before. I'll have an officer drive out right away to the TGV station, note down all of the motorcycle license plates, and run a check. Just a minute while I call Flamant over."

Verlaque waited while Paulik explained the situation and sent Flamant off to the TGV station. Paulik came back on the phone and Verlaque said, "I don't suppose it would help to have an officer watch the motorcycles?"

"I imagine that the thief has gotten rid of your bag," Paulik said, remembering the expensive-looking leather duffel. "And most people, even motorcycle drivers, will be getting off the TGV with some kind of small bag. They've just been traveling, after all. No, I think it best that Flamant calls in the license plates and we look for owners' names. Lydgate, for example. Schultz could have rented one; we can check the moto rental places in Aix; there aren't very many."

"I can't imagine either of them riding a moto," Verlaque said. "And the name of a mafioso isn't going to ring a bell."

"Unless he's been here before," Paulik said, meaning the Palais de Justice. "Besides, motorcycle enthusiasts come in all shapes and sizes," he went on, speaking as a former motorcycle owner. "They're not necessarily young, virile men with a death wish. Although I agree he or she would have to be an experienced rider to keep up with Caromb."

Verlaque wasn't convinced. He pictured just that: a young, virile, male rider. He said, "I've canceled my appointment with Hippolyte Thébaud, but I'm still going to see an officer named Commendante Barrès. She's a specialist on stolen art."

"Good luck," Paulik said.

"Thank you," Verlaque said, setting down his cell phone. He looked at his hand and saw that it was shaking. He felt useless; he'd lost a precious piece of evidence, and his own clothes to boot. He now had to rely on other people, which always stripped away a bit of his ego and self-confidence. The day began with saying thank you—to his father, then Hortense, and now Bruno Paulik—and he knew that he would continue to thank people all day long until he went to bed that evening.

Chapter Twenty-three

❧

Alain Flamant's Frustration

"*Daube au vin blanc!* Can you imagine?" Alain said as they walked up the rue Mistral. "My mother always makes beef stew with red wine. Lisa does, too." He was telling Jules of the amazing (though overpriced) meal he and Lisa had recently shared for their anniversary.

"Sounds like you're a convert," Jules said.

"Eh, I still think I prefer my mother's recipe. But don't tell Lisa."

"My lips are sealed."

"So why the sudden interest in Bar Zola? Doesn't seem like your type of place."

"I met the bartender the other night, with Verlaque. If no one else in this town is talking, he might," Jules said.

They crossed the Cours Mirabeau, busy despite the fact that it was after 11:00 p.m., and a Monday night. "What do you make of Verlaque?" Alain asked.

Jules shrugged. "I hadn't given it much thought, until the other night when we ran into each other and went out for a drink. But you know, he's just like anyone else—"

"Except he's rich," Alain offered.

"Yeah, but he also has the same worries, and hopes, and dreams that the rest of us have."

"*Hyperphilosophique*," Alain said, nudging Jules on the shoulder.

"I'll try to tone it down," Jules said, laughing. "Especially at the Bar Zola."

They walked up the rue Clemenceau in silence, Alain trying to guess how much per square meter a downtown apartment cost, Jules perplexed that the shop owners had to pile flattened cardboard boxes outside their storefronts every evening, waiting for garbage pickup, instead of being able to recycle them, as they did in Colmar.

As they approached the Bar Zola, Jules heard the same Rolling Stones song that had been playing the night he came with Verlaque. "After you," he said, opening the door.

Flamant made his way to the bar, and Schoelcher could see that, here, his colleague was at ease. Flamant walked slowly and purposefully, smiling slightly as he passed pretty young women. They got to the bar and Jules was relieved to see the same barman, wearing a different Harley-Davidson T-shirt. "Hey, Patrick," Jules said. "Good evening. How are you?"

"Excuse me?" Patrick said.

"It's me," Jules said, poking his thumb to his chest. "I was here the other night—"

"What will you have?" Patrick asked.

Jules looked at Alain, who pretended to be interested in studying the collection of bottles behind Patrick's head.

"A rum," Jules said.

"And a lager for me," Alain said.

"I guess you don't know me anymore," Jules said.

"That will be nine fifty," Patrick said, staring over Jules's head at a poster on the wall.

Jules paid and he and Alain took their drinks to a small round table that had just been cleared. "Wow," Alain said. "He's been told not to talk."

"Obviously," Jules said. "And I only wanted to say hi."

Chapter Twenty-four

≥

A Meeting in a Japanese Garden

Verlaque stared at the small Japanese house and thought of Fabrizio Orsani. *Dedans/dehors*. Inside/outside. He regretted never having visited Japan as he looked at the features the best 1960s Western architects had borrowed from the Japanese: sliding wood and parchment doors that could be opened to their fullest capacity, letting the garden come inside; no furnishings save a low wooden table, cushions, and a shelf or two where Verlaque knew the inhabitant would have displayed small porcelain bowls. The opposite of his parents' stuffy, closed-windowed, well-appointed home. Would his parents' relationship have been different if they had lived in a house like this one? Can architecture influence people's happiness? Yes, he thought. He imagined a series of color photographs of his parents—part of an exhibition in a modern-art museum—an artist's sociological experiment: *M. et Mme Verlaque in their Japanese-inspired home. Mme Verlaque pours out the tea. M. Verlaque prunes bonsai in the garden.*

"Right," Verlaque mumbled in English and he walked on, listening to the crunching noise his shoes made on along the pebbled path. Even in winter the garden was delicious; the path meandered around Japanese plants and led up over small arched footbridges painted red. The traffic noise reminded him that he was in a museum on the edge of Paris, and not in the Japanese countryside. He followed the path up a small hill; from there he could see the conservatory and a rose garden before it. A woman appeared at the edge of the rose garden, pushing a baby buggy, and Verlaque walked down the hill and made his way toward her.

She was arranging a small woolen blanket over a sleeping baby as he approached. "Commandante Barrès?" he asked, leaning down.

"Yes," she answered, standing up and shaking his hand. "You don't have to whisper; Jeanne can sleep through anything."

He smiled and said, "Jeanne. Lovely name." *Joan of Arc.*

"Thank you for coming down to Boulogne," she said as they sat side by side on a wooden bench. "I'm on maternity leave, but I was . . . intrigued . . . when your call came through to the precinct. A colleague called me at home right away."

"Really?" Verlaque asked, looking at sleeping Jeanne. "I had no idea that you're not working at the moment. I'm so sorry."

She waved his apology away with a gloved hand. "No, no, don't be sorry," she said. "My colleague called me because he knows how obsessive I can get. You see, Cézanne is my favorite painter. And given the sunny day, I thought we could meet here. I live around the corner. Jeanne is now six months old, so I'm just about to start back at work."

"It's lovely here, even on a cold day," Verlaque said, looking at the pruned climbing roses. "It's my first visit."

"Ah. Albert Kahn was one of those great nineteenth-century philanthropists," Barrès said. "He was interested in a bit of everything: plants, as you can see; photography; science and medicine. He lost it all in the crash of 1929. We're lucky that the city of Boulogne-Billancourt bought the estate in 1940. Kahn's houses on the Riviera, where the gardens were even bigger, are now lost."

He looked at the policewoman. She was tall and slender, although it was hard to see her figure as she was wrapped in a bright-pink woolen coat. She wore her brown hair cut short, which showed off her dangling silver earrings that looked handmade, a one-off. "How long have you been in the art theft division, Commandante Barrès?" he asked.

"Eleven years total," she answered. "And I've been commandante for five. Our office is a mix of gendarmes and police; we work together."

"Were you an art student before joining the force?"

"No," she said, laughing. "I studied languages, which comes in handy on the job. But I'm studying art history now, part-time. I'm working on my MA at the Sorbonne. It's a challenge, though, with Jeanne."

Verlaque had almost forgotten about sleeping Jeanne and looked at her tiny hands clutching the top of the blanket. "I'll tell you why I'm here," he began. "We're investigating the murder of a man, René Rouquet, who lived in Paul Cézanne's former apartment in downtown Aix. About a week before Rouquet died he found a canvas that had been rolled up and hidden somewhere in the apartment. A portrait of a young woman—"

"And you think it's a Cézanne?"

"A local doctor who's an amateur art historian thinks so, yes," he said. "But a retired art auctioneer from Sotheby's thinks it's a fake, although he seemed to me to be very taken with it."

"You think he's lying?"

"Yes. But I don't know why."

"What's his name?" Barrès asked.

"Edmund Lydgate."

She wrote the name down in a small notebook and frowned. "His name rings a bell, but I don't know why. I'll look it up when I get back home."

Verlaque refrained from telling the commandante that he had lost the canvas. "How easy is it to sell a stolen Cézanne?" he asked. "I'm trying to understand why Rouquet was killed, and if the killer was someone experienced in selling stolen art."

"It would be impossible to sell a stolen Cézanne in the legitimate art market. That's why the Ashmolean Museum Cézanne has never been recovered. Paintings like a Cézanne, or van Gogh, or an Old Master, when stolen, go underground. They disappear."

Verlaque leaned forward, resting his elbows on his knees. "Tell me about the Oxford theft."

"We police who specialize in art theft share files, across the globe," she said. "If I remember correctly, the Ashmolean theft took place on New Year's Eve, while all of Oxford was celebrating. The thief took advantage of some scaffolding on the building's façade and used it to get up to the roof. He broke one of the glass panes of a skylight and then lowered himself down using a rope ladder. On the way down he threw a smoke bomb on the floor, which set off the alarms, but the police officers who arrived on the scene weren't allowed to go in."

"Because of the smoke."

"Right," she answered. "So he, or she, took one Cézanne, a landscape, and went out via the skylight."

"Just one Cézanne?" Verlaque asked. "Was the theft an order from a collector?"

Commandante Barrès shook her head back and forth.

"That's a common misconception," she said. "Because of the movies, art thieves are imagined to be glamorous, sophisticated, and cunning. That couldn't be further from the truth. They are professional criminals, many of them very hardened. They, for the most part, steal whatever is most convenient, or whatever paintings they have seen on television. In 2003 two thieves stole two of van Gogh's early dark paintings from the Van Gogh Museum in Amsterdam."

Verlaque looked at her. "I've been to that museum," he said. "They didn't take the sunflowers?"

"No," she answered. "I would have taken a self-portrait myself."

Verlaque laughed. "So why two of his early works?"

Commandante Barrès smiled. "They were the first two paintings listed in the museum's catalogue."

"You're kidding."

"No, I'm not. So you can see, there's seldom a rich, cultured patron paying these men to steal. They're just thugs, often involved in organized crime."

"What in the world would these guys do with a Cézanne landscape, or two van Goghs?" Verlaque asked. "They can't possibly sell them at Sotheby's."

"The Mafia is a perfect place to 'get rid' of masterpieces," she replied.

"I read your article 'To Catch a Thief,'" Verlaque said.

"Thank you!" she answered. "Well then, as I said in the article, stolen masterpieces are used as currency. Criminals use artworks to pay off fellow criminals—for example, to pay off debts. The Mafia has connections all over the world—"

"Making it so easy to use priceless artworks to pay for arms, or drugs," Verlaque said. He thought of his quick dismissal from Orsani's house.

"Yes, and they have a built-in system of transportation. Crossing borders is usually no problem. Some of the objects *are* sold, and the quicker the objects are sold, the harder it is for us to trace them. We recently recovered a stolen gold clock from the seventeenth century; it was stolen from a château in Brittany on a Saturday night and on Tuesday morning was on the art market. But if it is sold illegally on the black market, an artwork can disappear forever."

She reached down into the bottom of the buggy and pulled out a padded case, unzipping it to reveal an iPad. She turned it on and opened a file, flipping through the photos to show Verlaque.

"Those are all stolen objects?" he asked.

"Yes, ninety-two thousand of them, to be exact."

He whistled. "What's your recovery rate?"

"Ten percent." She pointed to a lamp made in the 1960s. "This was a rare prototype made by Gae Aulenti," she said. "It was stolen from the minister of finance's office by one of his staffers. As elections come and go and ministers are changed, their staffs often leave with 'souvenirs.'" Commandante Barrès found a photo of a painting being held up by two smiling policemen. "In 2005 a security guard at the Pompidou stole this Picasso worth two and a half million. It proved impossible for him to sell as he didn't have the right connections, and so it was recovered."

Verlaque got a lump in his throat, thinking of the upcoming Soulages exhibition. "Do you have a photo of the painting you found in Aix?" she asked.

Verlaque got his cell phone out of his coat pocket and showed her the portrait.

"I don't recognize it," she said.

Verlaque was about to interrupt and say that it had just been found when the commandante said, "Have you done a background check on stolen Cézannes?" she asked. "A small Monet landscape was stolen from a museum in Le Havre in 1974 only to turn up at Christie's forty years later."

"The thief waited that long?"

"Yes; talk about patience. But we had photos of the painting on file, so it was easy to catch. A retired curator from the museum remembered it and called us when she saw its photograph in a Christie's catalogue. She still felt guilty, all those years later."

"It hadn't occurred to me that the canvas we found in Aix could have been a Cézanne stolen years ago," Verlaque said. Marine's father hadn't recognized it, but did he know *every* Cézanne painting? Lydgate he didn't trust; he hadn't even looked at it that long. And he now realized that they knew little about René Rouquet.

"What do you know about fakes?" he asked. Since he had canceled his meeting with Hippolyte and Hervé, perhaps the commandante could shed some light on the art of creating, and selling, reproductions.

"Ah, fakes are abundant and sold everywhere, from eBay to international galleries. Forgeries are getting better and better, which is why the provenance of your supposed Cézanne canvas is being disputed. These days it really *is* hard to determine the fakes from the genuine. The general public certainly has no idea, and even museum curators can be fooled. A Manet in a museum in Caracas was stolen and replaced with a copy. The copy was so good that the theft went unnoticed for years."

"And by then the real Manet was long gone," Verlaque suggested.

"Yes," she answered. "Last night I read an essay written in the 1930s by the art critic Walter Benjamin. Homework." She smiled and went on. "He predicted that in the new age of mechanical reproduction, the quasi-sacred quality of art would fade. He called it their 'aura.' Artworks would no longer be precious cultural treasures but just images circulating freely all over the world. Their value would drop."

"But the opposite's happened," Verlaque said. Jeanne made a gurgling sound, signaling the near end of their meeting. "Prices of original art are insane."

"Yes," she said. "But he was right about their images being everywhere . . . reproductions in books, on TV, posters . . ."

"T-shirts, calendars," Verlaque added. "It's as if all that reproduction drove the prices, and value, and desire, even higher. As Andy Warhol was all too aware of."

Commandante Barrès smiled, impressed by the judge with the streaked black-and-gray hair and the broken nose. "And because of the ready availability of images of the originals," she said, "fakes get better all the time."

"Yes, we all know what the originals look like, as we stare at them every morning on our coffee cups. We're intimate with them."

"And forgers are now using modern technology to make more-accurate copies. Digital scanning, for example. They can use those microscopic details to make exact reproductions. But there's something they can't reproduce—"

"The brushstrokes?"

"Exactly. Who can reproduce van Gogh's energetic brushstrokes? Or Rembrandt's?"

"The soul of the painting," Verlaque offered. "Benjamin's word 'aura' is apt."

"Yes. But enter the twenty-first century, and 3-D printing."

"*Merde.* I didn't think this would have a happy ending."

"*Ah oui,*" she said. "Even van Gogh's own museum in Holland offers—free of charge—massive amounts of close-up scientific information of Vincent's oil paintings. We may yet come full circle and prove Walter Benjamin correct."

"When reproductions become so good," Verlaque said, "that the originals no longer have any value."

"And at that moment the art market will collapse," the commandante said. "And I'll be out of a job."

She picked up a now-awake and yawning Jeanne and rocked her in her arms.

"Thank you for this meeting," Verlaque said, uncrossing his legs to get up.

"No problem," Commandante Barrès said. She looked down at his ankles and smiled. "Nice socks, by the way. I couldn't help but admire them."

"Thank you," Verlaque said, laughing. *They were a gift from my father, via Chiara, his Florentine girlfriend.* "My father gave them to me."

"Missoni, right?" she asked. She pointed in the direction of Albert Kahn's beloved Japanese garden. "Like that woman's coat over there."

Chapter Twenty-five

❧

Teppanyaki

Rebecca Schultz was standing on a Japanese bridge, looking down into the water, when Verlaque caught up with her.

He coughed and she swung around. "Oh my God!" she gasped in English. She then did a half laugh and continued in French, "You're the last person I expected to see here. You startled me, Judge."

He said nothing but held out his hand for her to shake.

"Have you been here before?" she asked, pulling off a green leather glove to shake his hand. "It's one of my favorite places in Paris."

He stared at her, bewildered by her genuine surprise. Either that, or she was a great actress. "You didn't follow me here?" he asked.

This time she burst out laughing.

"Why do I believe you, and yet I have this crazy hunch that if I were to call my commissioner he would tell me that you took the same TGV as I did?"

The professor stopped smiling. "I took the 7:05 last night."

"*Moi aussi*," Verlaque replied. *My turn to smile.*

She let out a bit of nervous laughter. "Well, at least we weren't on the same car. I would have seen you. I was in car eleven."

"I was in thirteen." Verlaque looked at Beauty. She was right; if she was in car 11 then he wouldn't have seen her, even on his way to buy the Cognac, as the bar was in car 14, right next to his. "You left your hotel without telling anyone."

"Isn't that all right?" she asked. "You told me not to leave France, that's all."

"You're to notify us of your movements."

"Oops."

It suddenly occurred to Verlaque that Rebecca Schultz may have gotten where she was partly due to her beauty. But it didn't work on him; he had seen plenty of beautiful women. His heart belonged to Marine. "Have you been in Paris the whole time?" he asked.

Schultz pulled her mohair scarf tighter around her neck. "No," she answered. "Listen, can we go somewhere warm to talk?"

Verlaque looked at his watch. It was 12:25. In an apartment around the corner, Commandante Barrès would be feeding Jeanne. Hortense was more than likely eating alone, or perhaps with another maid, as his father usually ate lunch at his men's club.

"Should we get something to eat? It's lunchtime," he said.

It had been years since he had been in a teppanyaki restaurant. The pure spectacle of it now embarrassed him, but as children, he and Sébastien loved it. He remembered their laughter as the tofu sizzled on the hot grill, then jumped up and flapped around, much like a fish does when it has been caught and thrown onto the deck of a fishing boat. He must have been smiling as Rebecca Schultz said, "I hope you don't mind that I brought you here. I used to love this place as a kid."

"You've been here before?" Verlaque asked as he looked around the simply furnished Japanese restaurant. *Today is a Japanese-themed day*, he thought.

"Many times," she answered. "We used to borrow the pied-à-terre of friends of friends that was on this street. My parents may have had a great art collection, but they were careful not to spend their money on frivolous things like hotels. I usually stay down here. Besides, there didn't seem to be any hotel rooms available in central Paris."

"That happens often," he said. "So that's why you know about the Albert Kahn museum."

"It was a favorite place of my mother's," she said.

Verlaque saw that although the professor was smiling, her eyes were moist. "Why did you come to France?" he asked. "And don't say for research."

She was about to answer when the cook appeared, both regal and frightening in his dark-blue kimono and leather knife holster. He bowed, drizzled oil onto the hot grill, and set six pieces of tofu down, which, as Verlaque remembered, began to jump and flip in midair. Schultz clapped her hands and then immediately brought them up to her face. "I'm sorry," she cried out. "But the jumping tofu always got me!"

Verlaque laughed, too. "It's just as funny now as it was when I was ten," he said.

"You're even more handsome when you laugh," she said in English.

The cook set aside the tofu and carefully placed thin slices of rolled omelette on the grill, and Verlaque realized that their conversation would be constantly interrupted by the spectacle of the teppanyaki chef. Had that been Rebecca Schultz's reason in choosing this restaurant? And here they sat, side by side. Verlaque had to turn most of his upper body to look at her; had they been sitting at an intimate table for two he still wouldn't have answered her flirtatious comment, but here he didn't have to, as they had the spectacle to watch. Slices of eggplant were now sizzling as the chef quickly flipped them back and forth, his spatula making rhythmic scraping sounds against the stainless steel grill.

"Sorry for being so brash," she said, twisting a large silver cuff, studded with turquoise, along her wrist. "Where were we before my ill-timed flirt?"

"You were going to tell me why you're here."

"I came because Cézanne had a mistress, and I'm fairly close to determining who she was."

"The affair in 1885."

"Well done," she answered. "And knowing what I know about the artist, I'm convinced he painted her."

Verlaque didn't reply but let her carry on. It was a trick that one of his law professors had taught him, and one of the only things about law school that he had retained. That, and an appreciation for whiskey that he had developed the semester he spent in Edinburgh.

"I had been to René Rouquet's apartment earlier in the evening," she said. "I lied before."

"Ah," he replied, turning to look at her.

"I arrived at René's apartment at around seven p.m. and rang his buzzer. To my surprise, he answered. I had expected Cézanne's former apartment to be owned by a pair of nobles, or by an obsessed artist, not him."

"Retired postman."

"Ah yes, that *is* what he looked like," she said. "I told him who I was, and that I was writing a biography on Cézanne, and he let me come up."

"Probably because he *was* a retired postman," Verlaque suggested. "And not a count."

Schultz smiled. "You're probably right. He made me a cup of instant coffee, and the more questions I asked about Cézanne, the more fidgety he got. Especially when I raised the date 1885."

"He didn't show you anything?"

"No, but I could tell he had more information. Or something he was hiding."

Verlaque leaned back as the chef served them their first course. "Do you like sake?" he asked. "I don't feel like drinking tap water."

"I loathe it."

"Good, so do I." He picked up the menu, motioned over a waiter, and pointed to a white Burgundy.

"My parents used to order the sake," she said, "until one evening my father made this funny face and said to my mother, 'Judy, I just can't stand this stuff!'"

Verlaque laughed again, taking a piece of tofu with his chopsticks and dipping it into soy sauce. "I've never been to Japan," he said. "But I would imagine there's great sake there."

"I haven't been there, either," she said. "It always surprised me that my parents never went, given the influence of Japanese prints on modern art. But they really couldn't stand being out of the East Village, especially my dad. Every Saturday they would do a tour of the small galleries, always on the lookout for new talent. It was more than a hobby for them; it was a passion." She smiled as she leaned her elbows on the lacquered counter, playing with her chopsticks, lost in thought.

"You have such palpable love for your parents." He took a piece of omelette, paused, and set it back on his plate. "It's admirable."

Rebecca looked at the judge and imagined she saw a cloud hovering over his barrel chest and wide shoulders. Family troubles? He seemed to her to be the classic wealthy Frenchman who had been ignored by his parents. "I'd do anything for them," she said.

The wine and the good food were having their effect on Rebecca Schultz; she was finally warm, and slightly dizzy. "I have another confession to make," she said as she watched the chef expertly cook her cod and Verlaque's tuna.

Her beauty had not gone unnoticed by the two young Japanese French waiters who hovered around her, at the ready with the wine bottle or carafe of water. Verlaque watched them, amused. "*Ah bon?*" he said, motioning to one of the waiters with his wineglass that had been empty for some time.

"I was upstairs, at Edmund Lydgate's, when you lunched there on Sunday. So I know about the painting."

Verlaque set his wineglass down and looked at her.

"I was going to tell you," she quickly said. She leaned back as the chef placed a rectangular ceramic plate in front of her, fish on one side and thinly sliced vegetables on the other. She asked, "What do you know about Mr. Lydgate?"

"Worked as a high-end art auctioneer for years," Verlaque said. "Now drinks too much in the Luberon. That's about it. My commissioner is looking into his history."

"He knew my parents," she said. "They were often called into Sotheby's to estimate the value of paintings. They didn't trust him, nor do I."

"Go on."

"He has this long-winded, emotionally charged version of why he quit the auction house," she said. "But I think it was because he was linked to an art theft. Though it was never proven. For years—no, decades—an extended family from Long Island has been in charge of the handling of art and antiques at the auction house," she went on. "It's a well-paid, comfortable job that these guys are sort of born into."

"*Les Cols Rouges,*" Verlaque said.

"Pardon?"

"We have the same system here, at Drouot. The men who handle and store the art are Savoyards. Always have been."

"And the 'red collars'?" she asked. "Is that their uniform?"

"Exactly. It's hundreds of years old."

"Well," Rebecca said, smiling, "I think these guys—most of them are from the Bolibar family—probably wear blue jeans. But they're French, too, or at least their origins are. Anyway, a few years ago a New York surgeon died and the Bolibars arrived, as they usually do, to pack up and catalogue the art that would be auctioned."

"And let me guess," Verlaque said. "They helped themselves to a few pieces?"

"Yes. They took some Raoul Dufy prints, a Picasso drawing, an Eileen Gray desk—the real thing, not a re-edition—and a small Degas sculpture. One of the ballerinas."

"How were they caught?"

"The surgeon had, luckily, shown his collection to a junior member of the auction staff just weeks before. It's hard to remember all of the art that passes through these places, believe it or not—"

"I believe it."

"But she had done her MA thesis on Eileen Gray's furniture, and so remembered the desk."

Verlaque wiped his mouth with his napkin and set it down, leaning back. "Where does Lydgate fit in?"

"My parents said that the Bolibars chose pieces that were valuable and that would be easy to sell," she said. "As if they had an advisor. Someone who would have seen the collection earlier, or who went with them."

"Someone from the auction house, and someone who could help them sell that stuff."

"Right," Rebecca answered, finishing what was left of her wine. "They'd been stealing for years, and in a warehouse on Long Island their 'holdings' were found. Crates and crates of art and antiques. Once they were caught, the trail of their sales was stupefying. One of them used his earnings to buy six studio apartments in Manhattan. Another sold two Picassos to open a chain of pubs. They drove Porsches and Lexuses."

"Were you hoping to meet Lydgate when you came to France?"

"Yes. I brought his number in Gordes with me. He knows a lot about art—my parents confirmed that for me, even if they didn't like him. So I called him and asked if I could visit. He told me that he was giving a lunch party for a judge, so I knew it was you."

"And was he able to shed some light on Cézanne?" Verlaque asked.

"Well, I couldn't see the painting," she answered. "But we talked about it after you had left. He didn't think it was a genuine Cézanne, and he talked about the canvas in vague terms, the kind of stuff my first-year students say."

"That sounds surprising."

"Yes. So either he's forgotten all he knows about modern art, or he didn't want to tell me."

"I'd go with the latter."

☙

Chapter Twenty-six

A Visit to Cézanne's Studio

Marine met her father outside the parking garage Pasteur.

"How was your class?" Anatole Bonnet asked his daughter after they had exchanged the *bise*.

"Fine," she answered. "I'm teaching History of the Civil State. I haven't done it in a while."

"Ah. I'm sure you'll make it more interesting than a bunch of dates and decrees."

"*Merci, Papa*," Marine said, putting her arm through his as they walked up the avenue Paul Cézanne. "Unfortunately, my methods are *too* interesting for some of my colleagues. Next week I'm showing the students the film *The Return of Martin Guerre*. Some of my fellow law professors think that a film is out of place in the classroom."

"Nonsense. It's very relevant, and if nothing else, you'll be showing the students something other than a vampire film."

Marine laughed. She was impressed that her father even

knew about the current vampire rage in young adult books and film.

"I'd forgotten how important the Martin Guerre case is to our history of law," he continued. "The beginnings of written documents used as identification, right? Seems so obvious now. When was it, exactly?"

"In Toulouse, 1560," Marine answered. "Before that, people's identities were acknowledged by their faces. Written IDs didn't exist. Until Martin Guerre decided to leave his wife and return twelve years later."

"Ah yes. In the meantime Martin Guerre had been replaced, by someone who looked like him," her father said. "An imposter."

"I remember going to see that film with you when it came out. It was the first Gérard Depardieu film I ever saw."

Dr. Bonnet laughed, remembering Florence doing her crossword a few nights previously. "Your mother was with us, too. But she's never been good at remembering actors' names. Well, it sounds like your semester is off to a good start."

Marine sighed. "It is, but I'm always a bit sad to have a smaller group after the Christmas break. So many kids drop out at midsemester."

"They'll find another path to take," he said.

"But they must feel so discouraged," Marine said. "You know, I'm not sure it's the best system we have, letting everyone who received a ten on the Bac—regardless of grades—into first-year law and medicine."

"It's *fair*." Anatole stared straight ahead. His daughter was picking up too many of Antoine Verlaque's nonsocialist ideas.

"And before you say that these are Antoine's ideas," she said, "it's something I've been thinking over for some time." She stopped to let her breathing catch up with her. "This road is steeper than I remembered. Well, let's not get upset about the dire straits of our university system and begin this Cézanne walk you've organized. I take it our first stop is his atelier."

"I thought it best to start there," Anatole said. "In my youth this was still the Chemin des Lauves, as it was when Cézanne had the studio built in 1902. Let's turn around and look at the view."

They turned and faced Aix, the father's arm gently resting on his daughter's shoulder. "He would have seen the same churches," Marine said, sheltering her eyes from the late-morning sun. "And the red-tile roofs."

"Fewer apartments in his day," her father said. "Look: you can see the green hills south of Aix, and Gardanne. I would have liked a house up here, but we thought it better to be south of the downtown, so your mother could walk to the university."

"The view is fantastic," Marine said. "But you'd have to walk uphill, back home, with your groceries."

"True enough."

They turned around and continued walking uphill, ten minutes later stopping at the gate of Cézanne's studio. "So sad that the studio is now surrounded by 1950s apartment buildings," Marine said, looking around her.

Her father shrugged. "Too many babies born after the war," he said, smiling. "We never had enough housing in Aix."

Marine said, "I know that Cézanne would have had a good view of the Mont Sainte Victoire from here, but I think it was perhaps more important that he be far away from the snotty Aixois."

Her father smiled and quoted Jean-Paul Sartre: *"L'enfer, c'est les autres."*

Marine usually got along with people, but her colleague Franck's snarky comment of her showing a film to law students made her think that the French philosopher may have been right. "Yes, other people can be hell," she said. "And here Cézanne would have been alone."

They passed through the entry and showed their IDs. As residents of Aix, they were admitted free of charge. They walked up the narrow flight of stairs to the painter's atelier, where an enormous north-facing window let in a subdued morning light. It gave the room a dreamy, filtered look. Hardly a noise could be heard except for the odd cough and shuffle of feet as the other visitors slowly moved around the room, looking at the objects Cézanne used for his still lifes: white ceramic bowls and pitchers, wooden chairs with cane seats, pewter carafes, and, of course, fruit, which Marine supposed the staff replaced every few days. "It's sad in here," Marine whispered.

"I've always thought so, too," Anatole said. "But Cézanne *was* sad here. His mother—to whom he was so attached—was dead, and Zola was, too."

"I thought they had a falling out."

"They did," he answered. "But all the same, when Cézanne heard of Zola's death in 1902, he locked himself in his rooms on the rue Boulegon and refused to come out for a day."

"Cézanne was sick, too, wasn't he?"

Anatole nodded. "Diabetes. He began using the atelier in 1902 but died four years later. One of my elderly medical professors was on the committee of citizens who tried to save the studio in 1952, when it was almost sold to developers."

"The same ones who built the apartments."

"No doubt. And the studio was full of paintings when they found it."

"Really?" Marine said. "What happened to them?"

"They were bundled up in lots of ten and sold to Americans."

Marine opened her mouth to protest.

Anatole put his index finger up to his mouth and then whispered, "The Americans *did* save the studio from developers. They bought it and offered it as a donation to the country of France, which refused. So they offered it to the region, which also refused."

"The city of Aix?"

"Also turned them down," Anatole said. They walked along, bending down to look at three skulls set out on a small wooden table. "The university finally accepted the studio."

A young man stood beside them, looking at the skulls, shaking his head. "This is it?" he asked them in broken French with what sounded like an Eastern European accent. He threw his arms into the air. "This is all Aix has of its most famous son? This small studio with hardly any paintings? Just some dusty bowls? A tragedy!"

"But Cézanne's here," Marine said. "Don't you feel it?"

The young man rolled his eyes toward the ceiling and walked on, shaking his head back and forth.

"I think that these objects speak for themselves, don't you?" Marine asked her father.

"Indeed," Anatole answered. "And my stomach is speaking to me right now."

Marine laughed. "Should we stroll downtown? We could pick up some cheese at André's, and a dessert at Michaud's, then eat at my place."

The walk downhill took half the time and Marine had to walk quickly to keep up with her father. He was not only six inches taller but, when hungry, walked at a determined pace. She pulled at his arm when they got to the cathedral. "Saint Saveur," she said. "Cézanne's funeral was here, right?"

"Oh yes," her father replied distractedly, "1906." Anatole pointed across the street at an elegant former mansion that now housed a political science university. "And that was the old law faculty where old Louis-Auguste Cézanne made his son study."

Marine thought of her students and wondered how many of them would prefer to study art, or nursing, or cooking, but had signed up for law to please their parents. "Let's buy some cheese around the corner," she said.

"I'm glad your cheese monger friends are back in Aix," her father said.

"Me, too," Marine answered. "The Marseillais just didn't buy their cheese."

"Marseille is a fish town, plain and simple."

"And the name of this street must remind André of that daily," Marine said as they turned right on the rue des Marseillais.

A bell rang as they entered the shop, and the handsome black-haired owner waved from behind a glass-and-chrome counter. "*Salut, Marine!*"

André walked around the counter and gave Marine the *bise*. She introduced her father; the elder Bonnets usually bought their cheese at the supermarket, which she didn't tell her cheese *affineur* friend. "André is Aix's only affineur, Papa," she said instead, turning to her father. "He has three different cellars for his cheese, each one with a different humidly and temperature, depending on the ripeness of the cheese. Is that right, André?"

"You've got it," André said, moving back behind the counter

and picking up a large piece of black-veined cheese. He cut two slivers and passed them to Marine and her father on a piece of butcher paper.

"I can smell it from here," Marine said.

"Truffle!" her father exclaimed, putting the cheese in his mouth and smiling.

"Pecorino laced with black truffles," André said. "I seldom get it."

"Too many people buying it?" Marine asked. "It's heaven!"

"Not *enough* people buying it," André answered. "I'm worried that the cheese maker isn't going to survive. People are unwilling to spend the money."

Anatole Bonnet looked at the price per kilo and whistled.

"But you only need a little bit when a cheese is this good," Marine quickly said, annoyed at her father. At least her mother wasn't with them; she'd have out her pocket calculator. "I'll take some for Antoine. He's in Paris but will be back tomorrow."

"Tell me how much," André said, posing his knife along the top of the cheese.

"About an inch, thanks," Marine said.

André cut along the pecorino and a sharp, musky, nutty smell permeated the shop. The bell rang as a new customer walked in. "Oh, André!" she exclaimed. "You need to put a warning sign outside the shop when you're about to cut the truffle pecorino."

"I'll take a slice, too," Anatole Bonnet said. He turned to Marine and went on, "It will be a surprise for your mother."

They quickly bought a selection of soft, runny goat cheeses for their lunch and left, in a hurry to eat but also to get to Michaud's. They walked down Aix's narrow medieval pedestrian streets without speaking, their feet taking them on a path that they had both known as youngsters. At times Marine wasn't even sure if she knew these streets' names, so familiar she was with their shops, their carved wooden doors, and the burbling fountains that appeared at almost every intersection.

They crossed the Cours Mirabeau and walked toward Michaud's, Anatole stopping in front of number 30. "Madame Cézanne lived here," he said, pointing to the upstairs windows, "after Cézanne's father died in 1886. She and Paul dined together almost every evening."

They walked farther down the Cours and into Michaud's, which was, mercifully, quiet. "What would you like?" Marine asked. She looked on lovingly at her father, who nearly pressed his long, fine nose against the glass, peering at each section of desserts. "A small lemon tart," he finally said.

"And I'll have a miniéclair," Marine told the black-uniformed salesgirl, who smiled shyly and had a head of thick red hair. "Café, not chocolate."

The girl carefully set their desserts into a small red cardboard box, then took a long piece of gold ribbon and wrapped that around the box, tying a bow.

Marine thanked the girl, who smiled again, her blue eyes sparkling. "Papa," Marine whispered, turning to her father, "that girl—"

"A relation of our mysterious sitter?" he asked, grinning.

Marine said, "She *does* have the same smile. But look: the gold ribbon. The girl in the painting is playing with one—"

"She worked at Michaud's!" Anatole Bonnet examined.

"What if?" Marine said, grabbing her father's coat sleeve. "Where could we find a list of employees from 1885? The archives? The library?"

Anatole Bonnet pointed into the air and whispered into his daughter's ear, "From Mme Michaud herself."

"She's still alive?" Marine asked, remembering the petite, blond Mme Michaud. Everyone in Aix referred to her using her maiden name—Michaud—when in reality she had been happily married for decades. Her husband, a busy notary, was never seen in the bakery and Marine wasn't even sure what his name was. Mme Michaud had always handled the cash, wore Chanel suits of varying pastel shades complemented by silk Hermès scarves, and had—simply by the glare she gave clients over the rim of her tortoiseshell glasses—frightened a young Marine Bonnet.

Dr. Bonnet said, "She's one of my most ornery patients."

Chapter Twenty-seven

❧

Breakfast, Alone, in a Banquet Room

Verlaque gasped for breath and sat up. He had drenched the sheets with sweat. "Thank God," he muttered, covering his eyes with the back of his arm. He now remembered why he preferred staying in hotels in Paris: the bad dreams he had on the rue des Petits Pères. Someone knocked at his door. "Come in," he said, more gruffly than he meant to.

"*Bien dormi?*" his father asked, stepping into the room and closing the door behind him. "You came home late last night."

Verlaque sat up, surprised both by the fact that his father was in his room and that he had noticed what time his grown son had come home. "Sorry," he said. "I spent the day in Boulogne, then last night having a mediocre, overpriced meal at Le Dôme."

"You were in Boulogne-Billancourt?" his father asked, sitting down in an armchair. "*All day?* What on earth for?"

Verlaque laughed. "A case I'm working on. Boulogne's not

that bad, you know. And God knows the real estate is almost as expensive down there as it is here."

"Perhaps—"

"Say," Verlaque said, "do you remember when we used to go to teppanyaki restaurants?"

His father surprised him, once again, by smiling. "You kids loved them," he said. "Speaking of restaurants, I thought, if you're free, we could have lunch together. Or dinner. There's this Basque chef—"

Verlaque rubbed his eyes and yawned. "In the eleventh—"

"That's right," his father said. "I just read a review of his restaurant in *Le Monde*. What do you say?"

It would be possible, if I work all day at trying to find the blasted stolen canvas. "Dinner would be possible," he answered. "Great, even."

His father made no answer, but Verlaque thought he saw him twitch and the slightest smile form at the edges of his small, narrow-lipped mouth.

Verlaque then added, "But I'm afraid we won't get a table."

"Leave it to me."

Verlaque smiled. His father, after all, had been a powerful Parisian businessman, the owner of one of France's largest flour mills.

"How is Mother?" Verlaque asked. "Will I be able to visit her?"

"I'm afraid not quite yet," M. Verlaque replied. "She needs as much rest as she can get, so the doctor has requested no visitors."

"But surely family—"

Verlaque Senior bent his head and then looked up. "She doesn't want you boys there," he said. "I'm surprised even I can go in. It would be shocking for you to see her. She's . . . changed. She's thinner than ever, if you can imagine, and has tubes coming and going—"

"I don't care," Verlaque said. "I want to see her."

"Her heart is weak," M. Verlaque explained. "She's been having abnormal heart rhythms resulting from the anorexia."

"Oh, I see." Verlaque tossed off the comforter and slowly got out of bed.

His father got up from the armchair and went to the window, making a mental observation: Antoine's short, muscular legs and huge back and shoulders were so dissimilar to his own long, thin legs and narrow chest. Sébastien had his build, and Antoine had his grandfather's.

"Next time," M. Verlaque said, pushing open the drape a few inches to look outside. "As soon as her heart rate gets back to normal."

"I'll come up again next week if I have to," Antoine said, walking toward the bathroom. "I'm serious about that." He turned on the shower and decided not to argue with his father. Not this time. "I'm surprised you'd try a restaurant in the eleventh," Verlaque called out. The 11th, 12th, and 19th arrondissements were the city's current hip neighborhoods, full of rowdy, packed bars and surprisingly good restaurants.

"So am I," Verlaque Senior replied, his trembling hand running up and down the soft velour curtain. "I haven't been north of the Place des Vosges in years."

Hortense once again served Verlaque breakfast. After he had finished, he asked her if he could spread out his papers and computer and work at the dining room table. She smiled, pleased that he would ask her permission. Lord knows she worked hard polishing all the wood and silver in that great room where guests rarely entered.

"Of course, Judge," she answered, looking out of the window at the rain hitting the panes in giant fat drops. "Would you like some tea while you work?"

Verlaque looked up at the maid and thought, *Here is a woman who enjoys taking care of others.* "Yes, why not," he answered.

"A green tea?" she asked.

Verlaque frowned. "That's supposed to be good for you, isn't it?"

Hortense smiled. She tried not to stare at Antoine Verlaque's paunch; he had put on weight since the last time she saw him. She hoped he had gained weight because he was happy, sharing dinners with someone he loved, unlike his parents. "I'll be right back with the tea," she said.

Verlaque thanked her and his cell phone rang. "*Oui,*" he answered, seeing Officer Flamant's name appear on the screen.

"Sorry to disturb, sir," Flamant said.

"Not at all," Verlaque answered. "It's raining cats and dogs here and I'm about to drink some green tea."

The humor was not lost on Flamant; he knew how much Antoine Verlaque loved coffee, and sun. "We're still working on the motorcycle licenses," Flamant said. "So far none of the owners' names ring a bell, and none of them have felonies, save for a lot of speeding tickets."

"No surprise there."

"But I have interesting news about a rental car turned back at the Hertz offices at the TGV station a half hour before your train left Aix."

Verlaque smiled, knowing what would come next. "Go on."

"Dr. Schultz," Flamant said. Verlaque could almost see the young officer's smile. "The Yale professor. She turned the car in at 6:30."

"*Ah bon*—" Verlaque had no idea why he wasn't telling Alain Flamant the whole story: that he had found Rebecca Schultz, that they had lunched together, and that they had walked around suburban Boulogne-Billancourt while Verlaque smoked a cigar and Rebecca had chatted on about New Haven, New York, and Cézanne's life. But something told him to hold off on telling the others that he had seen her.

"So I think we all know who took the painting while you were on the train," Flamant said. "Find her, and you'll find the painting."

Before Verlaque could reply, Flamant said, "Sorry, sir. That wasn't much help, my last comment. Paris is a pretty big city."

"It is, indeed." And in that big city he had found Rebecca Schultz, walking in a remote, gray winter garden, wearing a coat as bright and colorful as springtime. A coat he could have spotted from miles away. As if she had wanted to be found.

He set the phone down and banged the table with his fist. From her post in the kitchen, Hortense jumped. She had heard the judge on the phone, asking about a woman, and now he was angry. She had been about to go in and ask him about lunch, but now she'd wait.

Verlaque put his head in his hands and moaned. "Of course she's gone," he said. He could no longer hear Hortense; she had been opening cupboards and humming to herself. Now there was just the sound of ticking clocks, and the rain hitting the windows.

She didn't ask any questions about the painting, he wrote in his

Moleskine. *Wouldn't she have been curious? She didn't ask: What does the painting look like? What does the sitter look like? R.S., who has been researching Cézanne's life for years, and who was close to, as she claimed, finding the identity of his mistress . . .*

He sighed and looked around the crowded room. He was lost; here he was in his parents' house, after an absence of almost a decade, his only company a kind and bored maid who kept trying not to look at his stomach. He had lost a piece of evidence, been taken in by a gorgeous American, and was lying to everyone around him. Except Marine, but she wasn't here; she was in Aix, getting on with her life, taken in by no one.

Who could he talk to in Paris? Who could help him? He picked up his cell phone and scrolled down the address book until he got to the Ts.

Chapter Twenty-eight

Cézanne Paints Manon

• MARCH 17, 1885 •

*T*hat was the most thrilling ride I've ever been on!"

Cézanne frowned. "Keep still, Manon," he said. "That was also the *only* train ride you've been on."

Manon laughed and twisted the gold ribbon around her fingers. "When we went over the viaduct I thought I would faint!"

"I bet you could almost see your sister Isabella's house from up there," he said as he dabbed green paint on the canvas.

"I think I did!" Manon answered, pleased that he had remembered Isabella's name. "The train was so fast, but I'm sure I saw my nieces and nephews playing in the yard. Imagine, from Aix to Gardanne in thirty minutes!"

"I'm surprised to hear you so overjoyed by trains."

"What do you mean?" Manon asked. She stopped playing with the ribbon.

"Because the train tracks are wrecking the bloody landscape, that's why."

"That's better than roads zigzagging all over the hills," she said. "And soon the roads will all be paved."

Cézanne laughed out loud, setting his brush down and standing with his hands on his hips. He loved Manon's opinions; it reminded him of spending time with Zola.

"And, *Monsieur le Peintre*," she said, shaking a finger at him, "more people can travel on a train than by horse and cart. So one line of track can serve many more people than a dozen roads." She looked around the apartment that he had rented. It was small, but with a lovely view onto a small square that housed a fountain and two olive trees. She did not ask Paul, as she now called him, whose flat it was, or how he found it. She had told her mother that Michaud's needed her to work all day, and told Amandine, when asked if she could fill in for another girl, that her sister needed her to babysit. Amandine had looked at her with a smirk and then said, after a pause that seemed to Manon to last an eternity, "*Bon*. I'll find someone else."

Cézanne had picked his brush back up and was painting, frowning as he worked. Manon straightened her back and watched him, smiling. "Are you frowning because of the trains?" she asked.

"No," he answered, poking his head around the canvas to look at her. "I'm wishing that you'd keep still and stop grinning." He then smiled, giving her the sign that he was joking and not annoyed. With Paul, she sometimes couldn't tell the difference.

And then, before she could stop herself, she blurted out,

"Your usual sitters don't laugh?" She had not wanted to remind him of Hortense.

"No," he answered, seeming not to have noticed her blunder. "You know," he went on, "I learned to paint people at the Musée Granet, when I was young. Those Eustache Le Sueur and Jean Restout paintings of saints."

"I remember those," Manon said. "They're very melancholy." Once again, she bit her lip. She hadn't wanted to suggest that Paul's portraits were sad, or that she didn't like them.

"Well, this portrait of you won't be like those, that I'm sure of. You can't keep still, and you keep grinning like a fox." He wished he could show this portrait to his friends in Paris. Perhaps he would take it with him, on his next visit to Claude's in Giverny. His friends wouldn't ask questions about Manon, or judge him. "At least we have peace and quiet here," he said, continuing to paint. "Even Aix is getting too noisy for me."

Manon laughed and then began to cough, bringing her handkerchief up to her mouth. Cézanne looked up from his canvas. "I want you to see my doctor," he said. "I'll pay for it."

"Tell me about Paris," she said. "Please, Paul."

He turned back to his canvas, trying to hide the tears that were filling his eyes. "The women wear the most enormous hats," he began, "with broad brims, and some women look like they might topple over from the height of their hats, so piled high with silk flowers they are. Nothing simple like your lace bonnet."

"And their clothes?"

"Dull," he said. "None of our sunny colors. And if you are unlucky enough to be near Les Halles in the early morning, it is wretched for the eyes, and even worse for your nose." He tapped the side of his nose with his free hand. "The ground is covered in an ankle-deep filth that mingles with the steam that rises up from the animals' bodies. And there are people, yelling, everywhere: butchers, buyers, thieves, errand boys, vagabonds . . ."

"There *must* be some lovely things in Paris," she said. "I think you exaggerate all that is negative so I won't feel bad that I'll never have the chance to go."

He frowned, setting his brush down. "The bridges," he said. "Each one is beautiful. It's a good thing if you live on one side of the Seine but have business on the other side. That way, part of your working day involves crossing a bridge, and looking down the length of the river, watching the barges trudge past, and the fishermen . . ."

"I've never lived in a town with a river, or the sea, like in Marseille."

"That's why you're so sensitive to the countryside," Cézanne said. "Your color is green: the green of pine and olive trees."

"Amandine Michaud went to Paris last summer," Manon said. "She talked an eternity about a big department store—"

"Le Bon Marché," Cézanne replied as he began painting once again. "I'll loan you Zola's new book."

"Au Bonheur des Dames?" Manon asked. "Mme Michaud told us about it."

"Sit still, Mlle Solari! Yes, I have it at home."

Manon smiled, realizing that they still sometimes addressed each other in formal terms, especially if Cézanne was painting, or frustrated. "M. Zola based the store in his book on Le Bon Marché?"

"More or less," Cézanne said. "The big department store who buys up all the little buildings on the block, and it keeps getting bigger and bigger, like a monster."

232 · M. L. LONGWORTH

"And the little shops close?"

"*Oui, bien sûr.*"

"So the cities are changing as quickly as the countryside," she said.

He applied yellow to her forehead, and her mouth, and the wooden buttons on her blouse. "I wish you wouldn't be so wise," he said. "It can make an old man weary."

Chapter Twenty-nine

⤳

Visits to Two Well-Appointed Apartments

*H*ippolyte Thébaud's apartment was just as thrilling, and weird, as Verlaque had remembered it. It was every bit as busy as his parents' house, but he liked it here; the colors and textures interested him. He sat on an ancient sculpted wooden sofa, its cushioned back and seat upholstered in bright-red silk. Opposite was a blue chair whose base was made of fine stainless steel wires, like a cage. Verlaque thought it was American, and from the '50s, but he wasn't sure. Beside the chair was a backless green velvet sofa, all curves, and probably Venetian. The room's colors were bold, with accents in black and white.

"Say, Hippolyte," he called toward the kitchen.

"Yes, dear Judge?"

"Is this green sofa Venetian?"

"Yes, indeed!" Hippolyte answered. He arrived in the doorway, carrying a black lacquered tray with crystal flutes.

"The chandelier is Venetian, too. And later we'll drink the coffee out of Italian earthenware."

"Deruta."

"Ooh la la, I can't teach you anything."

"Sorry; I've been to Deruta," Verlaque said. "A few cases back. It also involved art."

Hippolyte set the flutes down on the table and gestured for Verlaque to open the champagne. He said, "I must say, I'm a little surprised that you'd show up here with chilled champagne."

"I passed a wine shop on my way over," Verlaque said, carefully turning the bottle as he held on to the top. "I can't resist a small, chock-full wine shop. And it's almost noon."

Hippolyte smiled. "Somewhere." He crossed his long, thin legs, dressed in a winter favorite: checked wool, but in bright colors—pink, orange, and green—that he could find only from one tailor, who worked out of a tiny studio in Batignolles, and who was covered in tattoos that bore the names of his favorite Saville Row mentors. They had been in jail together, the tailor having refused to pay income tax. "As much as I'm pleased for your visit," Hippolyte said, "and thrilled to be drinking a 1990 Pol Roger, you must be here on business."

The cork popped, and Verlaque filled their glasses. "I am," he said, sounding as serious as he could make it. He certainly hoped that Hippolyte didn't have a crush on him. "Will your friend Hervé soon be here?"

"He's on his way," Hippolyte said. *Oh dear God*, he thought. *Does the judge actually think I'm interested in him? He's gained so much weight. Not at all my type . . .*

Verlaque said, "I know that wine theft is—was—your domain—"

"Oh, it still is," Hippolyte said. "Chin-chin."

"Cheers," Verlaque replied in English, touching his flute to Hippolyte's.

"I'm still consulting with the Parisian police," Hippolyte said. He took a sip of the champagne and beamed. "*Très, très bon,*" he said.

"Well, I come to you with a question not about wine theft, but art theft."

Hippolyte sat back, a sign for the judge to continue.

"Last week, an old man in Aix was murdered, just days after he had discovered what may be a Cézanne in his apartment." Verlaque went on to explain that Rouquet had lived at 23 rue Boulegon, Cézanne's last dwelling. "The canvas has gone missing," Verlaque continued, "and I think it may be here, in Paris."

"And you want me, or Hervé, to suggest where the thief may have taken it."

Verlaque refilled their glasses, relieved that Hippoylte had not asked how the canvas had disappeared. "Yes, more or less. Where would a thief—perhaps a novice—take a canvas of questionable origins and try to sell it, or at least get it estimated?"

The doorbell rang and Hippolyte bounced up out of his chair. "Hervé will be able to answer your question."

Hippolyte opened the door and a middle-aged man walked in, every bit Hippolyte Thébaud's opposite. Hervé Lunel was balding, overweight, and dressed in dirty, baggy blue jeans and a well-worn blue overcoat. And yet the two men seemed overjoyed to see each other, Hervé removing his out-of-fashion gold-rimmed eyeglasses—which Verlaque could see, even from across the room, were filthy—to exchange the *bise* with Hippolyte. Hervé pulled at his overcoat as if desperate to get it off, handing it to Hippolyte. "The bloody metro was packed," he grumbled with an accent that Verlaque had trouble under-standing.

"Thank you for coming," Verlaque said, stepping forward and offering his hand.

Hervé Lunel looked at the judge's hand as if confused, and then shook it.

"Champagne?" Verlaque asked.

Hippolyte strolled back in, having disposed of the coat, and said, "Oh, Hervé doesn't touch the stuff, do you, Hervé?"

Lunel once again mumbled something, and Hippolyte re-plied, "Coming right up!" Verlaque had been able to make out only one word, and that was "Paris."

Hippolyte returned, carrying a glass with what looked like water, and handed it to his friend, who drank the liquid in one gulp. Verlaque then wondered if in fact it had been vodka, or gin, but this time he understood the accent: "Paris tap water is fine for me, always has been," Lunel said, placing the glass, roughly, on a delicate side table.

Verlaque asked, "Are you from Lille?"

"I'm a Ch'ti, yep," Lunel replied. "So is he," he said, point-ing at Thébaud. "Although he pretends not to be."

Hippolyte quickly drained his champagne and said, "Judge Verlaque has some questions for you, Hervé. They found a pos-sible Cézanne painting, down in Aix-en-Provence, but now it's gone . . . missing."

Hervé whistled.

"I understand that you once stole artworks, but now you've come clean," Verlaque said.

"Yep. I was tired." Hervé yawned and looked at the floor. Verlaque imagined that just getting out of bed made this man tired.

"And now you give advice to the police?" Verlaque asked, holding out his glass as Hippolyte served him more champagne. "Like M. Thébaud does with stolen fine wines."

Hervé nodded in the affirmative.

"Do you work with Commandante Barrès?"

Hervé smiled and slapped his knees with both hands. "She had a baby! A girl!"

Excited to have found the subject that might help the Ch'ti to talk, Verlaque went on. "Yes!" he exclaimed, trying to match Hervé's enthusiasm. "Jeanne! I saw her yesterday."

"Well, well," Hervé said, still smiling.

"So, if one had a Cézanne, a painting never having been seen before, how could one legally sell it?" Verlaque quickly asked.

Hervé replied, and Verlaque caught the word "loss."

"I'm sorry . . ."

Hervé spoke more slowly this time, and Hippolyte mumbled about finding something to eat. "If the painting has never been seen before, I'd report it. To. The Art Loss. Registry," he said slowly, as if Verlaque was simpleton.

"You'd report it?" Verlaque asked, confused.

"It's a database of stolen goods," Hippolyte explained. "Police use it all over the world. The new owner of a stolen painting, sometimes a reputable gallery, will send in a photo of the painting. If it's not in the database as being reported stolen—which the thief, or crooked gallery owner knows darn well it won't be—then the database folks send a letter that says, in brief, 'It doesn't match our archives.' It works especially well for artworks that have been stolen, literally, right out of the ground, like in the Middle East."

"And with that stamped letter," Verlaque said, "they can sell it legally."

"You've listed it as stolen, right?" Hervé asked. This time, Verlaque understood every word, and he was sure the look of panic could be seen by at least Hippolyte, who jumped up and poured the rest of the champagne in Verlaque's flute.

Marine had been reminded of Mme Michaud's legal surname—Bruissane—as it was written on a brass plaque beside the simple wooden entrance door, on the rue des Bernardines. They now sat in the old woman's living room, surrounded by Provençal antiques. Mme Michaud still dressed in vintage Chanel, and still dyed her hair a strawberry blond. It had been that color for as long as Marine could remember, and although she preferred that women let their hair go gray naturally, as her mother did, she admired the energy and discipline it took to get to the hairdresser's every four weeks, especially when one was so elderly. It hadn't been necessary to try to guess Mme Michaud's age, as the old woman had proudly announced it as soon as Marine and her father had taken off their coats and been seated. "I just turned ninety-two," she said to Marine, guiding her to a centuries-old sofa covered in a floral print. "But your father, and my children, thought it best I stop working when I began my tenth decade."

Anatole Bonnet smiled. "Madame, you could have kept working at the bakery," he said. "But you were standing all day, and worrying too much. Working is good for the mind and soul; I'm a firm believer in that. But your body was telling you differently."

She brushed aside his comment with her bejeweled hand. "Well, I've taken up painting," she said. "Since you won't let me run my business, dear Doctor, would you like to see my latest attempt at modern art?"

"*Bien sûr*," Marine and her father replied in unison.

"Come with me, then," she said. "I've turned my late husband's office into an art studio."

They followed Madame down a hallway that was lined with small oil paintings—mostly landscapes of Provence. Marine watched as the old woman walked, with the use of a cane; she worried that Madame Michaud might slip, as the bright terracotta floor tiles looked like they had just been waxed.

"These are impressively shiny tomettes," Anatole Bonnet said—what Marine had just been thinking.

"One of my grandsons just waxed them," Mme Michaud said, pausing to tap one of the hexagonal tiles with her cane. "He's having marital problems so comes here and gets focused on fixing things in the apartment. It didn't occur to him that I might slip. *Eh voilà...*"

Neither Bonnet replied, and Marine was fascinated and yet slightly shocked by the old woman's frankness.

"Here we are," Mme Michaud said, opening the door to her newly created studio. The walls were lined with built-in bookcases made in a dark wood that made the room look gloomy. But an easel stood in the middle of the room and a small wooden table had been set up that was covered with tubes of oil paints, oil pastels, and a glass jar of paintbrushes. "I have to use photographs to go by," she said, taking an old sheet off of a painting that rested on the easel. "I'm using old photographs to paint my family history. This one is of my aunt."

A Cubist-inspired painting stood before them and Marine looked at it in awe. It was not at all what she had expected from the tiny old woman who wore pearls and a pink Chanel suit.

"I didn't set out to paint Tante Amandine this way," Mme Michaud said. "I wanted to paint her, but nothing was working. My art teacher finally asked me to describe my aunt, and I told him: she was ornery"—Mme Michaud reached out her hand

and tapped Dr. Bonnet on the shoulder—"even more ornery than me."

Anatole laughed and said, "I would never say that about you."

"My foot." Mme Michaud looked at the painting and continued speaking. "Amandine never married, the poor dear, and took out her unhappiness on the salesgirls. My father was too busy to realize what was going on—he was the baker, so he was back in the kitchen—and Amandine terrorized the staff until she died in 1945 at a ripe old age. But she taught me the business—she was shrewd, even if half our product went into her mouth—and it was these conflicting ideas I had about her that made my art teacher suggest a Picasso-esque approach."

"He had very good advice," Marine said. "It's a wonderful painting."

"Yes, indeed," Anatole added. He was no fan of Cubism, even if, as Picasso had once famously said, it all came from *the father of us all*, Cézanne.

"So your Aunt Amandine would have been working at the bakery at the turn of the century," Marine said, glancing at her father.

"Of course," Mme Michaud answered. "She knew Cézanne."

"Mme Michaud, that's partly why we're here," Anatole said.

"Oh, not to look in at the health of your favorite patient?"

"That, too," he said. "But Marine is doing research on Cézanne at the moment—"

"I thought you were a law professor," Mme Michaud said, peering at Marine.

"I am," Marine replied. "But all academics are curious. I'm researching Cézanne as sort of a hobby. I'm interested in his personal life—"

"The nitty-gritty," Mme Michaud said, smiling. "That's a big seller. But I'm not sure Cézanne's personal life—as you call it—was very interesting."

"Your aunt never said anything?" Marine asked.

"As I said before, she was more concerned with the bonbons and éclairs. But why not have a look at her notebooks?"

"Notebooks?" Dr. Bonnet asked, leaning forward so much that his nose almost touched the top of Mme Michaud's wispy dyed-blond hair.

"I'm not promising anything." Mme Michaud shifted her tiny body toward the door, tapping the tomettes with her cane, and they followed her out of the studio. She kept speaking as they walked down the hallway. "Tante Amandine kept records of the business in dozens of notebooks . . . the sort they used for accounting back then. But I know she wrote down some of the comings and goings of the shop, too, busybody that she was. They're in a trunk in one of the bedrooms," she said. "Come with me into the kitchen. You can make us some coffee, dear Doctor, and the professor can help me find those books."

Chapter Thirty

M. Verlaque Senior Ventures Beyond the Place des Vosges

A young waiter came to their table and set down two small bowls of liquid. He rang out an impossibly long name for the liquid and then hurried away. The men shrugged at each other and lowered their soup spoons into the broth. "I didn't understand a word of that jargon, but I definitely heard the words foie gras," the elder Verlaque said.

"Me, too. Do you think it's at the bottom of the bowl?" Antoine asked, moving his spoon around.

"I found a piece!" his father exclaimed too loudly.

Antoine laughed and tasted the soup. "It's chicken broth."

"Yes, but with teeny-tiny chunks of foie gras," M. Verlaque replied. "I have two pieces."

"I haven't found any yet."

"Maybe this is where women who wear little black dresses come to eat."

Antoine laughed. "*Comme Maman.*"

"Your mother—" The waiter appeared and whisked away their empty bowls, setting down two more.

"Excuse me," Antoine said, "but we just had the broth."

The waiter adjusted his oversize black Ray-Ban eyeglasses and leaned back, as if Antoine Verlaque had just been extremely offensive, or even had taken a swipe at him. "This is a *second* broth, made from steamed winter vegetables, to cleanse the palate—"

"From the *first* broth," Antoine said, winking. The waiter rolled his eyes and walked away and the father and son burst out laughing. "Give me hearty Burgundian food any day," Antoine continued, sipping his broth.

"You were always such a good eater," the elder Verlaque said. "We had to practically spoon-feed Sébastien."

Verlaque looked at his father, trying to remember their meals together. Meals as a family had been infrequent; when he thought back to meals taken with his father, they were usually in restaurants, his father often accompanied by a "secretary." Antoine and Sébastien hadn't minded; the women were usually young and glamorous, and doted on the boys. Antoine thought about making a comment on memory, and how strange it was that certain events could be remembered in entirely different ways, depending on who was recounting the story. Who was the "we" in his father's memory of spoon-feeding Sébastien? Their mother? Emmeline, their grandmother? Or one of his father's girlfriends?

"Tell me," Antoine began, pushing his empty bowl aside and pouring wine into his father's glass. He had decided not to question his father about their family; they were having such a good time. It had been years since they had shared a dinner, and this evening Antoine had seen his father smile and heard his laugh. "Do you have friends who buy art? I mean expensive art—Impressionists, Old Masters, and such."

"My word," his father said, setting his spoon down. "I don't think any of my friends could afford that kind of art, not any more. But I did have a friend, Enrique de la Prada, who built up quite a valuable collection of what he called 'second-string Impressionists.' Enrique died a few years ago and his wife auctioned the lot at Sotheby's. Painters like Eva Gonzalès, Armand Guillaumin, and Stanislas Lépine. Quite a few stunning portraits."

Antoine listened closely, always impressed by his father's memory, especially for names. And the mention of Sotheby's, and portraits, made him think of Edmund Lydgate's home in Gordes.

The waiter reappeared with plates of guinea fowl, baked with pancetta and apples. Both Verlaques instinctively dipped their heads down toward their plates, smelling the roasted bird. "That's more like it," Antoine said. He took a piece of fowl and dipped it into the reduced juices that surrounded the meat and fruit.

"I had faith in our Basque chef," M. Verlaque said. "Although I do wish people could dine out *sans enfants*." He motioned to a table nearby where a man and woman ate with their young son and daughter.

"But you took us to restaurants," Verlaque reminded his father. "Plus, those kids are being well-behaved. The little boy yelped a bit, probably about the broth, but so did we. If I ever have—"

His father put his spoon down and looked up.

"Did your friend Enrique ever have a painting stolen?" Antoine asked, quickly changing the subject.

"Not in his Paris home," his father answered. "But he did

tell me the crazy story of his Empire-era eagle being stolen out of his Monte Carlo apartment."

"A gold eagle?"

"Yes, it was atop a dresser. Enrique was something of an amateur historian, with a keen interest in Napoleon. It was a former servant—a Corsican—who broke in one night. With all that art on the walls, some of it very pricey, the chauffeur took the eagle. Only that. He wanted to take it 'back home,' as he said, to Corsica."

"So not all art theft is done in order to make money," Antoine said.

"Honor. Ownership. Status," M. Verlaque said. "For some people, that kind of power can outweigh any monetary value." He looked past Antoine at the crowd that was waiting to be seated next. "There's quite a rush at the door. They do a second service here; I was told that when I called for a reservation. What's this country coming to?"

Antoine turned around and looked at the hungry clients waiting for a table. Some looked desperate, others tired, and a few joked among themselves, trying to make the best of it. Many of them were wet; it had started raining again. Others strained their necks, surveying the other diners who had booked earlier, trying to see which ones were already eating dessert, or having coffee.

"Not again! I don't believe it . . ." The restaurant's noise level was suddenly unbearable. "Papa, there's someone at the door whom I know," he said, pushing his chair back and wiping his mouth with his napkin. "I'll be right back."

From where M. Verlaque was sitting, he could see that his son was scolding the woman. The woman protested, throwing her hands in the air, and looked behind her, out the window. Antoine said something and put his hands on her shoulders, and they turned and walked toward the table.

"Father," Antoine said, "I'd like you to meet Dr. Rebecca Schultz. She teaches art history at Yale."

M. Verlaque quickly got up and shook Rebecca's hand. "*Enchanté.*"

"I'll get a chair," Verlaque said. "We'll squeeze you in, Rebecca. Father, Dr. Schultz speaks excellent French."

"But I'll never manage to lose my American accent," Rebecca said.

Antoine returned with a chair and Rebecca quickly sat down, not taking off her coat.

"Ah, like our charming Jane Birkin," M. Verlaque said. "She's lived in France for more than forty years and still has her accent. So, you're a university professor—" He stopped himself from continuing. Another professor? He had met Marine Bonnet only once, and was charmed by her. What was his son up to? He went on, "Some say that Ms. Birkin even fakes the accent a bit—" He stopped speaking, as he could see Ms. Schultz's face change from one of nervousness to one of fear.

"What is it, Rebecca?" Antoine asked, taking her hand.

"He's there," she sputtered. "I can see his red motorcycle helmet."

"Who?" Antoine asked, turning around to look out of the restaurant's wet, foggy windows.

"He's gone—"

"Rebecca, thousands of Parisians ride motorcycles."

"I'm scared—"

Antoine leaned in. "How did you find us?"

"You left me your parents' home phone number, remember?" she said.

"Yes—" He realized that he had put his cell phone on silent, so that this rare dinner with his father wouldn't be interrupted.

Rebecca played with her scarf, twisting the two ends around each other. "He was following me, but you didn't pick up your cell phone. So I called your house, from a taxi. Your maid told me where you were."

Thank you once again, Hortense. Antoine said, "I was followed onto the TGV in Aix by a motorcycle driver. Is that him?"

A couple who had been waiting for a table walked behind Rebecca, the woman's oversize purse bumping the back of Rebecca's head. "Can we go somewhere?" Rebecca asked, pulling in her chair. She turned to the elder M. Verlaque. "I'm so sorry to ruin your dinner."

"Nonsense," he answered. "But what *is* wrong?"

"Rebecca, does the motorcycle man have the painting?" Antoine asked, getting impatient.

"Is that what those questions were all about?" his father asked.

"Partly—" Antoine answered.

"No. I have it," Rebecca said. "Under my coat."

"What? Have you had it all this time?" Antoine hissed.

"Let's go back to the house," the elder Verlaque said, motioning for the bill, "if one of these tattooed youths they call staff can manage to call us a taxi."

"But the motoryole man will follow," Rebecca said, shivering.

"No; I have a good idea," Verlaque's father said, pulling a cell phone out of his jacket pocket. "I'll call Jamel, my usual taxi man. This will be his idea of fun."

Chapter Thirty-one

~

Jamel à la Conduite

"*T*ake rue de la Roquette," Antoine said, looking behind through the rear window. In the nighttime drizzle he could see a single light following them.

"One-way the wrong way," Jamel barked.

"Wait a minute," Antoine said, turning around to talk to Rebecca, who was in the backseat with his father. "Didn't motorcycle man follow me to my parents' house the other night? When I got off the train?"

"No, no," answered Rebecca. "He followed me, because I had your leather bag."

"Of course you did—" *What an idiot I am*, he thought.

Antoine looked over at Jamel, who was driving dangerously fast and talking on his iPhone. He was about to say something about safe driving when Jamel set his cell phone down in the cup holder between them and said, "I've just sent out a request for help to some other taxi drivers. I'm going to head south of the river to confuse this guy, and my buddies are going to try to separate us from him."

"Excellent notion, Jamel," M. Verlaque said. "Now you can stop giving directions, Antoine."

Antoine turned around, and in the dark he could just make out his father's smile. "So, if you were on the train in car eleven and I was in car thirteen, how did you get past me to take my bag?" Antoine asked Rebecca. "I would have seen you."

"I had no idea you were on the train; that part was the truth," she said. "But toward the end of the trip I wanted a coffee, so I got up to go to the bar car. I walked through my car, then through car twelve, and when I got into car thirteen I saw you get up from your seat and walk toward the bar. I froze."

Jamel raced to make a green light. The car swerved to the left, into a lane that would take them onto Pont d'Austerlitz, and Rebecca fell into the elder Verlaque's arms. "Sorry, sir," Rebecca said, sitting back up.

"Not at all, dear, not at all . . ."

"And then what?" Antoine asked. He turned around and saw the single light behind them, as Jamel looked in his rearview mirror and muttered, "*Merde*."

"I was going to try to catch up with you. I wanted to talk. And then I saw your bag," Rebecca said. "On the luggage rack. I knew that you had the painting—"

"Because you had been upstairs at Lydgate's."

"Yes. And I figured you were taking it to Paris, for an estimation. I saw my chance to grab the bag. When I got up close to it I saw your monogrammed initials in the leather."

"I know that bag," M. Verlaque said. "I think I gave it to you—"

"*Oui, Papa*," Antoine replied.

The car swerved to the right, heading west onto the multi-lane Quai de la Tournelle that hugged the Seine. At each intersection two or three other taxis turned onto the Quai, and by the time they had passed Notre Dame there were at least a dozen taxis beside and in front of them. "Here we go," Jamel calmly said as he picked up speed. "This is where we lose this moto guy."

"Hold on to your hats!" M. Verlaque called out in heavily accented English.

The car sped along, faster and faster, as the other taxis slowed down and got behind Jamel's car, cutting the motorcycle man off. Antoine turned around and could see only a blur of lights.

Verlaque's cell phone rang and he saw that the caller was Jean-Marc. "*Oui, Jean-Marc,*" he said into the receiver.

"Are you free to talk?" Jean-Marc asked. "We need to talk about the next cigar club meeting. It's at your place."

"Actually, I'm in a taxi in Paris being chased by a maniacal motorcycle driver. Can it wait?"

"I'll let you go," Jean-Marc said, laughing. "When I first met Pierre I told him that I'd date him under one condition: he stop driving his motorcycle! Say hello to Paris for me. Ciao."

Jamel turned right onto the Pont Royal and soon the car's tires made a repetitive thudding noise as they made their way over the cobblestones in the Louvre's courtyard. "*Mademoiselle, le Jardin des Tuileries,*" Jamel announced, slowing down the car.

Rebecca laughed, appreciating the taxi driver's humor. "The pyramid is loveliest at night," she said, looking toward her right.

"Mmm. I've always liked it," M. Verlaque said.

Antoine swung around to challenge him; he distinctly remembered getting into arguments with his father when I. M. Pei had unveiled his drawings: M. Verlaque had railed against its daring modernity while his sons had argued in favor of the Chinese-born architect's plans. But he let it go and smiled. "Home again, home again," he said in English, trying to remember the next bit of the rhyme that Emmeline had sung to him while she played with his toes.

"Jiggety-jig," Rebecca finished.

"You'll have to thank Jamel for us," Antoine said, handing his father a whiskey.

"Oh, I will," he said. "I also gave him a handsome tip, which I'm taking out of your birthday present fund."

Antoine laughed; had he forgotten that his father had a sense of humor? Or was it newly acquired? Was his father—now that his mother was in a hospital—finally at ease, after all these years? He had been having such a good time with his father that he had almost confided in him, but Verlaque Senior's comment about the children in the restaurant had stopped him. Rebecca coughed and both men turned to her. She was sitting beside the lit fireplace, wearing camel-colored leather pants and a tight gold sweater. "Sorry; I'm not used to whiskey," she said, "but this is good."

"Liquid sunshine," Antoine said.

"Even on a rainy Parisian night," Rebecca said, holding the glass up.

"Especially on a rainy Parisian night," M. Verlaque said.

"Yes," she said, "you're right." She looked at the judge's father; she liked his fine gray hair and thin nose and lips but most of all his dull blue eyes. They were wise, and could be funny, and were very different in shape and color than his son's big puppy-dog brown eyes.

"Once we've all warmed up and gotten over Jamel's Formula One racing tryout, we'll look at the painting," Antoine said. "In the meantime, Hortense is preparing us some snacks, and she's found you, Rebecca, a nightgown and some toiletries, since you don't have your suitcase with you."

"I forgot my bag in a café," Rebecca said. "I was terrified of the motorcycle man. I saw that he was outside, watching me, waiting—"

"It's all right now," M. Verlaque said. "You'll be safe here."

"And my leather bag?" Antoine asked.

Rebecca grimaced. "In the hotel in Boulogne. Sorry."

"I'll have Jamel pick it up tomorrow," M. Verlaque said, "after he takes you two to the Gare de Lyon."

"*Merci, Papa.* About the motorcycle man," Antoine said, getting up and walking across the room toward Rebecca, "did he follow you to the park?"

Rebecca shook her head back and forth. "No," she said. "But he was waiting at my hotel after our lunch. He had taken his helmet off because he was talking on his cell phone, so I could see his face better and I recognized him as someone I had seen in Aix, but I still can't remember where. I ran upstairs and double-locked the door. In the morning I paid the bill and then slipped out a back door, via the kitchen. Luckily a taxi was idling on the corner, and so I jumped in, but he must have seen me, because by the time the taxi dropped me off at the Café de Flore, he was there, across the street." She looked at Antoine and said, "You're probably wondering why I chose the Café de Flore."

"It *is* a little obvious," Antoine said, smiling. "Not exactly a hidden spot."

"An ex-boyfriend," Rebecca said, taking a sip of whiskey. "Funny, it doesn't burn anymore," she added, looking at the gold liquid. "Anyway, I fell in love with a French exchange student when I was in my early twenties—"

"That's why your French is so good," M. Verlaque said, smiling.

"It's the best way to learn a language," she said, winking at him.

"And you were meeting your old boyfriend there?" Antoine asked.

"No, good Lord, no," she answered. "He's married with three kids. I just went because I felt so . . . lonely. It felt safe; he used to take me there and we'd spend all our money on two *cafés crèmes* and one overpriced *croque-monsieur*. My parents may have collected Cézannes, but I was on a strict student budget, even when traveling."

The elder Verlaque's eyes lit up. "Are you serious? Cézannes?"

She nodded and smiled. "We even had a still life in the kitchen."

Antoine said, "We'll fill you in later, Papa, if that's okay with you, Rebecca?"

"My family history is no secret," she said. "That would be fine. But now I think you both want to look at the painting."

M. Verlaque set his empty glass down and got up. He walked across the room and reached out his hand to Rebecca, who took his hand and got up. "*Merci, gentil monsieur.*"

"I'm eager to look at this painting," M. Verlaque said as they walked arm and arm. "But I'm more curious to get your opinion of it, especially from someone who ate—what are they called . . .

peanut butter and jelly sandwiches?—under Cézanne's apples and pears."

They moved to stand beside Antoine, who had his hands in his corduroy pants pockets and was looking down at the portrait, lost in thought.

"*Elle est magnifique*," the elder Verlaque said, looking at the painting and then looking at Rebecca.

"But is she the real thing?" Antoine asked, looking at Rebecca.

"Oh yes," Rebecca said. "Edmund Lydgate told me it wasn't, but I didn't believe him. And having spent a full twenty-four hours with her, now I'm convinced he was lying. Why, I don't know."

"I've thought about that," Antoine said. "He could have been hoping to get his hands on it one day. But it would have been locked up at the Palais de Justice for years." He made a mental note to tell his secretary to see about hiring a law student as an intern to organize the room.

"So, how much do you know about Cézanne?" Rebecca asked, looking at father and son, her hands on her hips.

"His wife was named Hortense, like our maid," Antoine said, smiling.

"Yes, I noticed the coincidence right away," Rebecca said. "And he painted his wife very unlike this woman. Hortense was stern, with crossed arms, pining for her native Jura. Cézanne was uncomfortable with women; even those monumental nudes he did were all about form and color. The women are distorted, like his trees, like his apples."

"Wouldn't that fact make this painting *not* a Cézanne?" M. Verlaque asked. "This one is so realistic. The woman is of central importance."

"Good point. But Cézanne had an affair in 1885, with an Aixoise," Rebecca said. "It comes up a few times in correspondence, but nobody knows who that woman was. I think we're looking at her. It's realistic, yes, and different than his other portraits, yes, but he was in love. And it's definitely a Cézanne. Here, look—" She pointed at the young woman's bright-blue blouse. "Look at the careful, parallel brushstrokes. Some of the canvas is even left bare; it's all about artifice. As if Cézanne is telling us, 'This is not real.' My parents used to say that forgers—and they saw a few in their day—would never leave bare bits of canvas; they would have filled it all in. They weren't looking closely enough at Cézanne."

"Horror vacui," the elder Verlaque said.

"Right," Rebecca said, trying not to look around the medieval-inspired room. "The compulsion to fill everything in; Cézanne didn't have that. Now, you two, please stand back about two meters." Antoine and his father followed her order, and stepped back. Rebecca picked up two clean linen napkins that Hortense had just delivered with their snacks, and using them as makeshift gloves she picked up the canvas. "This is what my dad called 'The Judy Test,' named after my mother," she said. "Look at the colors; and the rhythm of curves, horizontals, and verticals. Keep looking, keep looking—" She then flipped the canvas upside down. "It works better with landscapes," she said, as if to apologize.

Antoine gasped, as did his father. "It's beautiful, even upside down," he said.

"There's still an incredible energy," M. Verlaque said. "It's full of patterns and shapes, dancing all over the canvas."

Rebecca poked her head around the canvas and beamed. "When you look at a Cézanne with fresh eyes, even upside down, you see all of the abstract elements at work: bands of color, warm and cool colors that bump up against each other. The whole thing vibrates. *C'est de la musique.*"

"You sound pretty convinced of its authenticity," Antoine said.

"I'm sure it's authentic," Rebecca answered, setting the canvas down. "I grew up looking at these, and my doctorate is on Cézanne. But you'll want another opinion, I'm sure." She tried not to smile, but Antoine heard the sarcasm in her voice.

"We have to take it back to Aix tomorrow," he said. "An expert can come down to Provence; I'm not moving it anymore."

His father snorted and then pretended to cover it up with a cough. "Shall we eat a little of this snack Hortense has arranged?" he asked, gesturing to a table that had been laid out with a watercress and orange salad and a small cheese plate.

"I'm ravenous," Rebecca said. "And you didn't get to finish your dinner."

"You should have told us you were hungry,," the elder Verlaque said, taking her by the arm. Antoine Verlaque stood by the fireplace, watching his father and Dr. Schultz across the room, laughing. He wished he could be as lighthearted as they were, but he still had so many nagging thoughts. Two unsolved murders. An unidentified nineteenth-century woman. A menacing motorcycle driver from Aix, someone whom Rebecca thought she recognized. And Jean-Marc's innocent phone call that had brought such unwelcome news: that Pierre had a motorcycle permit. Had Rebecca recognized the motorcycle driver because Pierre was there the night they found René murdered?

An hour later the trio made their way upstairs, politely wishing one another a good night's sleep before entering their respective bedrooms. Verlaque showered and then dressed for bed.

Before turning off the light he texted Marine, wishing her a *bonne nuit*, telling her he'd be home tomorrow. He then texted Paulik, informing the commissioner that he had recovered the painting, and Dr. Schultz, and that they'd both be returning with him to Aix the next day. Marine didn't answer, but Paulik did, saying that he'd be at the TGV station to pick them up, and that they'd also have a Parisian officer escort them on the train ride home. Paulik added that Flamant and Schoelcher were cross-checking the names of motorcycle owners who left motos outside Aix's TGV station with those who rented motorcycles at rental companies within walking distance of the Gare de Lyon, sometime after their arrival in Paris at 9:00 p.m.

Antoine Verlaque fell asleep within minutes, as he usually did. He woke up a few times in the night, listening to the rain tap against the windows, and once he heard a door open and close in the hallway, but he rolled over and fell back asleep.

Chapter Thirty-two

❧

Poring Over Amandine's Notebooks

*M*arine cleaned up after her grilled-cheese-sandwich lunch. She washed off the dining room table and put a stack of *Le Monde*s, which always seemed to take up half the table, in the recycling bin. Half of them were left unread; she felt bad for the trees but she would have felt worse not having a newspaper subscription. It was her way of supporting the dying world of print journalism.

As the front door buzzer rang, she set four pencils and a stack of paper, along with two bottles of sparkling water and four glasses, on the table, and then walked across the room to buzz in her parents. She could hear them chatting as they almost ran up the three flights to her apartment.

"Hello, chérie," her mother said, a bit breathless from the conversation rather than the climb. She gave Marine the *bise*.

"How was your movie night with the students?" her father asked, embracing his daughter then closing the door behind him.

"They loved it," she answered. "I could hear some of the sniffling."

"*Le Retour de Martin Guerre*," Anatole explained, turning to his wife. "Marine showed it to her first-year students. It's—"

"I know, I know," Florence Bonnet said, waving her hands in the air. "The film about that soldier—wasn't he?—who takes another one's place. We saw it at the cinema when Marine was young."

"Maman," Marine said, winking at her father, "who played Martin Guerre?"

"Now I know, judging by that big smirk on your face, it must be the same actor who played Cyrano." She looked at her daughter, and then her husband, as if searching their faces for clues. "Oh drat. I can't remember his name."

Marine and her father burst out laughing. "Well, you're great at research," Marine said, "and that's what we're doing today. Thanks so much for coming."

"Glad to help," Anataole said.

"And I'm intrigued by these notebooks," Florence added. "You say that Mme Michaud never looked at them? Unbelievable . . ."

"That's what she claimed, right, Papa?" Marine said. "By her own admission, she was too busy with raising kids and running the business, which I believe. Come, sit down in the dining room. I have them set out here."

"Is Antoine coming?" Anatole asked. "There are four spots."

Marine's heart sang. She loved that her parents—at least her father—liked Antoine's company.

"No," Marine said, "he's on his way back from Paris, with Dr. Schultz."

"Noted Cézanne expert," Dr. Bonnet explained to his wife.

"I know that, Anatole," she answered. "Just how forgetful

do you think I am? I may not remember movie stars' names, but I do remember what you and Marine have been getting up to this past week."

The buzzer sounded again and Marine said, "That will be Sylvie. She has only morning classes on Thursdays, like me, so offered to help."

As Marine went to buzz Sylvie in, she saw her mother look at her father and roll her eyes.

"*Coucou tout le monde!*" Sylvie announced a minute later as she walked in and gave everyone the *bise*. This week Sylvie had her short, spiky hair dyed with henna and wore a pleated green Issey Miyake tunic, with matching pants, one of her first designer purchases. It was also the only outfit that had survived two seasons in Sylvie's closet.

"Hello, Sylvie," Florence Bonnet said curtly. "How is little Charlotte?"

"Fantastic," Sylvie answered, handing her fur coat to Marine. "Don't worry, Mrs. B, it was my aunt's coat. I didn't buy it." She winked and saw that Marine's father was stifling a laugh. She didn't tell Marine's mother—whom she knew was an animal rights activist—that she did have another fur coat at home, which she had bought in Rome after a particularly successful gallery show of her photographs. "Let's get down to business, shall we?"

"All right," Marine said. "I've set the notebooks in the middle of the table. I had a quick look late last night, and Amandine seemed to have dated some of the pages, but very few. And in some cases she gave the day, or month, but not the year."

"One of my pet peeves!" Sylvie said, raising her hand in the air. "A Parisian gallery last year printed the month of my exhibition *chez eux*, but not the year! What about posterity? I asked them. What about the archivists, years from now?"

Florence Bonnet let out a tiny squeak, which Marine tried to cover up with moving the stacks of notebooks around. She knew that her best friend had been being sarcastic; while she enjoyed the financial success, Sylvie was in fact quite shy about her rising-star status in the art world.

"What are we looking for, exactly?" Florence asked.

"Well, any reference to Cézanne," Marine answered.

"And any references to the girls who would have worked with Amandine around 1885," her father added.

Marine agreed. "Mme Michaud told us yesterday that her aunt was born in 1860, so she would have been twenty-five when Cézanne painted our mysterious woman. He did go into the shop; Mme Michaud confirmed that for us. Papa and I have a hunch that the sitter in the portrait is a girl he was in love with, and that she worked at Michaud's in 1885."

"But we have no idea what her name is," Sylvie said.

"Correct," Marine answered. "She had red hair and green eyes, if we are to believe the painting."

"And perhaps—" Anatole then stopped speaking, and rubbed his chin.

"Perhaps what?" Florence asked.

"Perhaps," he continued, "she had some scars on her face . . ."

"Did you get that idea from the painting?" Sylvie asked. "Because Cézanne put colors and patterns everywhere . . ."

"I know," Marine said, "but this painting is more realistic than others. And I agree with Papa; there's some unusual patterning on the girl's face."

"It's just an idea," Anatole said. "I may be wrong."

"Well, call out when you read anything of interest," Marine said. "Or write it down and we can check over everyone's notes later."

"*Bonne chance!*" Sylvie called out as she opened her purse and got out a new pair of leopard-print reading glasses she had just bought.

The drapes had been pulled closed, so Rebecca Schultz had slept in well past 10:00 a.m. She sat up and rubbed her eyes as someone gently knocked on the door.

"Come in," Rebecca said.

"*Excusez-moi, mademoiselle,*" Hortense said, setting a breakfast tray on the night table. "Judge Verlaque asked me to wake you."

"Judge? Oh yeah, Antoine. Thank you."

Hortense took her time walking across the room to open the drapes so that she could study the guest. She did not like the look of her. Never mind how thin she was—so was Mme Verlaque, and look where that got her. Nor was it her big Afro—not at all pretty hair, like that of America's First Lady, also an African American—that bothered the maid the most. It was more the *comportement* of this *professeur* (as they had introduced her): the way she sat last night by the fire, her giraffe-like legs stretched out as if she owned the place. And the smile she had seen pass between—

"Is everyone up?" Rebecca asked.

"Judge Verlaque is working in the dining room," Hortense said as she finished opening the drapes. "He asked me to tell you."

Rebecca mumbled a thank-you and poured coffee from a small press into a porcelain cup. Hortense walked back across the room toward the door. She took one last look at the professor and tried to see if she had tattoos, but the professor had pulled the comforter all the way up to her chest. *She probably has one*, thought Hortense as she walked out and closed the door. *And I can easily guess where.*

"Flamant and Schoelcher have been calling motorcycle rental places near the Gare de Lyon all morning," Paulik said. "They have three hits already. I'll keep you posted."

"Thanks," Verlaque said, trying to sound more enthusiastic over their detective work. It didn't surprise him that moto enthusiasts would rent motorcycles in Paris when they got off the train; it was the easiest way to get around. Alain and Jules would probably find a dozen more names by the time they were ready to go grab some lunch.

"Can you check the Interpol archives for a Long Island family named Bolibar?" Verlaque asked. "Dr. Schultz told me about them; they used to collect the artifacts about to be auctioned at Sotheby's, until they were caught with crateloads of the stuff hidden in a warehouse. I'm expecting a call from Commandante Barrès, too, about Edmund Lydgate. Dr. Schultz's parents didn't trust him."

"I'll see what I can find," Paulik said. "Roussel is yelling that we're taking too long on this."

"Let him yell," Verlaque said of Aix's often-hysterical prosecutor. He thanked Paulik and hung up. He hadn't told the commissioner that Rebecca had been the one to steal his bag— and the painting—off the train. He hadn't seen the point, as he could keep an eye on her himself, and now the motorcycle man seemed more threatening, and urgent to find. Verlaque hadn't told anyone about the coincidence that Pierre rode a motorcycle, and had keys to the building on the rue Boulegon. And on the night of René's murder, Pierre seemed to have reached the rue Boulegon in record time. Verlaque picked up his cell phone and dialed Fabrice's phone number. "Yo, Judge!" Fabrice answered on the first ring.

"Fabrice, I have something that's nagging me that I need to talk about. Are you free to talk?"

"I'm sitting in the sad, underheated trailer that Julien calls his office," Fabrice replied. "I'm buying a used Mercedes for my wife off him."

"Does Julien have a speakerphone?" Verlaque asked. "I could use his advice, too."

A crackling noise came over the phone and Verlaque could hear shuffling and the men arguing in the background. "Let me guess: Julien has only one armchair?" he asked.

"Yeah, and he won," Fabrice said after a few seconds. "So what's this all about?"

"It's about Pierre, in our club," Verlaque began. "How long have you guys known him?"

"I met him first!" Julien yelled into the phone.

"No, I did!" Fabrice said. "My company redid the plumbing in the bookstore."

"Liar!" Julien said. "I met him years ago in the bookstore. I was asking him questions about guidebooks on Cuba, and we got to talking about cigars—"

"You bonehead," Fabrice said. "I'm the one who bought that guidebook for our first trip to Cuba."

"Last of the big-time spenders!" Julien called out.

Verlaque heard another scuffling noise and held his head in his hands. "Are you two finished fighting?"

"Hey!" Julien said. "We met him together!"

"I think you're right," Fabrice said. "We were both in the bookstore that day. What is this all about, Antoine?"

"I can't say right now," Verlaque said. "But what are your general impressions of him?" He waited for an answer but there was silence. "You guys?"

"We're lighting cigars," Fabrice said.

"Well," Julien said, puffing, "I've always wondered how a bookstore employee can wear such fancy clothes."

"*Julien,*" Fabrice said. "It's important to—"

"Gays?" Julien asked. "That's what you were going to say, isn't it? You're being homophobic!"

"How do you *spell* that, Julien?" Fabrice asked.

"Listen, Mr. Fancy Pants," Julien said, "you're no better than me! You may own plumbing stores all over Provence, but it's really all about backed-up toilets."

"Okay, I'm going to let you guys go now," Verlaque said. "Thanks for—"

"Are you going to tell us what this was about?" Fabrice asked.

"Later," Verlaque said. He hung up and thought about what Julien had said of Pierre's ability to buy expensive clothing; he himself had wondered the same thing, Pierre had dressed like that long before he began dating Jean-Marc. He was about to call Commandante Barrès when Rebecca appeared, looking fresh and awake despite the fact that she was wearing the same clothes from the previous evening. His father stuck his head around the door and said, "Good morning, Antoine; good morning, Rebecca. Jamel is here to take you to the station."

Verlaque looked at his watch. "*Merci, Papa.* I lost track of the time."

"I'm coming with you," the elder Verlaque said.

"Really?"

"Jamel sometimes drives me around the city," he said. "It clears my head. That way, after we drop you off, Jamel and I can go to Boulogne and get your bag at the hotel; and, Rebecca, where did you leave yours? Café de Flore?"

"Um, yes," she answered.

"It will be long gone!" Antoine said. "Okay, let's go. There's an officer meeting us at the station. My commissioner doesn't trust me with the painting."

"Well, he could now," his father said, "since the thief is now with you." He winked at Rebecca and she laughed.

Jamel drove remarkably slowly, and the city's buildings and bridges rolled by as if in slow motion. Verlaque could hardly remember growing up here, and yet back then he knew every street by heart. But the blues skies of Provence were his home now, with Marine.

The car pulled up in front of the station and they got out, bagless except for the painting of the girl, wrapped in a pillowcase, which Verlaque held on to. A tall, wide-shouldered bald man, dressed in a suit, suddenly appeared beside them and introduced himself as Officer Morice, quickly showing Verlaque his ID. Verlaque's father gave Rebecca the *bise*, and she politely turned toward the station, pretending to admire the building, so that father and son could say good-bye.

"Thank you for the bed, and the clothes," Antoine said. "I had a good time, Papa."

"So did I, Antoine."

"Please give Maman my best," Antoine said. "And I'm planning on coming back up to Paris next week, and I intend to see her."

Verlaque Senior looked up at the giant clock above the station's main entryway. "You should go. I'll keep you posted."

Antoine grabbed his father and hugged him for the first time in years. He felt his father's hands on his back, and then felt them gently pull away. Verlaque let go and looked over at Jamel, who was leaning against the car, smoking. "Jamel's a great guy to have around."

"Indeed," Verlaque Senior replied. "I'm thinking of giving him the ground-floor flat. It's half empty; we just use it for storage."

"That sounds like a fine idea." Verlaque called out to Jamel, "Take good care of my father."

"Yes, sir," Jamel answered, smiling.

"Thanks for everything!" Rebecca called out. She blew M. Verlaque a kiss and he put his hand on his heart.

Chapter Thirty-three

❧

Just Answer Yes or No

F ascinating," Florence Bonnet said, setting down her pencil and rubbing her eyes.

Sylvie stretched. "I agree, Mrs. B," she said. "At first glance, there's nothing here but the weather and price of flour, but then—"

"The more you read on, the more interesting all the little details become," Marine said.

"Exactly," Sylvie agreed.

"It was windier back then," Anatole said, "according to Amandine's notes. More days of mistral."

"Climate change," Florence said, tapping her pencil on the table.

Marine looked at the blue sky and the sun streaming in her dining room's large window. From here she could see the tops of the enormous bare plane trees that filled the shared gardens down below, and across to rears of the buildings that were on the rue Cardinale. This view hadn't changed much since Amandine's time, she thought. Saint Jean de Malte's spire was still here, separated from her top-floor apartment by the garden and a row of red-tile rooftops. A dozen or so illegally constructed balconies and terraces, including her own, had been built in the later half of the twentieth century, and the plastic, wood, or wrought-iron (in her case) furniture that sat out on those balconies brought the image back into the modern era. As did, of course, the satellite dishes and telephone wires. And her mother's voice.

"Marine?"

"*Oh oui, Maman,*" she answered.

"Earth to Marine," Sylvie said, smiling.

"So, I've jotted down the names of women whom I think are other shopgirls," Marine said, looking at her notes. "Clara comes up a few times."

"Ditto," Sylvie said. "Clara seems to be a whiner."

"Yes!" Anatole agreed. "Amadine writes, and I quote, 'Clara is always complaining about her sore back.' "

"I've got some references to a Manon," Mme Bonnet said.

"Me, too," Marine added. "She comes in late on the sixth of January."

"Fête des Rois," Anatole said. "That would be a busy day at Michaud's."

"Some things never change," Sylvie said.

"In my notebook Amandine says that Manon is a poker face," Florence said. "Do you think that could mean—"

"Perhaps," Anatole said, pausing. "She might be referring to this girl Manon being sad, or angry, but it could refer to a skin imperfection . . ."

"Suzette, anyone?" Sylvie asked. "Amandine says of Suzette, quote, 'Poor orphan girl . . .' "

"I didn't find any Suzette references," Marine said. "There's a funny mention of the wedding cortège of Countess Émilie de Saporta passing by Michaud's."

"I found a reference to a Mme Frédéric buying cakes for the priests," Florence said. "But it hardly seems that Cézanne would have an affair with the priests' housekeeper."

"Stanger things have happened," Sylvie said, winking.

"*Mais non!*" Florence tried to argue.

"Amandine certainly loves her job," Anatole quickly said. "The lists, and tastes, and even textures of their cakes and candies are described with such detail—"

"Yes!" Marine agreed. "Even lovingly described." She carefully turned one of the delicate pages of Amandine's notebook and read aloud: " 'Michel'—that must have been the baker, the current Mme Michaud's father—'has had the idea to add the zest of precious, plump grapefruit to our calissons.' "

"Lovely," Anatole said. "I've marked a passage—where is it; oh, here—where Amandine writes of 'chantilly whipped like a cloud,' and 'sunshine-yellow butter.' "

"There's a passage where she writes of caramels," Sylvie said. "And she says, quote, 'There's nothing quite like the smell of thick cream and sizzling butter, bubbling away in Michel's favorite copper pot.' "

"She could have been a food writer," Marine said, smiling.

"Or a professional cook," Sylvie said.

"Of course, as a woman, she never would have been allowed to," Florence said.

"Absolutely," Sylvie agreed. "Even today there are few female chefs in professional kitchens."

"It's sad, thinking of Amandine's life," Anatole said, setting down his reading glasses. "Here is a woman with a passion, but she has to amuse herself by ordering supplies—"

"And watching other peoples' weddings pass by," Sylvie said.

"On that sad note," Marine said, "I took the liberty of buying some candies at Michaud's on my way home from school." She got up and opened a drawer in the buffet and pulled out two small bags.

"Research!" Anatole said, rubbing his hands together.

"Caramels," Marine said. "And candied lemons."

Verlaque and Rebecca sat across from each other, both being careful not to touch the other's knees. Officer Morice sat beside Verlaque; the seat opposite him was mercifully free, so the pillowcase and its contents lay there, reminding Verlaque of all he had to do when he got back to Aix.

Rebecca looked out of the window and then said, "We should have a fast train on the East Coast. Connecting NYC and Washington to Boston."

"We're lucky here," Verlaque answered. "And as many times as I take this ride, it's never boring." They spoke in English, as if, unconsciously, they had decided to be secret, so that Officer Morice wouldn't understand. The policeman flipped through a TGV magazine, pretending to read an article about Bordeaux, but he was listening to every word. He had taught himself English watching Clint Eastwood movies.

"Unless it's at night," she said. "Then there's no view."

He laughed. "You're right. My favorite part is exactly halfway to Aix: Burgundy."

"Ah," she said. "Rolling hills and vineyards."

"And cows. I like cows."

She looked at his eyes again. In Aix she had been frightened of their blackness, but in Paris they had turned wet, and sad. Cow eyes, she thought.

"If the painting is really a Cézanne," Verlaque said, "you know it has to be turned over to the state. Rouquet had no living relatives." He thought of his dinner conversation with his father, and Enrique's stolen eagle, stolen for honor, prestige, not money.

"I know," she answered. "I wasn't planning on stealing it. I just wanted to be with it . . . her . . . for a while."

"Who *is* she?"

Rebecca leaned forward, putting her forearms on the small white table that separated them. "I have it narrowed down to a few possibilities. Cézanne was nervous around women, right?"

"That's what everyone says."

"I think he would have been introduced to this mysterious Aixoise somehow," she explained. "He wouldn't have met her in a café, say, or in the park. He would have needed an excuse to strike up a conversation with her."

"A maid?" Verlaque asked. "That's someone he would have seen every day, and felt comfortable around the working classes, *non*?"

"That's a good guess," she replied, "and I've gone that route, too. But he was a thinking man, and unhappy with Hortense, so I think his mistress would have understood him, and his art."

"Sounds like a good theory. A fellow painter?"

Rebecca shook her head back and forth. "There were very few female painters back then, and they were all in Paris, not

Aix. Besides, Berthe Morisot was already the mistress of Manet."

"Really?" he asked. "I didn't know that."

"It's common knowledge," Rebecca said. "At least we're 99 percent sure." She smiled. "No, I think our sitter was a sister of a friend. Cézanne was incredibly loyal to his buddies. Zola was an only child, but Jean-Baptistin Baille and Philippe Solari, both solid friends, and both from Aix, had sisters. Baille, Zola, and Cézanne called themselves the Inseparables."

"Sounds like the title of a Hollywood movie."

Rebecca laughed. "But my bet is on Solari. He was a sculptor, and had six sisters. So they would have grown up with an artist brother. Like Cézanne, Solari died in 1906, also of pneumonia, but unlike Cézanne, he died a pauper. On his way to the hospital he muttered, 'What a pity about the weather.'"

Verlaque thought about his mother, and wondered if she were dying. "Why is her identity so important to you?" Verlaque asked.

"Oh, for many reasons," she said. "I'm sure it's partly because I always feel like I have to prove myself to my colleagues."

"Because you grew up wealthy?" he asked, thinking of his own personal history.

"Not wealthy," she corrected, "but surrounded by priceless art. And then I go and get my doctorate in art history, so colleagues mumble—I know they do—about how lucky I was growing up."

"So by identifying Cézanne's mistress—"

"I prove myself, yes."

"But you couldn't have imagined that Cézanne painted her," Verlaque said, trying to go over the events of the evening of René Rouquet's murder in his head.

Now you're getting somewhere with all your questioning, thought Officer Morice as he turned a page of the magazine.

"I had fantasized about that," Rebecca said. "And when I saw how nervous M. Rouquet was whenever I said the year 1885 . . ." Her voice trailed off and she looked out of the window, then at her watch. "Almost in Burgundy."

Verlaque's cell phone rang and he answered it, trying to whisper. Cell phone conversations were forbidden in the train's cars, but he didn't want to have to squeeze past the policeman to go out into the hallway to speak. "*Oui, Marine*," he said. "*Ça va?*"

"We're taking a break from going over all of those notebooks that Mme Michaud loaned to us," she said, "the ones I told you about this morning on my way to class."

"Any luck?"

"Not yet," she answered. "But we have some possibilities. But listen, there's something more important. On our break, my father and I have been going over some of the aspects of this case, and the various people involved. Just answer yes or no, okay?"

"Yes."

Verlaque could hear her say, "*Oui, Papa, oui!*" "Are you sitting across from Dr. Schultz?" she asked, trying to stay calm.

"Yes."

"Do you remember the case of Martin Guerre?"

"Yes."

"That's what my father and I have been talking about," Marine said.

"Martin Guerre or Gérard Depardieu?"

"Antoine! Yes or no only!" She went on, hurriedly, "Martin Guerre was an imposter."

"Yes . . ." He looked up at Rebecca Schultz, who was now leaning back in her seat with her eyes closed.

"Antoine, Anatole Bonnet here," Marine's father said. Verlaque could hear Marine protesting in the background. "This is very important," the doctor said. "We've been duped by an imposter."

"Yes," Verlaque answered.

Chapter Thirty-four

❦

Le Fou Is Identified

Marine grabbed the phone back. "Antoine," she said, "I wanted you to only reply yes or no because I'm still not sure of Dr. Schultz's honesty. But it's Edmund Lydgate we're talking about. It's been bothering us how little he actually looked at the painting."

"Yes."

"You, too, right?"

"Yes." He remembered that Rebecca hadn't been impressed by Lydgate's art knowledge.

"Good. My father and I had been going over what Lydgate said about the painting, and it was all very vague, and in fact Lydgate kept agreeing to everything Papa said, using Papa's knowledge to make it sound like *he* was the expert. So we've been looking up images of Lydgate on the Internet. There are very few, only two rather blurry ones, both of Lydgate officiating at auctions. He *sort* of looks like the man we met in Gordes, although in these photos he's not wearing a moustache. But what's really important, more than what he looks like, is the fact that Edmund Lydgate is in a New York hospital. He just had his appendix out."

"Yes?"

"*Yes*," Marine said proudly. Verlaque could hear people clapping in the background. "I phoned his apartment in New York," she continued. "His number was listed! Using my best English—"

Verlaque then heard Sylvie laughing.

"I spoke to his great-niece—she's a student at NYU so lives with him. She's lovely; we had a nice chat. She told me that Edmund had an emergency appendectomy last week and is still recovering in the hospital. There's no way that man we met in Gordes is Edmund Lydgate. I've called Bruno and told him everything. He said that he's picking you up at the station, but he's sent some other officers up to Gordes."

Verlaque once again heard clapping in the background.

"That brings me to the motorcycle man you told me about," Marine said. "Our imposter must have an accomplice, as I can't imagine the man we met in the Luberon being an ace motorcycle driver."

"No." He once again thought of Pierre. But how could they possibly know each other? Or did they make a deal after they met that first night at René's? He had been so busy he hadn't had time to go over the notes he had taken when talking with Mme Chazeau. Pierre hadn't told him about the argument with René.

Marine asked, "So is Rebecca Schultz his accomplice, and did she just make up that story about the motorcycle? Or is there a third person in all of this?"

Verlaque looked over at Rebecca, who had fallen asleep. But he had seen the motorcycle following them. But was it the motorcycle man? Had they been hysterical over nothing? It might have been someone paid by Rebecca to follow them, or even a random Parisian. Thousands of people drive motorcycles in Paris.

"I'll leave you with that thought," Marine said. "And I'll see you later. I love you."

"Yes," he answered once again before setting his phone down.

They were now zipping through Burgundy, where every village seemed to have a Romanesque church, surrounded by roughly hewn stone houses that hadn't been garishly renovated as many had in Provence. The vineyards that stretched out over hills and held his favorite grapes—Pinot Noir and Chardonnay—were dormant, but the sun was shining on them.

"I have two more hours before I have to pick Charlotte up at her drama class," Sylvie said.

"Okay, let's get back to work," Marine said. She cleared up the teapot and cups they had used during their break; she didn't want the notebooks to be anywhere near liquids, or food. By the time she got back from the kitchen, her parents and Sylvie were hovered over their notebooks: Sylvie with one hand under her chin, the other hand playing with her hair; her father leaning on the table with his elbows; and her mother, back straight, hands on her lap, staring over the book. They stayed like that for almost thirty minutes, the only noise the gentle turning of the frail pages, until Sylvie said, "This is the second reference I've come across to Baronne de Montille." She wrote the baronne's name down on the sheet of paper beside her.

Anatole Bonnet frowned. "No," he said. "I don't imagine Cézanne ever having an affair with a noble."

"We keep saying 'affair,'" Marine said, setting down her pencil. "This was Provence in the nineteenth century. Who says they actually slept together?"

"He was an *artist*," Sylvie argued.

"He was *Cézanne*," Marine countered. "Not Manet. And certainly not Picasso. And his sitter probably had the fear of God instilled in her. This wasn't Paris; it was tiny, backwater Aix. The Provençaux were very pious."

"I agree," Anatole Bonnet said. "Cézanne was interested in ideas; perhaps this woman shared those. Perhaps that was enough to base a relationship on; that's *all* there was."

"But Cézanne was devastated after the affair," Sylvie went on. "He says so in his letters—"

"Here's something," Florence said. "Quote, 'I paid Manon 4 francs for her perfume. Lavender.'"

"Now, that's interesting," Anatole said.

"What's a Buddha's Hand?" Sylvie asked. "She mentions it a few times. Here she says, 'Michel bought five Buddha's Hands.'"

"*Un citron*," Anatole said. "A funny, knobby, elongated lemon."

"He would have used them for making candied lemon," Florence added. "I think they still do."

"Ah!" Marine said, picking up her pencil. "Amandine writes here, 'M now selling another scent. Verbena.' That must be Manon again."

"Enterprising Manon," Sylvie said. "I wonder if she made the perfumes herself."

"That suits Cézanne, doesn't it?" Marine asked. "Especially if Manon was collecting the plants and making the scents on her own. It's like what Papa was just saying; their relationship may have been platonic, based on ideas, or common interests."

"Listen," Florence said. " 'I caught Suzette sneaking a brioche. She said it was for her brothers. I let her have it; it was a day old.'"

"That's heartbreaking," Marine said, "Suzette was the orphan."

"Could it be Suzette?" Anatole asked.

"I'll write down Suzette and Manon," Marine said.

"Who's Le Fou?" Sylvie asked. "Amandine writes that he bought two galettes des rois, without boxes. Why note that detail about the boxes?"

"Saved the bakery money," Marine suggested. "Mme Michaud said what a good business head Amandine had. And Le Fou could be someone like Cézanne; everyone thought he was crazy."

"Or it could just be a crazy person," Florence suggested.

"But a crazy guy off the street couldn't afford two cakes at Michaud's," Marine pointed out.

"You're right," her mother said. "He'd have to be a rich fou."

"Like Cézanne," Anatole said.

Sylvie stood up and stretched, then touched her toes. "That's a good idea, Sylvie," Florence said. She got up and did the same, while Marine and her father kept reading.

"Whoa!" Marine said, jumping up a few minutes later. "Listen to this everyone: 'Manon and Le Fou meeting outside the shop. Secret RDV???' And Amandine's added two hearts in the margin."

"Put a star beside Manon's name," Florence said, rubbing her hands together. "This is getting so exciting."

They went back to reading, Sylvie checking her watch. She had another thirty minutes.

"Wait a minute!" Marine said. "I've got more here: 'M took some ribbon again. She thinks I don't notice. Ha! But it was just a little scrap off the floor.'"

"The ribbon!" Sylvie exclaimed. "That's how you got onto the Michaud track, right?"

"Exactly," Marine said. "The girl in the painting is playing with a piece of gold ribbon."

Anatole hit his forehead.

"What is it, Papa?" Marine asked.

"My time to make a phone call!" he said. "I should have thought of it an hour before. I'll call Mme Michaud and ask her if her tante Amandine had any nicknames for Cézanne."

"Brilliant, Dr. B!" Sylvie shouted.

He took out his small, out-of-date cell phone and slowly went through its address book until he found his ornery patient's number.

"Use my landline, Papa," Marine said.

"It's a free call that way," Florence added.

Dr. Bonnet quickly walked over to the telephone and dialed Mme Michaud's number, while the three others turned in their chairs to watch him. Mme Michaud seemed to have answered on the third or fourth ring, and doctor and patient spoke of her aching legs and the weather. "Madame," he finally said, "I'd like to thank you for loaning us your aunt's notebooks. I just have a quick question, referring to some of Amandine's notes. She doesn't refer to Cézanne by name, even though you say he was a customer. Did she have a nickname for him? Do you remember it?"

Anatole looked down at the floor while the old woman answered. He turned to Marine, Florence, and Sylvie and gave them a thumbs-up, thanking Mme Michaud and hanging up.

"Le Fou is Paul Cézanne!" he cried.

"Manon and Cézanne, that's it!" Marine said, clapping her hands.

"We did it!" Sylvie said.

"Not quite yet," Florence said. "We don't have her last name."

"Right you are," Anatole said. "Keep reading, everyone."

"Amandine doesn't seem to give the salesgirls' last names," Marine said.

"Yeah, that's not important to her," Sylvie said, snorting.

"Well, you never know," Anatole said.

They kept reading for another twenty minutes until Sylvie looked at her watch again. "Just ten more minutes," she said. "I can't stop reading this stuff."

"I know; it's addictive," Marine agreed.

They read on in silence until Sylvie shouted out, "*Quel dommage! C'est horrible!*" She tore off her reading glasses and put her head in her hands.

"What is it?" Anatole asked.

"There's finally a date," she said, shaking her head back and forth and running her fingers through her short hair. "And a year." She put her reading glasses back on and read, "'April 3rd, 1885. Morning off for Manon's funeral.'"

Rebecca woke up and rubbed her neck. "Did I sleep long?" she asked. "My sore neck certainly feels like I did."

"Yes," Verlaque answered. "You slept through Burgundy and most of the Drôme. We're almost in Avignon, so we'll be in Aix soon." *Home.*

While she had been sleeping he had been trying to connect to the Internet on his cell phone to look up photographs of Dr. Rebecca Schultz of Yale. The signal was finally strong enough somewhere south of Lyon, and he found three photos of her, taken for the Yale directory. It was definitely the woman now asleep in front of him. He took out his notebook and wrote, *Why steal a Cézanne? R would have (1) a painting of C's mistress, her pet project, but also (2) a Cézanne for herself, having been forced by the tax man to sell her parents' collection.*

He put his book down and mused, looking out the window at what was now very Provençal vegetation: white limestone cliffs, rocky sandy vineyards, groves of silvery olive trees. But why did Rebecca show up at the restaurant, painting in hand, terrified? Had it been a hoax? Was the painting still not safe? Was she planning on stealing it a second time? Or was the painting now sitting across from Officer Morice a fake? But she hadn't seen the painting while she was in Aix; how could she have had a replica made in twenty-four hours? Unless she had an accomplice in Aix. Lydgate. Or his imposter, rather. He had seen it, and Verlaque had stupidly let him take photos. But she hadn't known he would be going to Paris on the 7:05 train, so he had believed her when she said that the fact they had been on the same train was a coincidence. Unless she, too, had been on the motorcycle.

It was a good, very good, motive for murder, and one that had to do with honor: a tribute to Judy and Isaac Schultz.

Chapter Thirty-five

❧

Love and Loss

*B*runo Paulik was waiting for them on the quay. They said good-bye to, and thanked, Officer Morice, who handed Paulik the painting and turned around, walking toward the stairs that would take him up over the tracks to catch the next train back to Paris. Morice passed halfway on the overhead walkway and watched the judge and beautiful black woman walk toward the commissioner's car, which was double-parked in front of the station. From here he could see Mont Sainte Victoire. He had once walked to the top of it, on a vacation with his Scout troop from Paris, when he was fifteen or sixteen. His troop master, still a friend, was a Cézanne freak and had told the boys that Cézanne painted the mountain more than one hundred times, never feeling like he got it right. "When you look at the mountain from afar," he had said, "and the afternoon sun shines on it and breaks its rough surface into planes of color, you see that he did." Morice grumbled to himself, *Back to gray Paris*, and walked away.

The police car was driven by a young moustached officer Verlaque had seen around the Palais de Justice. Paulik sat in the passenger seat and Verlaque sat in the back, next to Rebecca. Paulik's cell phone rang and he mumbled yeses and nos, taking notes as he listened. "*Parfait, Alain, merci,*" he said, hanging up and turning around to face Verlaque. "Bingo on the motorcycle drivers," he said. "Officer Schoelcher wasn't making much headway until he thought to cross-check the owners' names with their addresses."

"And?" Verlaque asked, dreading hearing Pierre's name.

"One moto owned by a guy named Eric Legendre fits the bill."

"You're not serious?" Verlaque asked. He thought of Mme Chazeau, who had referred to Eric Legendre as a bully.

Paulik turned to the driver and added, "We'll drop the judge and professor off at the Palais de Justice and then head to twenty-three rue Boulegon."

Rebecca grabbed Verlaque's arm. "That's where I'd seen him! He's the neighbor! The night of M. Rouquet's murder—"

"The guy who made us tea," Verlaque said.

They passed a shopping zone full of oversize billboards, neon signs, and a McDonald's. Rebecca watched it with interest, leaning on the car's window ledge. "Wow," she said. "This is worse than New Jersey."

"You wouldn't know," Verlaque said. "You grew up in the Village and teach in Connecticut."

She laughed. "Touché."

Verlaque looked out the window at a block of apartments built so close to the highway he wondered how the residents could even carry on a conversation in their own flats. He thought of his parents' luxurious life, so different, and so privileged that they didn't even have to rent out their ground-floor one-bedroom apartment. "Bruno," he said.

"Yes, sir?"

"Who rents the storage space at twenty-three rue Boulegon? I know you told me . . ."

"The shop next door." Paulik's phone rang and he answered it.

"You know," Rebecca said, turning to Verlaque, "that couple on the rue Boulegon—the neighbors—they were hanging around when M. Rouquet let me in to his apartment. They were at their door when I went in, and when I left I felt like they were watching me, as if—"

"They were watching through the door's peephole?"

"Exactly."

Paulik snorted into the phone, laughed, and then said, "You made my day, Alain," before hanging up. "That was Flamant," Paulik said, turning back around. "They've got the guy pretending to be Lydgate."

"Fantastic!" Verlaque said. "I was worried he had flown the coop."

"He couldn't have," Paulik said, smiling.

"What do you mean?" Rebecca asked.

"Remember Lydgate's alibi?" Paulik said. "The old farmer?"

Verlaque said, "Elzéard something."

"Bois," Paulik said. "Elzéard Bois. Well, the night of Rouquet's murder, when he went to check on the man he thought to be Lydgate, Elzéard had been standing on the front steps, and Lydgate stood in the doorway and hadn't invited him in. That bothered Elzéard, because he was usually invited in, for a nightcap, plus he really couldn't see Lydgate—the imposter—very well."

"Because of the dark," Verlaque said.

"Right. So Elzéard's been watching the place, becoming more and more suspicious, until he finally walks right up to the house, goes in, takes one look at the imposter, realizes he isn't Edmund Lydgate, and knocks him out by hitting the back of his head with his hunting rifle. When Alain and the others got there, the imposter was tied up, sitting on a kitchen chair, swearing in English. Elzéard was sitting across from him, his rifle across his lap, drinking a fine Burgundy."

"Does the imposter have a name?" Verlaque asked after he had stopped laughing.

"I don't know yet," Paulik replied.

"Bolibar," Rebecca answered. "I'd bet my life on it."

"I thought they got caught," Verlaque said as they drove into downtown Aix. He quickly explained the story of the French American art handlers to Paulik.

"Only some of them went to jail, a few brothers and first cousins," she answered. "The kingpin, Henri Bolibar, got off."

"What did he look like?" Verlaque asked. "Enough to impersonate Lydgate?"

"It could work," she answered. "He'd be about the same age, too."

"Our motorcycle guy, Eric Legendre, doesn't have the same name," Paulik pointed out.

"What about her? His wife?" Verlaque asked. "The nosy neighbor."

Paulik got back on the phone. "*Salut, Jules,*" he said. "Can you check the passport of Mme Legendre, please? What's her maiden name?"

"They actually put maiden names on your passport here?" Rebecca whispered. "How archaic."

Verlaque did his best Gallic shrug. "*Mais oui.*"

Paulik hung up. "Bolibar," he announced. "Françoise Bolibar."

"Our firm is representing the Bolibars," Jean-Marc said, handing Verlaque a glass of whiskey.

"You're kidding?" Verlaque asked.

"I wish I were. I'm having nothing to do with the case because of Pierre's involvement," Jean-Marc said. "The owner of my firm finally figured out that Pierre's my partner."

"Is that a problem?"

"It might have been," Jean-Marc said, taking a handful of peanuts, "but I reminded him that I may be gay but I'm also faithful to my partner, unlike him at our last Christmas party. That ended the conversation. I'm also no longer with Pierre."

Verlaque put his glass down. "I'm so sorry. It's all my fault."

Jean-Marc waved a hand in the air. "No, it isn't. Pierre should have been honest with me."

"You had no idea he was collecting rent on the storage room?"

"No," Jean-Marc replied. "Although I had wondered how he could afford Prada." He managed a smile.

"How did he manage to rent the storage space that legally belonged to René?" Verlaque asked. "One of my officers looked up the deed."

"Pierre told me he began using it years ago, to store his bicycle, and some boxes, and gradually took it over. René had no idea that he could be renting the débarras out. It didn't occur to him that an empty room of four hundred square feet is worth some good money in downtown Aix. That's what Pierre and René were arguing about after their last apartment owners' meeting. At least he was honest about that."

"I'm sorry."

"Me, too," Jean-Marc replied. "But there were other problems in our relationship. Anyway, he's gone back to Toulouse to live near his family."

Verlaque asked, "So what else can you tell me about the Bolibar clan?"

"Henri Bolibar, the old guy pretending to be Lydgate, is uncle to Françoise, but he claims he didn't know that Eric and Françoise killed René. Henri was a part-time actor in New York; did a few television shows and theatre."

"Then I don't feel so bad for being duped," Verlaque said. "He's a fine cook, too."

Jean-Marc laughed. "Eric Legendre and Françoise Bolibar moved to Aix a few months ago, hoping to stay cool after the fiasco in Long Island, but also hoping to make a few small thefts; there's a lot of money, and antiques, between here and the Luberon. It was sheer coincidence that they landed at twenty-three rue Boulegon, although they admitted being charmed by living at Cézanne's former address. As Pierre can confirm, the walls are paper thin between the two apartments, and they overheard René when he found the painting. He was jumping around and yelling—"

"Poor René," Verlaque said, shaking his head back and forth.

"Françoise tried charming him," Jean-Marc went on, "to get more information out of him, hoping to see the painting, but he wouldn't budge, so last Friday night when he was out at the Bar Zola they broke into his apartment."

"And he came home?"

"Yes," Jean-Marc said. "There was a struggle; René threatened to call the police, and Eric Legendre threw him against the wall. René hit his head on the side of the fireplace—"

"And died."

"In the meantime, they looked for the painting, but of course Momo had it. But they did find a spare set of apartment keys."

"So they could go in and out of the apartment even when it was a crime scene."

Jean-Marc poured them each some more whiskey. "Françoise had called her uncle Henri in New York and told him that René might have found a Cézanne. In the meantime, Henri found out that Lydgate was in the hospital—"

"Dr. Schultz's parents never trusted Lydgate," Verlaque confirmed. "The real one, that is."

"That day you were in the apartment, with Pierre and Bruno Paulik," Jean-Marc continued, "and you found the painting . . ."

"Across the street."

"Right. Françoise Bolibar heard you guys run down the stairs, and watched you out her living room window run across to Momo's and then walk out five minutes later with something rolled up under your arm, grinning like lunatics."

"I thought we had been more discreet than that," Verlaque said, wincing.

"So she immediately called her uncle, who caught the next flight over here," Jean-Marc said. "It was easy to break into Lydgate's house, or maybe he even had a key—we're checking the locks on the farmhouse. It's an isolated house, and Lydgate wasn't there very often, and kept to himself—"

"Except for Elzéard Bois," Verlaque said, laughing. "Wait a minute . . . what about Lydgate's phone number that we found in René's apartment?"

"Planted by Eric and Françoise the night they killed René, after you had all left. They had a spare key, remember?"

"They wanted to get us up there, to Lydgate's," Verlaque mused.

"Right," Jean-Marc said. "None of them had seen the painting at this point. It was a perfect way for Lydgate to try to get his hands on it. What will happen to the painting now?"

"Professor Schultz is examining it," Verlaque said. "She believes that it's a Cézanne. And then it's being taken back up to Paris . . . not by me—"

Jean-Marc didn't hide his smile.

"To be examined by more experts," Verlaque went on. "This could take months, or years."

"In the meantime," Jean-Marc said, "we can have another sip of whiskey."

"What are you doing this summer?" asked Verlaque. "July?"

Jean-Marc shrugged. "In August we were planning to visit Pierre's sister who has a beach house in the Vendée. Now I have no plans. Why?"

"I'm hoping to throw a big party," Verlaque said. "With Marine. I'll keep you posted."

Marine, her father, and Rebecca had been looking at the painting, not speaking, for almost thirty minutes. A fourth-year law student, recruited by Marine, was silently working at a nearby desk, cataloguing objects used in past investigations that had been left in the small windowless room, forgotten.

Rebecca Schultz had surprised Marine. She was beautiful, yes, but also friendly, open, and moved by the painting. Anatole Bonnet finally broke the silence by saying, "Now I know why Cézanne's studio at Les Lauves always feels so sad."

Rebecca said, "He had lost Manon, then his mother, then Zola. Zola sent Cézanne a copy of *L'Oeuvre*, Cézanne sent him a short thank-you note, and they never spoke again; he never forgave Zola for basing the unhappy artist in *L'Oeuvre* on himself. Three weeks later Cézanne married Hortense."

"They weren't married?" Marine asked. "They had a teen-age son."

"We refer to her as Mme Cézanne, even in the early portraits," Rebecca said. "It just makes it easier. But no, they weren't marrried."

"How thoroughly modern," Marine mused.

Rebecca said, "*Trahit sua quemque voluptas.*"

"'Each has his dear delight which draws him on.' Right? Who said that?" Marine asked.

"Virgil," her father answered.

"Cézanne also wrote that in a letter to Zola," Rebecca explained. "In 1885."

"Manon Solari," Marine said. "There are still Solaris in Aix. Rebecca, Antoine told me that you had suspicions Cézanne's mistress was a Solari."

"Yes, but it was only a hunch," Rebecca said, "until you and your father linked the gold ribbon to Michaud's. Once we had the name 'Manon,' thanks to those notebooks of Mme Michaud's, and her death date, it was easy to confirm her identity."

"It will add a great chapter to the Cézanne biography you're working on," Anatole said, looking at Rebecca.

"No doubt," she answered. "It may even change the whole direction of the book."

"A story of love and loss," Marine said.

"There's your book title, Rebecca," Anatole said, smiling. "*Love and Loss.*"

"There's something that's been bothering me," Paulik said to Jules Schoelcher. "Do you have time to go to the rue Boulegon before it gets dark?"

Jules put his pen down. "Let's go."

They walked through Aix in silence, but Jules had guessed why they were going back to René Rouquet's apartment. When they turned onto Boulegon, Jules said, "We never found where the canvas was hidden."

"Hidden for all those years," Paulik answered. "And you guys thoroughly checked the place."

"Yes we did, sir."

"I want to ask Momo if he knows anything."

"Is he the fruit and veggie guy?" Jules asked. "Judge Verlaque showed me all the Manchester United paraphernalia he bought."

"Yes. And there he is."

Mohammed Dati was fussing with a bunch of bananas that he had hanging on an ancient crooked vine trunk. "Very nice," Paulik said as they approached Momo. "That looks great."

Momo turned around and Wayne Rooney stared at them.

"Nice apron," Paulik said.

"*Merci*," Momo replied. "Everyone likes it."

Paulik smiled and introduced Jules. "Momo," he began, "we still don't know where René found the Cézanne painting." He reached up and scratched his head for effect, and Jules added a perplexed face, his brow furrowed. "Could you help us?"

Momo excitedly waved his hands in the air and called for his uncle. "I'll get a flashlight," Momo said.

"Can we finally get in the apartment?" Momo's uncle asked as he introduced himself to Paulik and Schoelcher, shaking their hands. "Momo's been wanting to, but he couldn't as you guys have it marked off. René gave him a key, but Momo isn't one to break the law. René told Momo that there's something important for him there. In the same spot where he found the painting."

"You can come with us," Paulik said.

"Thank you, but I have to stay and guard the shop," the uncle said. "It's almost closing time."

Momo returned, waved a flashlight in the air, and crossed the street, not waiting for Paulik and Schoelcher. "Let's go!" Paulik said. "Momo, wait!"

They ran up the stairs, following Momo, who was already at the door of René Rouquet's former apartment, opening it with his key. "Trapdoor," Momo said, pointing toward the ceiling in the hallway that led to the bedroom.

"We looked up there," Schoelcher said. "With a flashlight, too. You pull on the latch and one of those folding staircases—"

Momo pulled on the latch and the three men ducked.

"Comes down," Schoelcher said, finishing his sentence.

Momo ran up the rickety wooden stairs and stuck his head in the crawlspace, turning on his flashlight.

"You can't stand up in there," Schoelcher said. "So we did what he's doing. Just shone the flashlight around."

"The wood beam," Momo said, turning around and looking down at the two men. "René told me to reach up and feel along the top of the beam." He set his flashlight down and, balancing himself with his left hand so that he could stretch, he felt along a beam with his right hand. "Got it!" He turned off his flashlight and lowered himself down the stairs, carrying a manila envelope.

"When did he tell you about the beam?" Paulik asked, giving Schoelcher, who was now red in the face, a stare.

"When he asked me to keep the painting," Momo answered. "And he told me that he was afraid, and that if anything happened to him, there was something for me on the beam. The same spot where he found the painting. This!" He held the envelope up and shook it, looking disappointed. "Papers? Is that what's in here?"

"Let's take this down to your uncle," Paulik said.

Momo flew out the door while Jules struggled to put the folding staircase back up. "Hurry up, Schoelcher," Paulik said, hiding his smile. By the time he and Jules were downstairs, Momo had ripped open the envelope and his uncle was reading aloud the document. The uncle reached into his pocket and pulled out a handkerchief, wiping his eyes.

"What is it?" Paulik asked.

"It looks like M. Rouquet's will," the uncle answered. "He's left everything to Momo. Including the apartment."

"We'll buy the store," Momo said. "Then we don't worry about the high rent."

His uncle turned to him. "How did you know that the rent was going up?"

Momo smiled and pointed to the side of his head.

"Not much gets by Momo," said Paulik.

Chapter Thirty-six

❧

Verlaque Visits Cézanne's Grave

*I*t didn't take very long to find the painter's grave. Most members of the Cézanne family were buried there, including the painter's son, also named Paul. Someone had taken the liberty of adding a small ceramic painting, poorly done, of a Provençal landscape. Verlaque certainly hoped that it hadn't been someone in the surviving Cézanne family, and he whispered his apologies to the painter.

Fittingly, there was a view of Mont Sainte Victoire. He reached into his coat pocket and took out an apple, placing it on the grave, beside a small blue paintbrush that another visitor had left.

Someone coughed and he saw, a few graves over, the old woman with whom he had chatted on the Cours the day of the Fête des Rois. Today she was wearing a gray wool coat, old-fashioned in its cut, but impeccable, with a matching gray hat trimmed in fur. She smiled and waved at Verlaque, bowed toward the grave in the front of her and whispered something, then walked toward the judge. "*Mon mari*," she said, gesturing toward the grave. "He died of cancer in 1982. I still miss him." Before Verlaque had a chance to reply, she said, pointing to Cézanne's grave, "You brought him an apple."

"Yes," Verlaque replied. "It seemed more appropriate than flowers."

"Nice spot here," she said.

"Quieter than downtown. A good place to . . . think."

She smiled and looked at the view of the mountain, then looked at the judge. She took her gnarled right hand out of a glove—these too were gray, and new—and tapped Verlaque's breast with the back of her hand. "You're trying to decide something," she said.

"I think I've just decided," he answered, smiling and looking down at her. "Thank you, Mme—"

"Solari," she replied. "My husband was a Solari." She straightened her shoulders and smiled.

Verlaque felt his thick body almost falling backward from the shock. Aix was indeed a small town, he thought.

"It's going to rain," she said, looking at the slate-colored clouds. "Have a nice evening."

"*À vous aussi, Mme Solari*," Verlaque said.

He watched her slowly walk down the cemetery's pebbled path, her gray coat and hat blending in with all of the gray stone around her. He felt inside his suit jacket pocket, making sure the small velvet Cartier bag was still there; he had been carrying it around with him since January 6. Emmeline had willed it to him. He stayed for almost an hour, looking at Cézanne's grave, and those nearby, bending down to look at faded black-and-white portraits of middle-aged men and women, or read inscriptions and dates. It gradually became dark, and the cemetery's custodian walked by. "We're closing, sir," he said.

Verlaque said, "I'm sorry. I hadn't noticed the time. Good evening." He headed toward the cemetery's gates, walking quickly and purposely down the narrow Traverse Saint-Pierre, then onto the busy Cours Gambetta that would turn into the rue d'Italie. By the time he got to the rue d'Italie, the streetlights had come on, and he looked down the length of the narrow street, its small shops lit up as if they were in Dickensian London. He walked on, sometimes stopping to say hello to a colleague or a friend, or simply nodding and smiling to someone he recognized but couldn't quite place. It was still a small town, Aix, no matter what anyone said.

Halfway up the rue d'Italie he saw Rebecca Schultz coming out of a shop, and he ran to meet her. After a few seconds of awkwardness, they gave each other the *bise*, their friendship now confirmed.

"I'm glad I caught you," Verlaque said. "I wanted to say good-bye."

"Even though you thought I was guilty," she said, smiling.

"Only for the briefest of moments," he said. "But you did flee, twice."

"Temporary insanity," she said. "I missed my parents." She thought of Marine Bonnet's words: love and loss.

"Well, good luck," he said. "Safe travels back to the US."

"I'm not going back right away," she said.

Verlaque looked confused. "You're not staying in Aix, are you? I thought you didn't like it."

"A town petrified in the sleep of ages," she said in a low, dramatic voice, as if reciting a poem. "Indifferent to everything."

Verlaque laughed. "Surely Cézanne didn't say that?"

"No," she replied. "Edmond Jaloux, a nineteenth-century writer."

"Where are you going then?"

"Paris," she answered flatly. "I'm taking a sabbatical year. Maybe more. Who knows. I'm buying an apartment, the one my parents should have bought years ago."

"In Boulogne?" he asked.

"Heavens no," she replied. "Too far from—"

"The center?"

"Yes. Too far from the center."

Verlaque looked at his watch. "Good grief!" he said. "I've got to buy something at Hédiard before they close. Good-bye. Perhaps we'll see each other in Paris."

"Most certainly," she replied, waving good-bye and winking.

Verlaque walked across the street, wondering what Rebecca meant by "most certainly" and the wink. He turned around. "Rebecca," he called out, and she walked toward him. He suddenly realized what was happening. The wink he had seen in the living room that night on the rue des Petits Pères. The opening and closing of the bedroom door in the middle of the night. Hortense's obvious discomfort the next morning at breakfast.

"Are you in a relationship with my father?" he asked, staring at her, his eyes stinging from the dry, cold night air.

"Yes," she said. "He's in my hotel room right now. He took a TGV down last night to meet me, and we're heading back up to Paris together. Don't look so shocked—"

"Don't tell me what to think," he said, turning his back.

"May I explain?" she asked.

Verlaque turned around.

"That night in Paris with you and your father," she began. "I haven't felt that . . . free . . . in years, even though I was frightened. Your father is wonderful."

"He's twice your age," Verlaque said. "And married."

Rebecca held her hand up, her palm facing Verlaque. "I know," she said. "Your father has wanted a divorce for years, and now with your mother sick—"

"If my mother were to die, my father would be free, without a messy divorce."

Rebecca went on, ignoring his comment. "I've suffered such loss. Our art collection, my mother, my father. And before you start, your father is not a replacement for my own. He and Isaac are polar opposites. If you must know, I've always dated older men. I was surrounded by them as a kid, I guess. Painters, art dealers, art historians—"

"Listen, Rebecca," Verlaque said as he waved to a woman he recognized rushing down the street, shopping bags in hand. The January sales had started, he realized. "Who am I to judge?" he asked. "It's just that my father has a bad track record. He's stayed married to my mother all these years, yes, but he's—"

"A philanderer," she answered. "I know. He told me. Who knows what will happen? But I need a change, and Paris was looking good."

Verlaque managed a smile. "It always does at night." He reached out his hand and she quickly took it in both of hers.

"Thank you for understanding," she said. "You'd better get into the shop."

Verlaque refrained from saying "but I don't understand." "Perhaps I'll see you next week. I'm coming back up to Paris."

"Your father said. Good-bye, Antoine."

"*Au revoir.*" He quickly opened the door to Hédiard then closed it, leaning against the glass. He couldn't wait to get to Marine's. Nice normal Marine, with her nice normal parents. Parents who had visited their daughter frequently when she was studying in Paris. Parents who kept track of how she was doing, kept an interest in her friends, in her work. In her lover. Never mind that in the winter they kept the house at a freezing 17°C and drove the ugliest car in the world.

"*Bonsoir, Monsieur le juge,*" the manager of the shop said. "Nice to see you."

"Thank you," Verlaque said, walking toward him and shaking his hand. "Nice to see you, too. I need a bottle of the usual champagne," he said. "I have an important declaration to make this evening, to a beautiful woman who lives around the corner."

"Ooh la la," the manager said, smiling as he opened the wine refrigerator. "*Félicitations!*"

Hédiard was a chain, so Marine had been enraged when the red-awninged shop had opened on the rue d'Italie, a street she considered her own little village. But Verlaque rather liked it. The shop had Pol Roger, and it was always chilled.

AVAILABLE FROM PENGUIN

A Verlaque and Bonnet Provençal Mystery

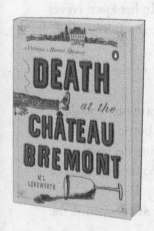

Death at the Château Bremont

Set in charming and historic Aix-en-Provence, France, this lively whodunit introduces readers to the chief magistrate, Antoine Verlaque, and his love interest, professor Marine Bonnet, who investigate the death of a local nobleman.

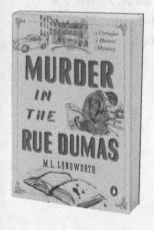

Murder in the Rue Dumas

When the Director of Theology at Aix-en-Provence's university is found dead, Verlaque is stumped. With Marine's help, Verlaque uncovers a mystery that proves even more complicated than university politics.

AVAILABLE FROM PENGUIN

A Verlaque and Bonnet Provençal Mystery

Death in the Vines

The owner of Domaine Beauclaire winery is devastated when he discovers the theft of priceless vintages. Soon after, Monsieur Gilles d'Arras's wife, Pauline, vanishes. As Verlaque and Commissioner Paulik investigate, they receive an urgent call: Bonnard has just found Madame d'Arras—dead in his vineyard.

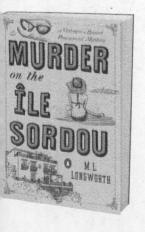

Murder on the Île Sordou

Just off the coast of Marseille, Judge Verlaque and Marine are vacationing among an amusing international crew of guests. But a shocking death and a sudden electrical storm jolts everyone. Verlaque and Bonnet spring into action to find the killer before another guest goes *morte*.

PENGUIN BOOKS